"My job is to keep you safe. T[...] to trust me. I know that's aski[...] first time less than ten hours ago, yet we're going to be alone in an isolated cabin for I don't know how many days. I'm going to use that time to earn your trust, which means I'm not going to take advantage of you. You have my word. Your safety depends on that. My family's reputation depends on that. Do you have any questions for me?"

Symone searched his wide midnight eyes beneath his thick black eyebrows. He was so earnest as he waited for her response, as though her answer was vitally important to him. Her muscles relaxed. She hadn't realized how knotted they'd been. Her eyes moved over his sharp sienna features. She could trust him.

Dear Reader,

Thank you for continuing The Touré Security Group journey with me. I'm having a blast and hope you are, too.

We first met the Touré brothers—Hezekiah, Malachi and Jeremiah—in *Down to the Wire*, my October 2023 release. That was Mal and Dr. Grace's reunion story. I hope you enjoyed it. I loved writing it.

I loved writing *Her Private Security Detail*, too. This is Jerry and Symone's story. Jerry's impulsive and doesn't believe in planning. Symone's compulsive and doesn't trust people who don't plan. They're opposites who must work together. I love opposites-attract stories. I love reading about their differences and following their journeys. What compromises are they willing to make? Will working together change them? If so, how?

Are you ready to discover the answers to these questions for Jerry and Symone?

Thank you so much for taking a chance on The Touré Security Group series. I hope you enjoy Jerry and Symone's story.

Warm regards,

Patricia Sargeant

HER PRIVATE SECURITY DETAIL

PATRICIA SARGEANT

Recycling programs
for this product may
not exist in your area.

ISBN-13: 978-1-335-59409-9

Her Private Security Detail

Copyright © 2024 by Patricia Sargeant-Matthews

For questions and comments about the quality of this book, please contact us at CustomerService@Harlequin.com.

TM and ® are trademarks of Harlequin Enterprises ULC.

Harlequin Enterprises ULC
22 Adelaide St. West, 41st Floor
Toronto, Ontario M5H 4E3, Canada
www.Harlequin.com

Printed in Lithuania

MIX
Paper | Supporting
responsible forestry
FSC® C021394

Nationally bestselling author Patricia Sargeant was drawn to write romance because she believes love is the greatest motivation. Her romantic suspense novels put ordinary people in extraordinary situations to have them find the "hero inside." Her work has been reviewed in national publications such as *Publishers Weekly*, *USA TODAY*, *Kirkus Reviews*, *Suspense Magazine*, *Mystery Scene Magazine*, *Library Journal* and *RT Book Reviews*. For more information about Patricia and her work, visit patriciasargeant.com.

Books by Patricia Sargeant

Harlequin Romantic Suspense

The Touré Security Group

Down to the Wire
Her Private Security Detail

Visit the Author Profile page
at Harlequin.com.

To My Dream Team:

- My sister, Bernadette, for giving me the dream.
- My husband, Michael, for supporting the dream.
- My brother Richard for believing in the dream.
- My brother Gideon for encouraging the dream.

And to Mom and Dad, always with love.

Chapter 1

"I can't." Jeremiah Touré jogged with his two older brothers, Hezekiah and Malachi, early Thursday morning. They'd started the last of their five laps around Antrim Park in the northwest part of Columbus, Ohio's capital city.

It had been dark when the trio had started their six-mile/five-lap workout. Moisture from the air joined with the sweat forming on Jeremiah's brow, cheekbones and upper lip. The weather was comfortable—for now—but July in Columbus could be brutal.

On his left, past the bushes and down a grassy slope, lay a pond in an imperfect oval. Its serene surface mirrored the sky, shifting from black to gray and more slowly to blue. The birdsong grew louder and more energetic as the sun rose.

In front of him, the narrow dirt trail led to a broader blacktop. A row of trees and bushes lined the asphalt on both sides. Those on the right shielded the woods beyond the park. Leafy branches formed a canopy over the path, sheltering the handful of other joggers and walkers who were getting in their early morning exercise. Several had dogs or strollers. Some had both. A few were on their own.

Starting the day jogging with his brothers was the best. What wasn't to love? He was with his brothers, his friends.

They were outdoors, getting exercise. They pushed each other to keep up a good pace—no slacking!

Jeremiah and his brothers had been doing these runs since they were teenagers. Jogging was one of his favorite hobbies, which was fortunate since physical fitness was a job requirement. But opportunities for him to workout with his brothers were becoming more infrequent. Business was booming for Touré Security Group, his family-owned company. He and his siblings had inherited the agency from their deceased parents. It figured Hezekiah, the human manifestation of a killjoy, would bring up work during one of their increasingly rare opportunities to enjoy each other's company.

"You *can't* do it? Or you don't want to?" His eldest brother's response came from behind him. This part of the path was too narrow to jog side by side.

They all wore black running shorts with dark jogging shoes, but their moisture-wicking pullovers were different colors. Hezekiah's crimson red jersey commanded attention—sort of like the man.

Hezekiah had gotten his wish to expand their company to attract bigger clients, in large part thanks to publicity from a case they'd closed two months ago. They'd protected a scientist from a serial killer who'd been after her formulation. Their success had attracted a lot of new clients, from small companies to midsized businesses and larger corporations. They'd even secured a contract with Midwest Area Research Systems, the scientist's employer.

"Can't." The answer was at the same time easy and hard. "I can't take on new cases. I'm leaving the company at the end of the month, remember? I've got my hands full, wrapping up the cases I'm overseeing now. But I'll gather a few of our personal security consultants and bring them up to speed."

With their increasing client list, maybe his timing could've been better, but Jeremiah was ready to pursue his own plans. Hezekiah, however, wanted him to take on a new case protecting a high-level executive with The Bishop Foundation, but he couldn't do this anymore. He needed to walk away from the company. Staying was putting everyone and everything at risk. Leaving was the right thing to do. But, crap, did it have to be so hard?

Jeremiah took a deeper breath, meant to soothe him as he led his brothers past the first curve on their fifth lap around the pond. The air was heavy with the musty, damp scent of the earth beneath his running shoes and the sharp, dew-laden grass that rimmed the pond.

"The client asked for you personally." Malachi sounded so reasonable. The medical research scientist they'd protected, Dr. Grace Blackwell, had been his ex-girlfriend. The case had helped rekindle their romance. "They want the best."

His second-eldest brother's leaf green jersey helped him blend into the foliage. Malachi was playing to his ego. He'd give his sibling credit for that. The tactic would've worked on the old Jerry. He missed that guy. Without realizing it, his steps had sped up. It was like his subconscious knew he was running away. He made an effort to slow down. "Why does The Bishop Foundation sound familiar?"

"It came up during our case with Grace." Malachi's voice came from Jeremiah's right. This wider section of the path allowed his brothers to jog beside him. "The foundation chair contacted her for the recommendation."

Jeremiah's body filled with pride for his family and their company. Their parents had founded Touré Security

Group on qualities that were important to them: integrity, excellence, professionalism. His brothers followed the example they'd set—another reason he was quitting. He couldn't live up to those standards any longer.

A rustling from the undergrowth on his right drew his eyes to the woods beyond the park. A pair of chipmunks disappeared beneath the shelter of the nearby bushes.

"You did a great job protecting Melba." Hezekiah kept pace on Jeremiah's left.

Having his eldest brother on his left and middle brother on his right made Jeremiah feel like they were ganging up on him.

Still, thinking of Grace's grandmother, Melba Stall, made him smile. "We've kept in touch." He wiped the sweat collecting on his upper lip with the back of his right wrist and pulled together the tattered remnants of his confidence. "I know I did a great job protecting her. I also did an excellent job training our personal protection consultants. I know each one's strengths and weaknesses. We don't have any bad apples. I'll identify six of the best of our best, two agents per shift for twenty-four-hour security. I'll get the estimate to you by end of day."

"That should work." Hezekiah's sigh was louder than necessary. Typical. He was lathering on the guilt. "The client meeting's tomorrow morning. Early. We didn't expect you to guard the executive on your own, but we'd feel better knowing you were at least overseeing the job."

"The guards are well trained, thanks to you." Malachi used the back of his hand to remove the sweat from his chin. "But this is a high-profile case."

Another wave of restlessness washed over him. Jeremiah struggled to keep his steps even and his tone casual.

"All of our cases are important, Mal. Don't worry. I won't leave you hanging." *This time.*

Their silence suffocated him. He knew they didn't mean for it to. It wasn't their fault. Jeremiah blamed his guilt. He didn't *want* to leave the company. He *had* to. His brothers didn't make any secret about their concern over his decision to walk away. He didn't want them to worry about him. He wanted them to be proud of him. He wanted them to be confident in his abilities, as confident in him as he'd always been in them. He wanted things to go back to the way they'd been before he'd made a mistake that could've cost a teenage boy his life.

Digging deep, Jeremiah faked a grin. He tossed it at his brothers. "Let's sprint to the end."

Malachi groaned. "I'm too old."

Hezekiah frowned. "I'm almost two years older than you."

Malachi arched an eyebrow. His look spoke for him. *Then we're* both *too old.*

Jeremiah gave the first real laugh he'd felt in weeks. "Come on, old-timers."

He sped up, setting a challenging pace, even for himself. He took long slow breaths, straining to control his breathing. He raised his arms, pumping them as he pushed himself to take faster, longer strides. His heart galloped in his chest. Still his two older brothers kept pace with him.

"Jerry, what are you about now?" He heard his mother's voice as though she was running alongside him. He brought her image to mind. She'd stayed slim and fit his whole life. Both of his parents had. Her face had remained smooth and her hair dark well into her sixties. *"Zeke and Mal aren't your competition. They're your brothers. The only person you should compete against is yourself."*

They rounded the fourth corner of the pond and flew the final leg of their last lap. Jeremiah's feet barely touched the dirt path. Slow breath in. Hold. Slow breath out. He forgot about Hezekiah and Malachi. Now he fought to push himself as hard as he could.

I competed against myself and failed, Mom. And my failure hurt Dad's and your legacy. I can't put the company in that position. Never again.

In his mind, she frowned. It was the loving, chiding expression she'd given him when she thought he was being a fool. *But is leaving Touré Security a bigger risk to you than your staying with the company would be to your brothers?*

"You'd remove me from the foundation my family built?" Seated at the head of the long oval dark wood table Thursday morning, Symone Bishop met the eyes of each of the nine other people—all with voting power—in the small conference room, seven board members and two administrators. Most didn't—or couldn't—return her regard.

"We wouldn't remove you entirely." Tina Grand, president of The Bishop Foundation Board, sat at the foot of the table. The sixty-something woman was businesslike in her dark blue pantsuit and white shell blouse. Her cap of salt-and-pepper hair framed her round, pale cheeks. "We'd find another, more suitable position for you."

Seriously?

Symone braced the tips of her fingers on the thin black frames of her glasses. She swept her eyes over the four women and three men of the board in addition to her stepfather and vice chair, Paul Kayple, and her administrative assistant, Eleanor Press. To her left, Paul looked as shocked and outraged as she felt. Okay, so it wasn't just her. This really was a waking nightmare. On her right, Eleanor looked like she was going to sob. She could go ahead. Symone would remain dry-eyed. Tears were a luxury she didn't have time for.

Masking her anger, she held the board president's cool gray eyes. "Please explain to me again exactly why the board believes a confidence vote is necessary."

Aaron Menéndez sat at Tina's right. Of average height and build, he was in his early sixties, Symone thought. "As we explained, we've been unhappy with the way you and your mother, God rest her soul, have been running the foundation since your father's passing. God rest his soul. You've become predictable."

Symone swallowed to clear the lump of grief—and anger?—from her throat. Her father, Langston Bishop, had inherited The Bishop Foundation from his father, Frederick. Langston had died almost six years earlier after a long battle with pancreatic cancer. She'd just buried her mother less than three months ago. Odette Bishop's death after a heart attack had surprised Symone and her stepfather, Paul.

None of the current board members had served with her father, but the foundation's records showed its growth under his skillful leadership. He'd been larger than life, not just to his doting daughter and adoring wife, but to everyone who came into contact with him. His board would never have even thought about removing him.

But her board seems to have been making plans to replace her.

Symone drew a breath to calm her voice. The large, shadowy boardroom smelled like a coffee shop. She could use another cup herself. "Under my family's leadership—my grandfather's, my father's, my mother's and now mine—the foundation has been steady and successful. Is that the predictability you find so concerning?"

Julie Yeoh was midway through the second year of her first three-year term with the board. Her cool pastel business suit emphasized her large dark eyes and chin-length ebony hair. She'd taken the chair to the right of Eleanor. "The foundation's funds would benefit from taking more risks with its investments and the projects that are approved."

Symone worked to mask her surprise. "The foundation's accounts are secure while they're making a strong return on investment. Do you want me to take risks for risk's sake?"

Did the board think the foundation's investments were a game? Not on her watch.

Tina raised her right hand, palm out in a Stop motion. "No one's denying that the foundation's finances are solid, but for some time now, we have thought they could be better."

"How much time?" Symone asked.

Tina shrugged. "What does it matter? A few years?"

Keisha Lord, the third-longest-serving board member, leaned into the table. Her shoulder-length micro braids swung forward, half obscuring her elegant profile. Her ruby red A-lined dress complimented her slender figure. "'They could be better' is subjective. What level of return on investment are you aiming for? Remember, this is a nonprofit foundation."

It was as though Keisha had read her mind. What was the board's goal?

Kitty Lymon shrugged almost flirtatiously from her seat beside Paul. Her cotton candy pink figure-hugging dress clashed with her deep red mane. "The more money the foundation has, the more money it could award in grants."

Symone couldn't argue with that logic, but there was always a flip side. "Conversely, if our investments lose money, we'd have less money to award." She addressed Tina. "I respect your business background. You and Aaron both have MBAs, but my background is in financial investments. Before returning to the foundation, I worked for one of the most prestigious investment firms in the country. The foundation has a strong balance of growth and middle investments."

The newest board members, Xander Fence and Wesley Bragg, hadn't contributed to the discussion. Both men had been appointed to the board a little more than six months ago. Paul had recommended Wesley. He and the lawyer had been friends for years. Like her stepfather, Wesley was in his sixties, and of average height and build.

A former board member had recommended Xander as her replacement. The banking executive was in his fifties and was also of average height and build. But whereas Xander was like a daytime drama star with his salon-styled, wavy golden blond hair and striking green eyes, Wesley's salt-and-pepper hair and dark blue eyes seemed as somber as the evening news.

Tina sniffed. "Yes, we're aware of your background in investments, but we're still concerned with the foundation's management style. The foundation has been stagnating for the past six years. The records support our assessment."

Symone once again searched the faces around the table. Xander and Wesley avoided eye contact, as did Kitty and Aaron. Tina, Julie and Keisha looked at her expectantly. "You've stated the board has had these concerns for years. Why didn't you speak up sooner?"

Tina looked like the question caught her off guard. What had she expected Symone to do, accept their decision without debate? Not a chance.

Tina stared at the pen she was rotating between her

hands. "Frankly, Symone, Aaron and I had hoped, over time, you and your mother would update your investment strategy."

Symone didn't believe Tina's answer. For now, she'd put a pin in it. She directed her next question to Aaron, who was still avoiding her eyes. "Are you unsatisfied with the investment company? We've had them for decades. Do you think it's time for a change?"

Aaron looked up, waving his hands. "We'll leave that decision to you. You're the one who has experience with investment companies."

They were frustrated with her investment decisions but entrusted her to choose an investment partner. Were they gaslighting her? "You've said you have concerns not only about the investment strategy but also our application screening. What types of projects do you believe we should be pursuing?"

Tina repeated her deer-in-the-headlights impersonation. "Our feedback isn't meant to be taken literally. We don't have specific projects in mind, but we feel the ones you've approved have been predictable. I hate to keep using that word. It's our strong belief that the foundation should be leading the way in health care innovations. We shouldn't be following the industry. The projects we support should be more imaginative."

Symone's cheeks filled with angry heat. "This is my family's foundation. My grandfather established it before I was born."

Tina inclined her head. "And, as you know, he structured the foundation in a way that allows the board to have a guardianship role over the administration. We have the authority to replace the chair if we believe management is destructive to the foundation."

Symone unclenched her teeth. "Are you accusing my leadership of being destructive to my family's legacy?"

Tina angled her chin upward. "Yes, I'm afraid we are."

Eleanor seemed stricken. Paul appeared concerned. Aaron, Wesley and Xander continued to stare at the conference table. Keisha and Julie looked troubled. Kitty returned her regard as though trying to read her mind. Symone hoped she couldn't. This wasn't a good time for others to have access to her thoughts. People's feelings would be hurt.

She met each board member's eyes. "Are you all in agreement?"

"I'm not." Keisha waved her hand. "Like Tina, I've served on the board for less than five years. We've never worked with Langston Bishop, but I've heard he was a dynamic force." She smiled at Symone. "He must've been to rebuild the foundation's investments after several of the funds collapsed. But we're not in a rebuilding state anymore. We don't have to take risks to save the foundation. Under Symone's leadership, the funds are secure. That's what matters."

Julie tucked a swatch of her ebony hair behind her ear. "You make a good point, Keisha, but do we want to be stagnant? I mean, I wouldn't mind seeing a proposal that showed us other options. I'm not in favor of a confidence vote, but maybe it's time for a shakeup."

Keisha and Kitty nodded, murmuring their agreement.

Symone shook off her irritation. "Xander? Wesley? I haven't heard from either of you. I realize you're the newest board members, but you have a right to be heard. What do you think?"

Xander adjusted the dark blue shirt he wore beneath his smoke gray jacket. As usual, he'd forgone a tie. "The foundation is solid, but perhaps Julie makes a good point. We all might benefit from seeing a projection of what the account would look like with more aggressive funds."

Wesley shrugged. "I don't need to see that, but if the others want it, I won't stand in their way."

Symone swept her arm around the table. "If you wanted to see funding options, you could've requested that during any of our previous monthly board meetings. There's no need to bring up a confidence vote."

Tina gave a tight smile. "Let's see your proposal first."

Symone considered the board president. *What was this really about?* She stood. "I'll submit the proposal prior to the next board meeting."

That gave her three weeks to learn the real reason behind the confidence vote. In the interim, there was one thing she knew for certain. The board would have to wrestle the foundation's leadership from her cold, dead hands.

Jeremiah reread the printout of The Bishop Foundation chair's bio at his desk late Thursday morning. He didn't know why he was reading it a third time. Or why he'd printed it, much less as a color copy. Yes, preliminary client information helped assess possible threats to her security. But he'd already made notes for that. Besides, she wasn't the target. Her stepfather was.

Still… Symone Bishop. He'd committed her cool, tan features to memory. There was something in her chocolate brown eyes behind those black-rimmed glasses that made him want to take a second, third and possibly fourth look at her.

"What's really keeping you from taking this assignment?" Malachi appeared in his doorway.

After their run, the brothers had gone to their respective homes to prepare for work. Malachi preferred business casual clothes. He'd rolled up the sleeves of his crisp white shirt and left his dark brown jacket—a match to his slacks—in his office. The sage green tie was a nice splash of color. Was that Grace's influence?

Like his brothers, Jerry favored darker colors for his wardrobe, but he refused to wear a tie.

Jeremiah looked away from Symone's image to consider his middle brother's question. "I'm not taking the case because I'm leaving. Really." He hated himself for lying to his brother, but he was too ashamed to tell the truth. He couldn't bring himself to tell them—to tell anyone—that he was walking away because he didn't trust his abilities to keep people safe anymore; not after what happened with the teenage rising pop star.

Malachi took a drink from his black coffee mug. The cursive white text on the side of the mug that faced Jeremiah read, "I'm not anti-social. I'm just not user friendly." It had been a joint birthday gift from him and Hezekiah and was one of the few times he and his eldest brother had agreed on anything.

"Tell me about your plans for your consulting business." Malachi gestured toward him with his mug.

There were obstacles between him and his brother, literally. A couple of chairs had been pulled out from under the conversation table. Boxes of personnel and case files and personal protection supplies were stacked halfway to his desk. To the layperson, his office appeared to be a disaster. His brothers didn't nag him as long as he agreed to keep his door closed during client visits.

Jeremiah leaned back against his black cloth executive chair. Thinking about walking away from his family and going out on his own made his heart dive into his stomach. It was the kind of feeling you got when you think you're making a mistake. He shrugged it off and dug up a cocky grin. "Like I said, a friend of mine is a manager at a fitness club."

"Adam, right?" Malachi took another sip of coffee.

"That's right." Jeremiah had known Adam since high school. "He sold the club's owner on having me teach self-defense courses a couple of times a week to start. We'll see how it goes from there. But I'm also going to offer one-on-one fitness training."

"Sounds exciting." Malachi watched Jeremiah closely. "I'm sure you're going to be successful. You're really good at marketing. You've done ours for years, and the results have always been great. But I still don't understand why you're leaving."

Jeremiah forced himself not to squirm on his chair. "I thought you'd be happier about my leaving. You're always complaining about how much Zeke and I argue. Now you'll have the peace you're always asking for."

Malachi gave a dry laugh. "Why do you always go on the offensive when Zeke and I ask you anything personal? Or ask you anything, full stop? We're just trying to understand why you're leaving, and don't say it's because you're tired of arguing. No one buys that."

Hezekiah's laughter sounded before he appeared in the doorway beside Malachi. "That's the truth."

The eldest Touré brother slipped past Malachi and strode toward Jeremiah's desk. Along the way, he nudged the chairs back beneath the conversation table and pushed the boxes of files aside with his black oxfords.

Jeremiah swallowed a sigh. "Am I the only one with work to do?" His tone was sour. He winced, realizing he sounded like Hezekiah.

"No." Hezekiah collected the stack of files from one of the visitor's chairs, turning to place them on the table behind him. He glanced at Malachi. "Don't let the chaos and disaster scare you. It's Jer."

Despite his visible doubts, Malachi stepped forward. He cleared the chair beside Hezekiah's. "If all your files are on your floor and furniture, are your cabinets and drawers empty?"

Jeremiah had heard that question before. He closed the folder, covering the printout of Symone's bio. "All right. Let's get this over with."

Hezekiah set his left ankle on his right knee. He'd also left his suit jacket in his office. Still, in his sapphire shirt and matching iron gray pants and tie, he looked like a model for a business magazine cover. "I'm not going to speak for Mal, but I want to know what's chasing you out of the company. And as Mal said, don't try to feed us the line about not wanting to argue with me anymore."

Malachi placed his right ankle on his left knee. His eyes, so like their mother's, bore into Jeremiah's. "You know that old saying, be careful what you wish for. I left the company—left Columbus—almost six years ago in part because you guys were arguing all the time. But I came back because I missed you pains in the neck. In the end, it's about family, the good, the annoying and the ugly."

Jeremiah rested his hands on the arms of his chair. "Look, I'm sorry you guys expected a different answer from the one I'm giving you, but it's the truth." Lying wasn't getting any easier. His stomach muscles were tied in knots.

Hezekiah narrowed his eyes. "Is this because of that pop star assignment?"

Malachi frowned. "Zeke—"

Hezekiah glanced at Malachi on his left. "We need to stop tiptoeing around this." He returned his attention to Jeremiah. "Is that the reason you think you need to leave?"

Jeremiah felt his fists tighten around his chair's arms. He forced his grip to loosen. "I just guarded Melba Stall, remember? I know I'm good at what I do. There's no problem there."

Guarding Melba had been a piece of cake. First, Melba hadn't been a rebellious teen. She'd been cooperative and taken the situation seriously. Second, she'd lived in a secure senior residence where there were security procedures and guards in place. All he'd needed to do was staff up with a few Touré Security Group consultants, including himself. He'd gone undercover as Melba's godson, visiting from out of town.

Hezekiah's coal black eyes were still clouded with doubt. "Jer, The Bishop Foundation's a very important new client. They asked for you based on Grace's recommendation. We need you on this."

Jeremiah dragged his left hand over his tight dark curls. "All of our consultants are our best. I've trained them myself and oversee their annual recertification."

Touré Security Group's annual personal consultant recertification was intense. He'd created the original course with input from his parents and brothers. Each year, they reevaluated it for improvement. It was designed to cull people who didn't take the responsibility of their clients' safety with the gravity it deserved. Testing categories included physical and mental fitness, medical care and weapons training.

Malachi raised a hand, palm out. "We know, Jer. We're not questioning your commitment to the program. And we know we're going to need more than one consultant to guard this client, but you're our best. Our client expects *you*."

Jeremiah shook his head. "That won't be possible. We agreed my last day would be July eighteenth, next Friday." And he really needed this fresh start. He needed time to clear his head before he began his business. "Have you guys started interviewing the consultants I suggested to replace me as director of personal security?" He thought it would get easier to say that over time. It hadn't.

Malachi ignored his question. Not a good sign. "You haven't committed to a start date at the gym."

Hezekiah caught and held Jeremiah's eyes. "Come to the meeting in the morning—"

Jeremiah interrupted him. "Of course I'll be at the meeting. I need that information to brief the teams."

Hezekiah shook his head. "No. Come to the meeting with an open mind. Hear directly from our client before making your final decision. You might agree you're perfect to lead this detail."

Jeremiah looked from Hezekiah's intent scrutiny to Malachi's watchful regard. "Fine." Anything to get them to drop the subject. "I'll keep an open mind at the meeting. But afterward, if I believe our consultants can handle this without me, I'm leaving on schedule."

"Fair enough." Hezekiah sprang to his feet as though afraid Jeremiah would reconsider his decision.

Malachi seemed to be searching for something else to say. Jeremiah returned his regard with as much self-assurance as he could collect.

Finally, Malachi stood, stepping back toward the door. "Thanks, Jer."

Jeremiah managed a half smile. "You got it."

As soon as his brothers disappeared beyond his doorway, his smile faded. He opened the folder. Symone's image stared up at him. His consultants could handle this case without him. Besides, she wasn't the target. "You're better off without me."

Chapter 2

"What are we going to do?" Eleanor's voice was tight with worry. It exacerbated Symone's irritation—and panic.

She'd led Paul and Eleanor into her office immediately after the board meeting to debrief late Thursday morning. There was only one thing they could do.

Symone settled onto her navy blue, ribbed, faux leather chair behind her heavy oak desk and took a steadying breath. She had to at least sound as though she was in control if she had any hope of maintaining her position with the foundation. "I'll revise my annual proposal to the board to reflect their feedback, making sure it isn't predictable." She turned her attention to her assistant. The other woman was a striking figure in a sky blue pantsuit, with sapphire earrings and matching necklace. "Ellie, I'll need you to pull new figures and forecasts. I'll send you an email with the adjusted parameters."

She was pleased that she'd been able to strip her emotions from her words. It hadn't been easy.

Eleanor sat on the dark blue cloth visitor's chair farthest from the door. She typed something into her electronic tablet. "I'll get right on it as soon as I receive your instructions."

"Thank you." Symone turned to her stepfather. Paul had taken the matching seat beside Eleanor. "Could you produce a proposal of recommendations for revisions to our application process? How can we reach a broader pool of applicants? What more can we do to encourage innovations?"

Translation: *How do you suggest we get the board off my back so I can continue to protect my family's legacy?*

Paul crossed his legs, adjusting the crease in his dark brown suit pants. "What about reconsidering the application from the exercise equipment entrepreneur?"

Symone drew a blank until she remembered the application her mother had screened out of consideration. "The pitch for the enhanced aerobic cycler?"

Paul balanced his elbows on the chair's arms. "We should take another look at that application. It was a very exciting idea, cutting-edge."

Symone adjusted her black-framed glasses as she considered Paul. One of them was confused. She was pretty certain it wasn't her. "My mother screened out that application. It doesn't meet the parameters of the foundation's mission."

The Bishop Foundation was created to support, fund and encourage innovative ideas in lifesaving pharmaceutical formulations, medical equipment and health treatments. The exercise machine didn't fit any of those categories.

Ignoring her explanation, Paul's voice raced with enthusiasm. His round, brown cheeks pinkened. "But the board is looking for riskier, more exciting projects. Mark's application fits that description."

Symone frowned. "Mark? Do you know him?"

Paul's dark brown eyes slid away from hers. "Only casually. He has exciting, revolutionary ideas about health and fitness. He just needs a chance."

Her stepfather wasn't breaking any rules by associating with someone who'd submitted an application to the foundation. Even one who'd issued a veiled threat when his application had been rejected. The award process was too stringent for that. Grants were awarded only to applicants who made it through the initial screening and received the supermajority vote of seven of the nine voting members.

"Paul has a good point." Eleanor's comment refocused Symone's attention on their discussion. "The project's different from anything we've ever done. It could help generate excitement among the board."

Symone lowered her eyes to hide her alarm. Paul's and Eleanor's attitudes were the reason she had to retain her position with her family's foundation. Both were in administrative positions, which meant the board could appoint either of them to replace her. But neither Paul nor Eleanor seemed bound to the foundation's mission.

She pulled a soft cloth from her top desk drawer, taking off her glasses to clean their lenses. "The reason the enhanced aerobic cycler is different from any other project we've approved is that it doesn't meet the application criteria. It's not an advancement in medical formulations, equipment or treatment. That's the reason my mother screened out the applicant." She put on her glasses before looking first to Eleanor, then Paul. "Our mission statement is the foundation's compass. It's the reason the foundation exists. My grandfather recognized the very urgent need to support medical research to ensure quality of life. That need still exists, and that's the reason we'll continue to use the mission statement to screen out applications."

"All right." Paul nodded, but Symone sensed he wasn't convinced.

"I'm sorry, Symone. You're right." Eleanor stood to leave. Her three-inch beige stilettos pushed her close to six feet. "I'd better get back to work. I'm still archiving this year's applications."

Symone offered her a smile. "Thank you, Ellie."

Paul raised his hand. "Yes. Thanks."

Symone waited until Eleanor had left her office before turning to her stepfather. "Do you remember we have the meeting with the Touré Security Group tomorrow morning?"

Paul's eyes widened with surprise before his brow furrowed with confusion. He pinned her with dark brown eyes beneath thick black eyebrows. "I thought you were going to cancel that meeting."

Symone blinked. "What would make you think that?"

Paul rubbed his eyes with his right fingers. He always did that when he was frustrated. Well, he wasn't the only one who felt that way.

He sighed before dropping his hand to meet her eyes. "Symone, I told you I don't want a bodyguard. I don't need a bodyguard. The detectives are investigating the threats. Let them do their job."

If only it was that simple. She wished she could hand over these worries to the Columbus Division of Police. She'd then go back to worrying only about the foundation, its investments and its applications. She hadn't been able to focus on just the foundation for a long time, though, not since her mother had died suddenly and now her stepfather was receiving threats.

Symone tamped down her impatience. "Paul, the police consider stalking complaints to be homicide prevention, but the detectives said they can't do anything unless an actual attempt is made on your life. I'd rather it didn't come to that."

Paul broke eye contact. "I don't want someone following me around."

Symone raised her eyebrows. "Apparently, someone's already following you and not in a good way. A bodyguard would keep you safe."

"Fine." Paul stood to leave her office. "We'll try a bodyguard, but if this person gets in my way, the deal's off."

Symone watched her stepfather march out of the room. She owed it to her mother's memory to help keep him safe. Why was he fighting her efforts to do that?

"Someone's trying to kill me." Paul nodded toward the woman seated to his right in the Touré Security Group's conference room. "Symone and I have already reported this to the police. They're investigating so I don't think I need a bodyguard."

It was early Friday morning. Symone sat opposite Jerry at the long, rectangular, glass-and-sterling-silver conference table. She projected understated wealth and was even more striking in person. Her golden brown hair was styled in a tousled bob that swung above her narrow shoulders. Her bangs ended just above thin, black-rimmed glasses that drew attention to her wide chocolate brown eyes beneath winged dark brown eyebrows. Her dove gray skirt suit and ghost white blouse were unassuming but probably expensive. Her thin rose-gold Movado wristwatch peeked from beneath her cuff. She'd accessorized with discreet pearl stud earrings and a matching single-strand princess-length necklace. A hint of wildflowers drifted across the table toward him. Jerry couldn't help himself. He drew a deep breath.

In contrast, the man she'd introduced as her stepfather wanted the world to know he was flush. In his early sixties, he had a full head of tight, dark brown curls. He was tall and slim in a tailored blue three-piece silk suit. His gold pocket watch was redundant to his black-and-gold Rolex. His black shoes looked Italian and handmade.

On Jerry's right, Mal sat in quiet contemplation. His middle brother was good at reading people. Jerry could feel Mal's mind working as he observed Symone's and Paul's body language and considered their words. He was interested to know what his brother was thinking.

Zeke's voice from the head of the conference table pulled Jerry from his thoughts. "Mr. Kayple—"

Symone interrupted. "Please. It's Paul and Symone."

Zeke gave her a warm smile. "Thank you." He turned back to her stepfather. "Paul, could you tell us about these threats?"

Jerry breathed a sigh of relief. They were finally getting somewhere. "When did they start?"

Paul's eyebrows rose toward his hairline. "I just told you, I don't need a bodyguard." His whiny tone brought back uncomfortable memories of the spoiled pop star Jerry had attempted to protect almost a year ago.

Jerry's brow furrowed. "You don't think these threats are real?"

Paul reared back against his seat as though Jerry had slapped him. "Of course I think they're real. Why else would I contact the police?"

"You believe the threats against your life are real, but you don't want protection." Jerry cocked his head. "Make it make sense, Paul."

"Jer." Zeke gave him a pointed look.

He sat back. "Tell us about the threats."

Paul regarded Jerry with wide, unblinking eyes. His lips parted but no words came out. Jerry turned his attention to Symone.

Anger darkened her pretty brown eyes, but her voice was

cool. "There have been two threats. My stepfather received the first one July third."

"Right before the long holiday weekend." Paul sounded irritated.

Symone continued. "It was a message painted on my mother's dining room table. It read, 'Walk away.'"

"Someone broke into your house?" Mal broke his silence. He directed his question to Symone.

"It's not my house." She gestured toward Paul. "It's the home my mother, Odette Bishop, shared with Paul. She passed away in April. I've been staying in the house while I help Paul settle her affairs."

"I'm so sorry." Jerry's heart clenched. His brothers echoed his sentiment.

He empathized with the heartache and grief she and her stepfather must be feeling. Their mother, Vanessa Sherraten-Touré, a retired marine, had died of heart disease two years and nine months ago. Their father, Franklin Touré, also a retired marine, had died two months before her. He missed them every day.

Symone inclined her head, accepting their condolences. Her voice was a little huskier as she continued. "The break-in triggered Paul's security system. When we got to the house, we saw the message. It was written in red paint." She pulled her cell phone from her silver faux leather purse and went through a series of taps on its face before passing her phone to Zeke on her right. "I took a photo."

Paul picked up the story, shifting again on his seat. Waves of impatience vibrated around him. "The police searched the entire house. Nothing else was touched. They didn't take anything and the only thing they left was that message." He gestured toward Symone's cell.

"They probably didn't have time to do anything else

once they triggered your alarm." Jerry took the phone Zeke passed to him.

He studied the image of the message painted onto a black laminate dining room table. The perpetrator—or perpetrators—had worked quickly. They'd shoved the table's centerpiece and crimson-and-dark-gold runner out of the way to make room for their warning. The two-word message had been written in all caps. The letters were different sizes, but the threat covered what appeared to be a third of the midsized table. The paint had dripped during the process, forming accidental links between the printed letters. The color was a deep red, as though the culprit wanted Symone and Paul to think it had been written in blood. It was an indication of the home invader wanting to heighten the sense of danger. Jerry offered the phone to Mal.

Paul continued, adjusting his cuffs. Had he meant to reveal his Rolex? "The police dusted the table for prints and took a sample of the paint. It was still wet. That's how quickly we got home."

Jerry frowned. His eyes bounced from Symone to Paul and back. "Did you notice anyone near your home or any cars that were leaving?"

Paul sat back on his seat, shaking his head. "I didn't see anything."

"I didn't, either." Symone reached diagonally across the table to accept her phone from Mal. Frustration creased her brow and tightened her voice. "I was focused more on getting to my mother's house as quickly as possible."

Paul rubbed his eyes with his right fingers. "The second event happened when Symone and I were leaving a restaurant in Granville. It was July eighth."

"Someone followed you." Jerry's muscles tensed. His eyes settled on Symone.

"I guess so." Paul seemed uncertain. "A dark car—black or blue or gray, I don't know—came speeding through the parking lot and almost hit us. We thought it was just a reckless driver, but the next day, someone put a photo of that attempted hit-and-run in my mailbox. They'd actually taken a photo of what happened and left a message that read, 'This wasn't an accident. Walk away.' Can you believe that?"

"Walk away from what?" Jerry watched as Symone once again tapped commands against the surface of her cell phone.

She offered the device to Zeke. "I took a photo of the picture and message they left for us."

Paul's brown cheeks flushed an angry red. His eyes darkened with emotion. "I believe these threats are coming from the company that made my wife's heart medicine or her doctor or both. I'm suing them for malpractice. They were negligent in my wife's care. Obviously, they think they can intimidate me into walking away from the lawsuits." He sat back, crossing his arms over his broad chest. "Well, they can think again. I'm not dropping the suit. I refuse."

Jerry took the cell from Zeke and studied the image. Something didn't seem right to him. "You think a doctor and a pharmaceutical company broke into your house and painted a threat on your dining room table?"

Paul scowled. "*They* didn't break in. They hired someone."

"You think a doctor and a drug company hired a criminal to threaten you?" Jerry handed the phone to Mal. "I can't see a doctor or a pharmaceutical manufacturer taking a hit out on someone over a lawsuit."

"I agree with Jerry." Zeke gestured toward him with his right hand. "Recent studies have shown doctors have won almost seventy percent of malpractice cases I think, even when the evidence against them is reasonably strong."

"The odds are in their favor." Mal studied the image on Symone's phone. "They won't go to the expense of hiring someone to harass and threaten you into dropping your suit. It's unnecessary."

Paul frowned at Mal. Jerry had the sense his lawyer hadn't shared those reports with him. He made a mental note to get more information on Paul's lawyer and the case. Something wasn't right there. He owed it to his personal security consultants to tie up these threads before assigning any of them to the case. Information like this would help make sure his consultants were well prepared to protect their clients and themselves.

Paul returned his scowl to Jerry and his brothers. "So who do *you* think's behind all this?"

Jerry caught and held Symone's attention. "Who knows you've been staying at your mother's house?"

Symone shrugged one slender shoulder. "Everyone. I haven't made a secret of it." She stiffened, giving Jerry an intent look. "You can't think those threats are meant for me."

All semblance of serenity had faded as Symone seemed to bristle at the idea that someone was trying to intimidate her. Did the unflappable Ms. Bishop have a temper?

Jerry cocked his head. "Why can't I? You're the new chair of a multimillion-dollar foundation."

Symone squared her shoulders. "These threats aren't connected to the foundation. What would I walk away from?"

She was hiding something. Jerry felt it like the hair twitching on his arms. He exchanged a look with Mal on his right and Zeke on his left. Their expressions told him they sensed it, too. He caught the warning glint in Zeke's eyes. He wouldn't voice his suspicions. Yet. But her secrecy was giving him flashbacks to the rebellious pop star. He was glad he'd told his brothers he was going to pass on this case. He didn't need a repeat of that botched assignment.

Chapter 3

Symone struggled to hold Jerry's eyes without flinching. She sensed his suspicions and doubts. They were wearing her down. Somehow, he knew she was withholding information. They all knew. Were they psychic or did she have the worst poker face on the planet?

It wasn't easy to meet the skepticism darkening Jerry's midnight eyes, which were set in one of the most classically handsome faces she'd ever seen. All the Touré brothers were strikingly attractive. Their family resemblance was strong. They were tall and athletic, with sharp sienna features, deep-set, unfathomably dark eyes and strong, obstinate jawlines softened by full sensual lips.

As she met with them in their agency's conference room early Friday morning, Symone also noticed their differences. The eldest, Zeke, had an unmistakable air of authority. Mal was the quiet one who took in everything with an enigmatic expression. His personality contrasted the most with Jerry's. The youngest Touré gave the impression of a live, ungrounded electrical wire. His brash personality didn't detract from his good looks, though. It made him even more compelling.

Symone pulled her eyes from his and sent them around the long, narrow conference room. The cloud-white walls displayed oil paintings in black metal frames. The art-work was incredible, as good as any she'd seen in muse-ums around the world. From this distance, she couldn't read the artist's signature, even with her glasses. The im-ages celebrated well-known Ohio landmarks, including the Ohio Statehouse, the Cincinnati Observatory, the Paul Laurence Dunbar House, the Rock & Roll Hall of Fame and The Ohio State University Oval. Sunlight poured in through the rear floor-to-ceiling window overlooking the front parking lot. The window framed the treetops and a distant view of the city's outer belt, Interstate 270.

"As I said when we first arrived, the police are inves-tigating these threats." Paul stood as though to leave. "I don't need, nor do I want, a bodyguard."

Symone strained to keep her temper from her words. "Paul, could you please give us a few more minutes?" She waited for him to sit before returning her attention to the Touré brothers. "I reviewed the estimate you sent yester-day." She adjusted her glasses before opening the folder she'd placed on the table in front of her. The TSG estimate was on top. "According to your description, there would be four teams of two guards. Why two?"

"One consultant would remain with Paul and the other would monitor the perimeter." Jerry braced his forearms on the table. The position brought him closer to her. Sy-mone caught his scent, a combination of soap and mint that was oddly erotic.

Zeke's voice helped clear her head. "Our security pro-fessionals are discreet. They're trained to blend into our clients' routines without being disruptive."

Jerry continued the explanation. "You'll have four teams in seven-hour shifts. The hour overlap is for a more secure transition. They'll monitor inside and out, even while you're sleeping."

Symone looked up from the document. "I'm moving out of my mother's house tomorrow morning." Her two bags were already packed. She hadn't brought much with her. "Your teams will only be protecting Paul."

Jerry's frown didn't diminish his good looks. Could anything lessen their impact? "It would be better for you to remain together until the police catch the stalker—or *stalkers*. They could try to hurt you to get to Paul."

Symone assessed Jerry. "Will you be stationed on-site with your consultants?"

Jerry shook his head. She thought she saw regret in his eyes. "No, I won't. But they're well trained and very experienced."

Why did she feel disappointed? This situation was serious. Lives were at stake. It wasn't time to be developing crushes, especially on someone who was so obviously out of her league.

Symone frowned. "Dr. Grace Blackwell had enthusiastically recommended *you* specifically. She said your quick thinking and excellent instincts saved her grandmother from a killer."

Jerry's cheeks filled with dusky color. His reaction surprised Symone. She didn't think someone so confident could be disconcerted by praise. His obvious embarrassment made him seem more approachable—more mortal.

He lowered his eyes to the table. "That's nice of her. It was a pleasure protecting Melba."

Symone struggled to control a smile. "I understand Melba enjoyed having you as her bodyguard."

"Our consultants will be just as effective keeping you and Paul safe. My brothers and I put them through regular, rigorous training." Jerry seemed to have shaken off his discomfort and was back to full cocky mode.

Symone glanced at Paul. She wasn't certain she could count on his cooperation. But she wasn't doing this for him. She was doing it for her mother.

She turned back to the Touré brothers and gave a decisive nod. "Let's get started."

Symone pulled into the concrete driveway of her mother and stepfather's home in Upper Arlington. It was about half an hour after her Friday morning meeting with the Touré Security Group. Paul didn't wait for her to put the car in Park before stepping out on the passenger side. Symone watched him stride toward the house as she waited for Jerry to uncoil himself from the back seat. At six-feet-plus, he'd had to sit sideways in her silver four-door compact sedan. It couldn't have been a comfortable ride for him.

He closed the rear door, then took a few moments to scan the neighborhood and the facade of her mother's home. Was he getting a feel for the neighborhood—or waiting for the circulation to return to his legs?

All the Touré men were handsome, intelligent and successful. But there was something especially exciting about the impatient youngest brother. He was built like a runner, long and lean. As he stood with his back to her, Symone's eyes traveled over his broad shoulders clothed in a sapphire blue, long-sleeved shirt. She paused on the black slacks hugging his slim hips and long legs. Jerry turned and she quickly lifted her gaze.

His loose-limbed strides brought him to her. "Beautiful house in a beautiful neighborhood."

Symone's cheeks were burning. Did he know she'd been staring at his butt? She'd never done anything like that before. "Yes. It's very clean and quiet. My mother liked living here. Most of her neighbors are—were—grandparents whose children and grandchildren visited every weekend."

Nervous chatter. She forced herself to stop and take a breath.

The houses in the area were similar. The modern Craftsman homes were dark brick with white, cream or tan siding and solid wood front doors. The lawns were in the same rich, healthy condition, which wasn't surprising considering most of the neighbors, including her mother, had the same landscape service.

Jerry tossed her a smile that made her knees tremble. "Did she use that to put pressure on you to settle down and start a family?"

For the first time, the memory of her mother made her smile. "My mother wasn't in a hurry to become a grandmother." Symone turned to lead him into the house.

Paul had left the mahogany front door open as though welcoming them in. He turned from the bay window overlooking the front yard as Symone and Jerry entered the house. Had he been watching them?

Jerry examined the locks and threshold before closing and securing the door. His eyes lingered on the security panel on the left wall. He must be trying to figure out how a stranger had gained access to a home with an alarm system and multiple sturdy locks.

Symone gestured toward the rear of the house. "The police believe the stalker got in through the door off the deck."

Jerry shared a look between her and Paul. "Thanks for letting me tour your home. I'm looking for information that could help our consultants protect you."

Paul stepped forward. The glint in his eyes was a challenge. "How do I know you're not casing my house?"

"Paul!" Symone gasped. This would be a good time for
the ground to open up and swallow her. Before she could say
anything else—like humbly apologize for her stepfather's
piggish behavior—Jerry laughed.

His smile was genuine. Lights danced in his midnight
eyes. "Are you suggesting my brothers and I use Touré
Security Group as cover for a burglary ring?"

Paul squared up to the younger man as though Jerry, who
looked like he worked out for fun and entertainment, didn't
have at least four inches on him. "That seem funny to you?"

"Paul!" Symone unclenched her teeth. "There's nothing
funny about your behavior. You're being extremely rude."

Jerry raised a hand, palm out. "No. Wait. We can give
you references in addition to Grace's, if that would make
you feel more comfortable about hiring us. You could even
talk with Detectives Duster and Stenhardt."

Paul scowled up at Jerry for a moment longer. Jerry's
smile never faltered. Finally, Paul stepped back. "No, never
mind."

Symone exhaled her relief. "I'm terribly sorry about
what just happened." She shot a glare toward Paul. He'd
never have behaved that way if her mother had still been
alive. "Grace's recommendation is enough for me. Are you
still willing to work with us?"

"Of course." Jerry seemed unfazed.

Amazing. If their roles had been reversed, Symone
would have been shattered. She would've walked away
from the assignment without looking back.

"I'm glad." Symone's gratitude eased her tension. "Let's
start that tour."

In addition to the two-car garage, her mother's home

had three floors and an attic. The main level was an open floor plan. Her mother had deferred to Paul, who'd hired an interior designer. The rooms on the main floor were heavy with crimson red and old gold accents, including wall-to-wall deep gold carpeting.

"How long have you lived here?" Jerry considered the bay window's locks and framing.

"Odette and I moved in shortly after we married almost two years ago." Paul's voice was still stiff with resentment.

Symone hadn't been surprised when her mother had told her she was selling the family home so she and Paul could have a fresh start with a house of their own. She could understand why Paul wouldn't have wanted to move into a home with so many memories. Her mother had understood as well. Odette cared enough to sell their family home to start a new life with Paul. It was out of respect for her mother's feelings for Paul that Symone was doing what she could to help keep him safe even if he was opposed to it.

She trailed the men as Paul led the tour, striding through the living room, dining room, kitchen and foyer. Jerry followed at his own pace. In each room, he examined the windows and tested their locks. He checked the entrance door in the garage, as well as the ones in the basement and kitchen. He spent extra time examining the French doors off the foyer that led out to the wide Honeywood deck.

"What are you thinking?" Symone watched as he stood outside, running his hand along the doors' threshold.

"None of your doors or windows were forced open." His attention was on the doorway. "There aren't any splinters or grooves in the wood or scratches on the locks." Jerry caught her eyes. "Have either of you lost your house keys?"

Paul's eyes stretched wide in surprise. "You think the intruder had a key?" His voice rose with horror.

Jerry reentered the house and secured the door. "I don't know how else to explain someone breaking in without damaging the doors, locks or windows."

"I've been using my mother's key." Symone turned to Paul. "You still have your key, right?"

"Of course." Paul sounded shocked. "And those are the only keys in existence, Odette's and mine. We've never made copies."

Jerry's eyes were dark with concern. "You should change your locks. Somehow someone got a copy of your keys."

Paul looked from Jerry to Symone and back. "Why didn't the police tell us this?"

Jerry shook his head. "I don't know."

Paul looked confused and suspicious, as though he couldn't bring himself to believe what Jerry was saying. Symone made a mental note to make sure Paul changed the locks.

She stepped back, preparing to leave the foyer. "We've shown you the basement and this main floor. Paul, could you take us upstairs, please?"

She followed Paul up the winding carpeted staircase. Her skin tingled with awareness of Jerry's presence behind her.

"May I ask how your wife died?" Jerry's voice was soft sympathy. Still, Symone's back stiffened.

Paul's voice was husky. "Odette had a heart condition. She'd had it for years and had been managing it with prescription medication." He reached the top floor and turned left, leading Symone and Jerry toward the room he'd shared with Odette. "Recently, she'd been feeling weaker. She'd called her doctor, who'd assured her she was fine. Everything was fine, including her prescription. Two days later, she had a heart attack and died."

"I'm so sorry for your loss." Jerry paused a moment before continuing. "You're suing her doctor because he said she was fine days before her heart attack?"

Paul crossed into his bedroom. "That's right. As well as the pharmaceutical company who made her medication. A friend who's also a lawyer and a member of the foundation's board suggested the lawsuits. He's representing me. It's taking a long time to wind through court, though, but I'm determined to make someone pay for Odette's death. This wasn't her time. She'd been taking her medication. She was exercising and watching her diet. She wasn't supposed to die now."

Jerry scanned the room before crossing to the window. "There's no way for anyone to sneak in through these windows. They'd need a ladder." He crossed to the windows on the other side of the room. "It's the same here. The intruder would've been noticed and one of your neighbors would've called the police."

Symone rubbed her arms to dispel a sudden chill. The image of intruders who were intent on harming her family climbing through their windows was alarming. "That's what we thought as well."

Jerry turned back to the room. "Did you have your mother's medication tested?"

Startled, Symone exchanged a look with Paul. "No, we hadn't thought of that."

Paul scowled, something he was doing more and more of since her mother's death. "Why hadn't Wes suggested that?"

Jerry addressed Paul. "Would you mind if I take a sample of your wife's medication and ask Grace to test it?"

Paul looked at Jerry over his shoulder. "What do you think you'll find?"

Jerry shrugged. "We might not find anything, but there's no harm in checking, is there?"

"No, there's not." Symone crossed to her mother's nightstand where she knew Odette kept her prescription. She took the bottle from the top drawer and gave it to Jerry. "Thank you for the suggestion. I'd like the tablets to be tested."

"I'll take care of it." Jerry scanned the label before putting the bottle in his front pants pocket.

"Great." Now that Jerry had brought up testing her mother's medication, Symone wanted answers yesterday. She turned toward the bedroom door, fisting her hands to contain her impatience. "If you're done here, we'll give you a tour of the foundation's offices."

The Bishop Foundation operated from a suite on the top floor of a four-story concrete-and-glass building off Riverside Drive near Interstate 670. Symone and Paul gave Jerry a complete tour starting with the parking lot before taking him into the building and up the elevator to the foundation's headquarters.

Jerry followed Symone and Paul from the elevator. What he'd seen so far hadn't impressed him. Why was security the last thing companies considered—if they considered it at all?

"There aren't any security cameras around the building's perimeter, in the parking lot, or in the lobby." He looked around the small elevator lobby between the two sets of glass doors leading to the foundation suite. Disappointing. "There aren't any here, either."

Symone spoke over her shoulder as Paul pushed open one of the glass doors. "The foundation doesn't own this building, but if you think it's important, we can address security with the property management company."

Jerry held the door as Symone walked through. "It's very important. At a minimum, there should be security cameras and guards. How many employees do you have?"

Symone paused just inside the suite. "We're a small organization. We have twelve full-time staff, including my mother, Paul and me. Well, Paul and me. There are seven board members, but they aren't staff."

Jerry paced beside Symone. She stopped several times to exchange greetings and a few words with employees. She asked after them and their family members. In response, her staff asked about her. More than one person hugged her. With each employee, her demeanor was warm and attentive as though there was nothing on her mind other than the person in front of her.

"Her mother was the same way." Paul made the comment as he watched Symone once again stop to speak with a member of her staff. "I told Odette she'd get a lot more done during regular office hours if she limited these distractions."

For some reason, Paul's words irritated Jerry. He'd noticed no one stopped to speak with Symone's stepfather. "Maybe Symone and her mother realize that these distractions contribute to employee satisfaction and the foundation's success."

The tour of the foundation's offices didn't take long. The open floor plan, bright colors and natural light streaming into the main room from the near floor-to-ceiling windows made the workplace feel like a cheerful and positive environment. The suite was laid out so the elevator lobby was in the center. This allowed people to access it by two sets of doors, one on the east side of the floor and the other to the west. They'd entered the offices through the glass doors on the east. But by walking around the office, they could return to the elevators using glass doors on the west.

Large pale gray cubicles grew up from the thin powder blue carpeting. There were four glass-and-wood-paneled offices, one in each corner of the floor. Other areas included a small kitchen-cum-lunch room, a small conference room, a large boardroom, a women's restroom and a men's restroom.

Jerry looked over his shoulder, scanning the area one more time. "Both doors to the suites should be keycard access only. People should only be able to enter through one of the doors, making the second door an exit only."

Symone narrowed her eyes as though trying to visualize the process he described. "We don't have security threats."

Jerry's eyebrows shot up his forehead. "You have one now. Think about what's already happened. The stalker broke into your mother's home without leaving a scratch. That's with a security system and all the doors and windows locked. Here, there isn't anything preventing them from getting to you and Paul."

Paul rubbed his chin. "Maybe he's right. We can do with a few cameras for our safety."

Jerry followed Symone and Paul into Symone's office. "Set them up in public spaces. Hallways, lobbies, the parking lot. But you need more than cameras. You should have security guards monitoring the grounds and the lobby. These are investments meant to keep you safe, especially since there's an active threat—"

"Symone! I was told you wouldn't be in today." A well-dressed, middle-aged white man entered the room.

The stranger's bottle green eyes scrutinized Jerry at the same time Jerry assessed the newcomer. The other man had perfect thick, wavy blond hair. Like Paul, he wore his wealth. The cost of his black Italian shoes, three-piece dark brown pin-striped suit and black silk shirt was probably enough to send a student to a four-year college.

Symone's smile didn't reach her eyes. Interesting. "Good morning, Xander. Is there something you need?"

"Hello, Paul." Xander offered Symone's stepfather a smile before responding to Symone. His grin revealed dazzling white teeth. "I wanted to ask if you need help preparing for the upcoming board meeting. If so, I'm happy to offer you my services."

Symone's smile remained fixed in place. "Thank you for your generous offer, but I can handle the report on my own."

Xander inclined his head in a gallant motion. "Well, my dear, if you change your mind, please feel free to give me a call. I know you have a lot of experience with finance and investments, but those are my areas of specialty as well. If you'd like us to put our heads together, I'm happy to brainstorm some ideas with you."

Symone stepped back from him and toward her desk. "That's very kind of you. Thank you."

"Of course, my dear." Xander turned to Jerry. His hand was outstretched. "Xander Fence."

Jerry accepted the handshake. "Good to meet you."

Xander's eyebrows, a darker blond than his hair, knitted at Jerry's refusal to identify himself. He hesitated as though he was going to say something more. Instead he released Jerry's hand.

Symone's manners were impeccable. Jerry suspected she had a reason for not introducing them. It wasn't up to him to satisfy the other man's curiosity if his client wasn't going to. Was he wrong? He glanced at Symone. Humor twinkled in her brown eyes as she observed their exchange. When she noticed him watching her, she lowered her eyes and sat behind her desk. She set her silver purse beside her keyboard.

Jerry waited until Xander disappeared beyond the doorway. "Who was that?"

Paul shoved his hands into his front pockets. "Xander's a banking executive and one of our newest board members."

Symone stood, adjusting her purse on her shoulder. "I don't have any messages that need to be returned right away. Let's—"

A woman hurried into the office. "Symone, I'm so glad I caught you." In her purple, figure-hugging, knee-length, polyester dress and three-inch, black stilettos, she looked like she'd walked out of a scene from a soap opera. Jerry waited for the theme song to roll. "There are some messages I need your input on before responding. One of the—"

Symone interrupted her. "Ellie, can those messages wait?" She checked her watch as she circled her desk. "Paul and I have an errand to run. We'll be right back."

Ellie followed Symone as she left the office. "I'm afraid they can't." She glanced over her shoulder, giving Jerry a curious look. "Hello."

Jerry inclined his head. It wasn't as gallant a gesture as Xander's. Symone didn't introduce him this time, either. Why not? He didn't think she was capable of bad manners.

Symone strode out of the office with Ellie hot on her heels. Paul and Jerry followed. "Then we'll have to walk and talk."

There was something exciting about seeing Symone in this environment where she was in charge, multitasking as people came to her with issues, comments and questions.

She'd dispatched Xander with grace and confidence. With Ellie, she was courteous and efficient.

The elevator came quickly. Ellie started talking as soon as they boarded it to return to the lobby. "There are several issues on the list."

"Take them one at a time." Symone's voice was patient.

Ellie tossed her auburn mane behind her right shoulder. "All right. The first one is those new numbers you wanted me to get." She glanced at Jerry before lowering her voice. "Are you certain it's okay to talk about this here?"

Symone frowned. "You said these issues couldn't wait. Either tell me what's going on now or wait for me to return."

Ellie shrugged. "All right." The elevator doors opened, and she followed Symone across the lobby. "The first issue is the numbers. I think the information the financial institution pulled for us is wrong."

Symone gave her a sharp look as she pushed through the exit. "What makes you think that?"

Ellie followed her from the building. "They seem too low based on the trending from the year-to-date prospectus we just received."

Symone dug into her purse and pulled out her car keys. "Ask them to rerun the numbers."

Ellie hurried to keep up with her boss. "That might delay our report and cause us to miss the board's deadline."

Symone paused on the sidewalk. "If the numbers are wrong, we can't use them. We'll worry about the deadline if it comes to that."

She was at least thirty yards away when she pointed her keyless entry device toward the tiny torture machine she called a car. Jerry wasn't looking forward to folding himself onto the back seat again. Symone pressed the device as she stepped off the sidewalk—and her car exploded.

The blast was loud enough to make Jerry briefly double over in pain. It shook the trees surrounding the parking lot. Red, orange and yellow flames engulfed the vehicle. Black smoke rose up, stretching toward the sky.

Symone gasped, jumping back onto the sidewalk.

Ellie screamed.

Paul shouted. "What the—"

Without stopping to think, Jerry leaped forward, pushing Symone and Ellie back into the building. "Come on!" His shout shook Paul from his trance.

Jerry stood behind Symone and Ellie, desperate to use his body to shield them. Was the car bomb the only attack? He didn't know, but he wasn't waiting to find out. The stalker could be close, waiting to strike while the explosion distracted them.

"What just happened?" Ellie's voice was strident with fear. "What's happening?" She kept repeating those questions as though waiting for someone to answer. No one could.

Symone was shaking. She was as pale as a ghost. Behind her glasses, her eyes almost swallowed her face.

Jerry scanned her features, neck and shoulders. "Are you all right?"

"Yes." Her response was a thin breath.

Jerry looked at Ellie and Paul. "Are you okay?"

They nodded, staring at him with wide clouded eyes.

His attention swung back to Symone as he pulled his cell phone from his pocket. "Remember I told you I thought you were the target?" He waited for her nod. "We need a new plan."

Chapter 4

"Are you all right?" Zeke crossed The Bishop Foundation's lobby late Friday morning. Mal was close behind him. Their approach was quick but stiff and jerky.

Jerry excused himself from the group he'd been speaking with and strode to meet his brothers halfway. Through the building's Plexiglas facade behind the two men, he saw the flashing red and blue lights of the emergency vehicles that had responded to his call about the explosion. Police and firefighters had arrived within minutes. He shouldn't be surprised his brothers had shown up seconds later even without the advantage of lights and sirens.

Zeke and Mal stopped in front of Jerry. Their spare features were tight. Their eyes were dark with fear, concern and anger. Both men looked Jerry over as though reassuring themselves the youngest Touré was safe and unhurt despite the danger he'd been in.

Jerry frowned at Zeke. "What are you doing here? I called Mal."

Zeke arched a thick eyebrow. "*Car bomb*, Jer? Did you expect me to sit at my desk, twiddling my thumbs?" He squeezed Jerry's right shoulder.

Mal gripped Jerry's left upper arm. "Did you think I wouldn't tell him?"

Zeke's dark eyes held him in place. "You may think you're invincible, but we know better."

Jerry felt the faint tremor in Zeke's and Mal's hands. His muscles relaxed. They were shaken, just as he would've been had the situation been reversed. He placed a hand on each of their shoulders and offered a small smile. "It's all good, guys. No one was hurt. We were far enough from Symone's car. Our clients are upset and scared, of course, but physically fine." He directed their attention over his shoulder. "Duster and Stenhardt just got here."

He turned to lead his brothers across the lobby to Symone and Paul, who waited with their administrative assistant and the two Columbus police department homicide detectives.

Eriq Duster's jaded ebony eyes twinkled and his stern, dark features eased into a welcoming smile as the Touré brothers approached. "Next time we get the band back together, let's make it a beer instead of a bomb."

The veteran detective was creeping toward retirement. He resembled an aging pugilist in his comfortable lightweight brown sports coat, pressed black pants, crisp white shirt and bolo tie with a bronze slide clip in the shape of a trout.

Zeke's smile was stiff around the edges. "I can get behind that." He turned to Symone and Paul. "We're glad you're both okay."

"I don't know if you could call us okay." Paul's tone was harsh. Anger seemed to be masking the fear that shook his words.

Eriq looked away from Paul as though giving him time to settle down. He turned his smile to Mal. Faint laugh lines bracketed his full lips. "How's Dr. Grace?"

Mal's expression brightened. "She's well. Thanks."

"Tell her we said hello." Detective Taylor Stenhardt had gathered her heavy, honey blond hair into a bun at her nape. It seemed too heavy for her long, slender neck. Her dancer's figure was clothed in a dark blue, lightweight suit.

Jerry gestured toward Ellie. "Eleanor Press, my brothers and business partners, Hezekiah and Malachi. Eleanor is Symone's administrative assistant."

Ellie seemed distracted as she greeted the elder Tourés. She hadn't been far from Symone's side since the bombing.

Eriq addressed Symone and Paul. "Is there somewhere we can talk privately?"

Symone glanced at Jerry. The uncertainty in her chocolate eyes triggered his protective instincts. He stepped closer to her.

"We can use the boardroom." She adjusted her glasses. "This way, please."

Symone led them to the two elevators at the rear of the lobby. Jerry braced his hand on the small of her back. Her muscles eased by degrees against his palm. A thick, tense silence followed them. Symone, Paul and Ellie seemed lost in thought. Did anyone have theories about the car bomb? Who would have planted it, and when, how or why?

As they waited for the elevator to arrive, Zeke, Mal, Eriq and Taylor surveyed the bronze-and-white-tiled area. He knew they were taking in the lack of security cameras and guards. At his first opportunity, he was going to talk with Zeke and Mal about submitting a proposal to the building owners for TSG's security services. He was leaving the company, but that didn't mean he didn't care about the family business any longer. Just the opposite.

An elevator arrived after a short wait. It was a cozy fit for the eight of them but a quick ride to the foundation's fourth-floor offices. Symone led them past the gauntlet of startled, curious and concerned employees into the board-room. She took the chair at the head of the long, oval, dark wood table surrounded by ten cushioned dark wood chairs. Jerry took the seat on her right, followed by Zeke and Mal. Paul took the seat on Symone's left. Ellie and Taylor filed in behind him. Eriq took the chair at the foot of the table.

The veteran detective opened his notebook. "Ms. Bishop, how long had your car been unattended in the parking lot?"

"Um." Symone adjusted her black-rimmed glasses as she took a moment to think. "Less than an hour. Paul and I gave Jerry a tour of the foundation. As you can see, our offices aren't very big. Then Paul and I were going to take Jerry back to his office. So, yes, less than an hour." She looked to Paul for verification.

Paul nodded. "I'd agree with that." He sounded much calmer now.

Taylor's piercing jade green eyes were wide in her fair skin. She gestured toward the large picture window at the back of the conference room. "That would give the bomber plenty of time to plant the device. And since there aren't security cameras around the perimeter of the building, the parking lot or the lobby, they could've done so without anyone noticing."

"You've reported previous threats." Eriq swung his pen between Symone and Paul. "We'll follow up with your wife's doctor's office and with the pharmaceutical company. Is there anyone else you can think of who might want to harm you?"

Paul glanced at Symone. "No, there's no one else."

Eriq's eyes narrowed just a bit. The seasoned detective seemed to sense Paul wasn't being honest. He lifted his chin toward Symone. "What about you? Can you think of anyone who'd want to hurt you?"

Symone blinked behind her glasses. "Me? I'm not the one being threatened."

Jerry's lips parted. From his seat on Symone's right, he shifted to face her. "You *still* think *Paul's* the target? *Your* car was the one they bombed."

Eriq waved his pen toward Jerry. "Jerry's right. Since it was your car, we have to ask who'd want to kill you. Or perhaps they want to get to you *and* your stepfather."

Symone frowned at Jerry. "The first threat was in Paul and Mom's home."

"With you in it." Jerry counted the threats on his fingers. "The second was in a restaurant parking lot after you and Paul had dinner. This third involved *your* car."

Paul interrupted. "Maybe they're right, Symone. Maybe the threats are for both of us."

Jerry had his doubts, but if the suggestion made Symone more agreeable, he'd go with it. He shared a look between Symone and Paul. "Pack whatever you need for the foreseeable future. Neither one of you is coming back here until the detectives have whoever's after you in custody."

Symone straightened on her chair. "I can't just walk away from the foundation. I have responsibilities."

Ellie leaned forward to catch Symone's attention. "Symone, really, your safety is the most important issue right now. The board will understand."

"No." Symone shook her head adamantly. "The board can't know that anything's wrong."

Mal nodded toward the boardroom door. "They've probably already heard about the car bomb." His tone was dry.

Symone scowled. Jerry sensed her mind racing. He felt her tension rising.

Ellie extended her arms toward Paul and Symone. "You both can work remotely until this stalker's caught. There's no reason you can't, and I'm sure this investigation won't take long."

Zeke addressed Jerry. "I've asked Celeste Jarrett to help us with this case."

Eriq somber expression eased into an uncharacteristic grin. "CJ's on board? That's great. She'll help you get to the bottom of this case in a snap."

Celeste was an ex-CPD homicide detective. Several years ago, she and her partner had left the department and opened a private investigation agency.

"I agree with Eriq." Taylor's tone was almost apologetic. "And I'm afraid you don't have a choice, Ms. Bishop. It's the only way to protect you."

Symone closed her eyes briefly. A red flush highlighted her cheekbones. "This doesn't make sense." She looked from Paul to Jerry. "Why would someone want to harm me?"

Jerry cocked his head. "I think we need to figure that out and fast. Don't you?"

"Welcome back, Tourés." Kevin Apple looked up from his U-shaped gray laminate reception desk as Jerry led his brothers, Symone and Paul through the agency's Plexiglas doors late Friday morning. "Glad you're okay, Jerry."

This was the twenty-something's fifth week as TSG's administrative assistant. It hadn't taken him long to fit into the company and prove his value to the team. After media coverage of the brothers' success protecting Dr. Grace Blackwell and finding a serial killer, their security company's new client intake email and phone lines had been overwhelmed. TSG wasn't the little-security-company-that-could anymore.

When their parents had launched the company, they'd replied to emails and answered calls themselves. They took pride in knowing long-term as well as prospective customers who contacted the firm were speaking with a member of the family. But after Grace's high-profile case, the brothers couldn't keep up with the flood of requests and new client inquiries. They'd needed help. Kevin was a quick study, efficient, organized and cordial. During his interview, he'd stated he wanted to be a personal security consultant. Jerry had put him on a training schedule, which was going well. TSG would need to find a new admin soon.

"Thanks, Kev. I appreciate your concern." Jerry gestured to his right. "These are our clients, Symone Bishop, chair of The Bishop Foundation, and her stepfather, Paul Kayple, the foundation's vice chair. Symone, Paul, Kevin Apple is our administrative assistant."

Kevin inclined his head. "It's nice to meet you." He looked again to Jerry. "Celeste Jarrett's waiting in the large conference room."

Jerry looked the younger man over. His eyebrows knitted with confusion. "Did you get a haircut?"

The admin had subdued his twisted high top to a curly low fade much more like Jerry's. He also was wearing a crimson long-sleeved cotton shirt with an ebony stripe down the left side. Jerry had an identical shirt somewhere in his closet.

Kevin's smile was sheepish. His cheeks filled with a hint of rose. "Yeah." He ran a hand over his tight dark curls.

Jerry turned his confusion to Zeke and Mal. His brothers shrugged their eyebrows.

Zeke turned to Symone and Paul. "This way, please." He led the five-member group down the short hallway to their large conference room at the back of their suite.

Celeste had taken one of the black cushioned chairs on the left side of the large, rectangular glass-and-sterling-silver table. She arched a straight dark eyebrow as they entered the room. "So is TSG going into investigations now?"

"Thank you for coming, Celeste." Zeke stopped in front of her and offered his hand.

Celeste took it. Her slightly irritated expression eased into surprise. Zeke's tense features relaxed. Celeste tugged free, and the moment was lost almost as though it had never happened.

But Jerry knew what he'd seen. His eldest brother had been shaken out of his comfort zone. Interesting.

Zeke took the seat at the head of the table, putting Celeste on his right. He cleared his throat. "To answer your question, no, we're not moving into investigations. That's why we're asking for your help." He made quick work of the introductions before starting the meeting.

"What's the case?" Celeste's piercing hazel brown eyes leaped from Jerry beside her to Mal at the foot of the table, and Symone and Paul across from her before returning to Zeke.

Celeste had launched Jarrett & Nichols Investigations with her former partner, Nanette Nichols. Rumor had it Celeste and Nanette had been detectives for less than two years when crooked cops had framed them for their criminal activities. They'd been kicked off the force and charged for the crimes. It had taken courage and strength of will for them to prove their innocence, restore their reputations and put the real criminals behind bars. The department had wanted to reinstate them, but the experience had been so bad, Celeste and Nanette had agreed to decline the offer and start their own investigative agency. Eriq had worked with both women. He never said much about Nanette, but he took every opportunity to talk up Celeste. He seemed almost paternal toward her.

Paul scowled across the table at Celeste. "Someone's trying to kill us."

"All right." Celeste pulled out a notebook. She looked from Paul to Symone and then Zeke.

The private investigator was dressed in a black cotton T-shirt beneath a gray blazer, black jeans and gray flats. There was a plain sterling silver ring on her right thumb.

Zeke gestured toward Jerry. "Jerry's taking point on this."

Jerry scanned the faces around the table as he collected his thoughts. Diagonally across from him, Symone looked distracted, as though she was developing arguments against Jerry's assertion that she was the real target. Beside her, Paul's frown was a indicator of his short temper. At the foot of the table, Mal's features were inscrutable to anyone who didn't know him. Jerry was certain his brother already had a strategy for the case but was waiting for everyone else to catch up. On Jerry's left, Celeste's serene expression was fake. He felt the vibrations of her impatience to get moving, to do something. Zeke sat back against his cushioned seat, waiting for Jerry to lead the discussion. Jerry brought Celeste up to speed with the timeline, the two previous threats, culminating with the bomb planted in Symone's car.

Celeste looked between Symone and Paul. "Walk away from what?"

Symone's breath was unsteady. "We'd thought the message was meant for Paul because of his malpractice lawsuit against my mother's doctor and the suit against the pharmaceutical company that made her medication." She threw a quick look toward Jerry before turning her attention back to Celeste. "But now I'm not sure." Her voice dwindled.

"We now think the threats are targeting Paul *and* Symone." Jerry's gut was telling him the threats were meant for Symone with the intent of separating her from her family's foundation. It was a theory worth looking into. "We need your help identifying who's behind these attempts on their lives. We've worked one investigation, but the scope was much narrower. We need your expertise."

"Of course." Celeste inclined her head. "You're right to be concerned." She turned her attention to Symone on the other side of the table. "The threats are intensifying. First, someone broke into your home and left behind a threatening message. Next, someone followed you with the intent of terrorizing you with their car. Did they intentionally miss you? We don't know. Today, they planted a bomb in your car while it was parked outside your place of employment. Their messages are clear. They're in charge. They can reach you whenever, wherever, however."

Paul scowled. "We didn't need you to tell us that. We figured that out ourselves." His voice was almost a growl. Jerry heard the fear underneath.

Mal spoke over Paul. "The timing's an issue as well."

Symone's eyes flickered toward Jerry before redirecting to Mal. "What do you mean?" Her question was cautious.

Mal spread his hands above the conference table. "The time between the attacks is shrinking. You received the first one July third. Five days later, on July eighth, you were almost run over. Three days later, today, your car was bombed."

"He's right." Celeste made another note in her book. "Whoever wants you to leave is getting impatient."

Paul swept his arm in a stiff, jerky motion toward Celeste diagonally across from him. "You're deliberately trying to scare us."

Jerry arched an eyebrow. "We shouldn't have to scare you

into taking these threats seriously. The car bomb should've been enough. This isn't—"

Paul cut him off. "The police are aware of these threats. They're doing their own investigation. We don't need a private investigator getting in the way nor do we need bodyguards."

Zeke's dark eyes flared in a way that people who knew him took extra care. "Celeste Jarrett will not be in the way. As you'll remember, the detectives spoke highly of her and were pleased that she'll be partnering with us on your case."

Jerry and Mal exchanged a look. Zeke had jumped to a stern defense of Celeste without hesitation. Interesting.

Symone touched the back of Paul's hand where it lay on the table between them. "Paul, they're right. My car's destroyed. We could've been standing beside it if not seated inside. The more experienced help we have to stop these threats, the faster all of this will be over, and we can get back to normal."

Her tremors were visible. Jerry's hands itched with the need to console her.

"No." Paul bit off his response. He took a deep breath and managed to regain his calm. "The message was clear. Whoever is sending these threats wants us to walk away. That's what I'm going to do. You should, too, Symone."

Jerry frowned at Paul. "Walk away from what?" The hairs on the back of his neck tightened. Why was Paul so opposed to their help?

Paul glowered at him. "I'm dropping the lawsuits. I don't want to, but they're playing hardball." He turned to Symone again. "And I'm leaving Columbus. I'm going to ask my brother if I could stay with him in North Carolina at least until things settle down here. You're welcome to come with me."

Symone's eyes were wide behind her black-rimmed glasses. "What about Mom? I thought the purpose of the lawsuits was to get justice for her?"

Jerry detected a thread of anger and something else under her words. Perhaps betrayal? He rubbed his chest, surprised by the pain that was like a tight grip on his heart.

Paul's jaw dropped as though Symone's questions surprised him. "Symone, our lives are in danger. Someone's threatening us. Do you think your mother would want that? Of course not. If we leave, the threats will stop and then you can come back or do whatever you want."

Her eyebrows knitted. "I can't leave Columbus. I have a responsibility to the foundation."

Paul glanced around the table before facing Symone again. "Your parents wouldn't want you to stay with the foundation if it was putting your life in danger. Your mother would be the first person to tell us to leave for our safety's sake."

"No, she wouldn't." Symone's objection was quiet but firm.

Jerry wondered what Paul saw as he searched Symone's face. If they were seeing the same thing, then Paul also witnessed her unwavering courage and unbreakable determination. It was in the stubborn tilt of her rounded chin and the fierce directness of her chocolate brown eyes.

Paul leaned back against the black cushioned chair. "We'll have to agree to disagree."

Symone shook her head. "My mother and father wouldn't want me to run away and abandon the foundation. They wouldn't want me to turn my back on the legacy my grandfather left us. They believed in his goal of improving the quality of people's lives." She gestured toward Jerry. "The Touré Security Group and Celeste can provide both of us with protection and help us find the person behind these threats."

Paul drew a deep breath, then blew it out. "Well, Symone, you can do whatever you want, of course, but I'm leaving."

Symone stared at him. Jerry sensed she wanted to say something more, but after several tense seconds she nodded, then looked away. Her grief drifted across the table to him.

He turned to Paul. "We could provide you with a bodyguard while you prepare to leave." He lifted his hand to stop the other man from interrupting. "The agent will be unobtrusive. He or she will keep you safe just until you're ready to leave."

Paul scanned the table. "No. Absolutely not."

"We'll respect your decision, Paul." Zeke stood, effectively ending the meeting. Jerry and Mal stood with him. He turned to Celeste. "Please send us your contract. We'll schedule a videoconference once we've secured Symone."

Celeste stood, setting her black tote bag on her right shoulder. "Sounds good." She addressed Symone. "You're in good hands with the Tourés. And I've worked plenty of investigations like yours, both on the force and with my agency. Let us do our jobs. We'll keep you safe and put this stalker behind bars."

Symone rose from her seat. Her eyes were clouded behind her glasses. "Thank you."

Celeste nodded, then turned to leave. Zeke escorted her from the conference room.

Jerry stepped away from his chair, pulling a small brown plastic bottle from his front pants pocket. He drew Mal aside and lowered his voice. "Could you ask Grace to test these pills? We need to know what's in them and what effect they would have on the user."

Mal examined the bottle. "What are they?"

"Odette Bishop's prescription medication." He inclined his head toward Paul. "He believes it might have contributed to her death."

Mal gave Jerry a sharp look. There was concern in his dark eyes. "I'll take it to Grace this afternoon. We're having lunch." He crossed to Symone, jerking his head toward the suite's entrance. "I need to get you set up with a burner cell and laptop."

Symone frowned her confusion. "I already have a laptop and phone."

Mal shook his head as he stepped back, gesturing for her to precede him. "These devices are clean. They're set up with VPNs to mask your location. That way, no one can track you while you're in the safe house."

Paul pushed himself to his feet. "And where will this safe house be?"

Mal glanced at Jerry before responding to Paul. "The location is confidential."

Paul scowled. "But I'm her stepfather. That information doesn't have to be confidential to me."

Symone faced her stepfather. "You're leaving, Paul. You have no reason to know my location. And I agree with the Touré policy to limit that information." She turned back to Mal. "Shall we go?"

Once Mal and Symone disappeared down the hall, Jerry held the door for Paul. "I'll ask Mal to drive you home. We'll meet you in the reception area. I need to get some things from my office."

He watched Paul stalk to the front of the suite before turning to his office a few steps from the conference room. He wound his way around the empty supply boxes and piles of old newspapers and magazines and supply catalogs. At his desk, Jerry shoved aside a few file folders and two dirty coffee mugs to get to his laptop. He powered down the machine and disconnected it from the surge protector before packing it into the laptop bag he'd found under his desk.

"Good grief! Is this your office?" The scandalized exclamation shattered Jerry's thoughts.

He looked up to find Symone swaying in his doorway. Her lips were parted in shock. Her eyes were wide and dashing around his office as though looking for a safe place to land.

Voices shrieked in horror in Symone's head. "How could anyone possibly work in this space?"

From Jerry's stunned expression, she realized she'd spoken that last part out loud.

"I'm in the process of packing up my office. I'm leaving the company." Jerry stopped speaking, as though he hadn't meant to confide so much to a client.

Symone stepped back in case gnats were congregating in that space. She was appalled, but she couldn't look away. The rest of the Touré Security Group's suite was impeccable, gleaming metal, polished wood, exquisite artwork. She hadn't expected to find a landfill in the center of a professional office. And what was that smell? She was going to have nightmares.

His response finally penetrated her shock. She tore her eyes away. "You're what? Why would you leave your family's company?"

Jerry jerked his laptop bag onto his shoulder. He circled his desk. Maneuvering the dark gray carpet like a minefield, he was careful to sidestep a stack of books. "We don't have time to discuss my future. We have to get you to the safe house."

Symone stepped aside, giving him room to join her in the hallway. "Are you going to be my bodyguard?" Did he hear the dread in her voice?

"That's right." Jerry stopped beside her, close enough for her to catch his clean-soap-and-peppermint scent. "Did Mal set you up with the burner tech?"

She nodded. "He said the stalker is probably tracking my movements through my devices."

"That's right." Jerry pinned her with his dark eyes. "So it's vital that you do *not* turn on any of your personal devices. Only use the burner cell and laptop Mal gave you. If you turn on your own equipment, the stalker will be able to track them again and we'll be right back where we started. You'll be in danger again—or worse. Do you understand?"

"Yes, I understand." Symone's eyes strayed back to his office. She tried to suppress a shiver. "It's just… I thought you were going to assign one of your contractors to the job?"

Jerry shook his head. "The assignment is dangerous and too complicated since it's both an investigation and protective detail." He shifted to face her. "So until the stalker is identified, we're stuck with each other."

Symone looked at Jerry's office again. *Oh, boy.*

Chapter 5

Symone's body had cried out for a nap by the time she and Jerry had entered their cabin in the wooded resort early Friday afternoon. This would be their temporary home until the police caught the stalker. But when Jerry had suggested lunch before giving her a tour of the cabin, her stomach had rumbled its approval. Either Jerry hadn't heard the noise, or he'd politely ignored it.

The safe house had stolen Symone's breath. It was a beautiful, two-story, dark-pine-and-red-cedar, post-and-beam log cabin. It stood in an idyllic spot at the back of a sprawling resort that one of Touré Security Group's clients owned. Symone had heard the pride in Jerry's voice when he'd informed her that TSG guards protected the resort's buildings and grounds. To the west and south, sturdy, old oak and evergreen trees sheltered the cabin from a distance. Symone wondered about the wildlife, fauna and hiking trails beyond the perimeter. A healthy, active river protected the cabin's eastern border. She imagined it would be a wonderful fishing spot. It seemed their cabin's closest neighbor was perhaps a mile or so north of them.

The cabin's great room was decorated in muted tones of warm tan, soft brown and moss green. An area rug in all three colors covered the pine flooring beneath the cedarwood coffee table. A stone fireplace was in front of the table. A matching overstuffed brown sofa and two chairs with ottomans were arranged around it. There was a dining area at the edge of the great room with a kitchenette beyond it. Both spaces picked up the colors from the great room.

The irony of the situation wasn't lost on Symone as she'd gazed around the cabin's warm, cozy interior when she'd first arrived. She was staying at a quiet, isolated cabin at an idyllic resort with the most attractive and exciting man she'd ever met. It would be so romantic—if someone wasn't trying to kill her.

Jerry was a surprisingly good cook. He'd made preparing their seared Cajun chicken, pasta and tossed salad lunch look easy. Symone could boil water for instant oatmeal and brew coffee, which explained her limited breakfast options. As she stared longingly at her now empty plate and salad bowl, she could still smell the sharp aromas of Cajun peppers and melted Parmesan cheese.

"I feel better now. Thank you." Symone drained the ice water from her glass and sighed. "I hate to sound like a broken record but truly, my compliments to the chef."

"I never get tired of hearing it." Jerry collected his dishes as he started to rise.

"No, please." She waved him back down. "You cooked. I'll clean. It's only fair." She stood, stacking his dishes and silverware on top of hers.

"You won't get an argument from me." His voice was thick with amusement.

Symone sensed him behind her. She set the dishes on the counter, raising her eyebrows as she looked from him to their clear acrylic glassware, which he set on the counter beside their place settings. "You won't argue. You'll just ignore me."

His grin was sheepish—and endearing. "I have a hard time sitting still."

Symone could believe it. Too bad he didn't expend that extra energy on keeping his office clean. She began packing the dishwasher. "Who do we have to thank for the groceries?"

"Zeke called the resort's manager to arrange to have the cabin opened and prepared for us with a week's worth of groceries and the rental car in the garage." He raised his voice over the sound of the running water as he scrubbed the pots and pans. His movements were confident and comfortable. Obviously, he wasn't opposed to washing dishes, just every other form of cleaning. Jeremiah Touré was a complex and complicated personality.

Symone wondered whether Zeke had made the call while Mal had taken her and Jerry to pack their bags before traveling on to the safe house. Jerry had accompanied her when she'd entered her mother and Paul's house to collect her two bags. She'd already packed her things since she's intended to move back to her place tomorrow. However, she'd been told to wait in the car with Mal while Jerry had packed his suitcase. Were those instructions for her security—or because Jerry hadn't wanted her to see the condition of his home? Would every room have been like his office? Her mind recoiled at the thought.

Jerry dried the last pan and stored it in one of the cupboards beside the oven. "Are you ready for the tour?" He waited for her nod before circling her to lead her from the kitchen. His scent, soap and peppermint, trailed after him. "You've seen this floor—great room, dining area, kitchenette. Let's go upstairs."

He swept up her two large suitcases, one in each hand,

as though they were beach towels. He held them as easily as he'd held the acrylic glass during their late lunch.

"I'll get the other bags later." His back muscles flexed beneath his amethyst shirt. Symone's eyebrows rose. Her fingertips tingled as though she'd felt the movement. She blinked, trying to break free of the sensation.

"Are you coming?" Jerry's question startled her.

Symone looked up to find him standing several steps up the staircase. He gave her a puzzled look. She blinked, then started toward him. "I'm sorry." She grabbed her laptop case, which held the computer Mal had given her.

His midnight eyes narrowed as they moved over her features. "This cabin is designed and reinforced as a panic room." Once again, in his voice, she heard the pride he felt for his family's company. She could relate. She felt the same way about her family's foundation. "There are security cameras on the cabin's perimeter and up in a few of the trees closest to the property."

"I noticed the camera above the door when we came in." She looked over her shoulder toward the entrance. "But what about the windows? Shouldn't the curtains be drawn?"

"There's a tint screen on every window in the safe house. We can see out in case someone approaches the cabin, but no one can see in." His words drew her attention back to him. "We'll be safe here—as long as you follow Mal's instructions. They're meant for your security. Don't use your personal cell phone or laptop. If you absolutely have to, you can turn them on very briefly, but don't leave either of them on for more than two minutes."

Symone paused on the step beneath his. "No electronics."

"There's a good chance whoever's stalking you is tracking you through your devices." He held her eyes. "If you leave any of your devices on for more than two minutes, they'll be able to track your signal to the cabin, which would defeat the purpose for being here."

"I understand." Her words came out on a breath as she felt the weight of his words.

Jerry held her eyes a beat longer as though reassuring himself that she did indeed understand how critical it was for her to follow those instructions. He turned to lead her up the rest of the stairs.

There were four rooms on the second floor. Jerry nodded toward the room to his right. "This is the office. All of our security systems are managed from the computers in that room. I'll go over it with you later. The narrow door beside it is the linen closet. Just a few bed sets and towels."

"Thank goodness." Symone's interjection was spontaneous. "I didn't bring any to my mother's house. I used hers."

He tossed her a crooked smile that trapped her breath in her throat. "We've got you covered." He took a few steps to the next door. "This will be my room. It's closest to the stairs."

Symone peeked in. "It's very nice."

The room wasn't very big but it seemed so comfortable. A patterned coverlet in moss green and soft brown covered the queen-size bed. It matched the area rugs that surrounded it. An ornate cedar carving of a landscape had been placed on the snow white wall behind the bed above the headboard. The bed frame, nightstand and dressing table were made of the same wood.

Jerry led her the few steps to the room next door. "This will be your room." He left her suitcases at the foot of the bed.

Symone entered the room, setting her laptop case with them. "It's also very nice. Thank you."

The room was almost identical to the one Jerry would be using. The patterned coverlet on the queen-size bed was warm tan and moss green as were the area rugs around it. The intricate cedar carving above this headboard depicted maple leaves. They seemed to be floating on an autumn breeze.

"I'm glad you like it." Jerry nodded behind him. "We'll be sharing the bathroom next door."

Alarm bells rang in Symone's head. She had a flashback of Jerry's office. There was no justification for that disaster. Would knowing he was *sharing* the bathroom with another being make him any neater?

Oh, boy.

She took a calming breath, detecting the slight scent of cedar in the room. "What are your plans for finding the person behind the threats?"

"Plans?" Jerry braced his shoulder against the threshold and crossed his arms over his broad chest. "I don't have a plan. Plans fall apart. I prefer to follow my instincts."

She blinked. "Oh." *Boy.*

Symone turned from him, pressing her hand against her chest. Her heart hammered against her palm. He didn't have a plan? How could he *not* have a plan? Wasn't it his *job* to have a plan? *She* was a planner. She had plans and schedules for every aspect of her life stretching months into the future. Plans brought her comfort. How could she face mortal danger with someone who flew by the seat of his pants?

Symone pulled the brakes on her runaway thoughts. She drew a deep breath of the cedar-scented air and reminded herself that Jerry had kept Dr. Grace Blackwell's grandmother safe in a similar—although not the same—situation.

"Why would someone want to kill you, Symone?" Jerry's question was muffled beneath the sound of the blood rushing in her head.

Symone forced herself to relax by degrees. She turned to him. "I have no idea. I hadn't even realized I had enemies."

Jerry crossed the threshold into the room. He leaned against the wall beside the door, slipping his hands into the front pockets of his black slacks. "Has anyone new come into your life? I mean, work-wise or in general." His words stopped abruptly.

"The past year?" Symone wandered to the dressing table. A simple rectangular mirror in a cedar frame balanced on top of it. "We brought on two new board members. And Ellie. But if you're implying any of those people would be behind these attempts on Paul's and my lives, you're wrong. It couldn't be them."

"Why not?"

She glanced at him over her shoulder. "We have a very reliable vendor who does background checks on all of our employees and board members."

"How many board members are there?" Jerry asked.

"Seven." Symone changed direction and wandered to the bed across the room. She trailed her fingertips over the coverlet. The cotton material was soft. "They sit for three-year terms that can be renewed. Two of our members chose not to renew this time around, but they'd already served several terms."

"The foundation does important work. I can understand their staying for multiple terms." He ran his hand over his hair. "What's changed in your life this past year—in addition to your mother's death? I'm truly sorry for your loss." His voice was thick with sympathy.

For the first time, she didn't feel as though she was experiencing her mother's death on her own. Paul had loved her mother. Symone was confident of that. But he didn't share his grief or even show it, at least not around her. The sense of isolation made losing her mother so much more painful. But the look in Jerry's eyes made her feel like she wasn't alone.

"Thank you." Her voice was husky even to her own ears. She cleared her throat as she collected her thoughts. "The only thing that stands out, of course, is the board's ultimatum. They've given me just over two weeks to develop a proposal for a more aggressive investment strategy both for the foundation's funds and the projects we support."

Jerry straightened from the wall. "What happens if the board doesn't approve your proposal?"

Symone shook her head. "They'll hold a no-confidence vote the last Monday of July. If I don't receive the support of a simple majority of the board, they'll schedule another meeting to elect a new chair."

"Really." His eyes were on her, but Symone sensed he was picturing someone or something else. "Your board would replace you. And I take it you replaced your mother."

Symone felt ice drop into her chest. Her lips were numb. "What are you saying?"

This time, his midnight eyes were laser focused on her. "It's too early to say anything. We don't have all the information. But I think it's curious that you became chair after your mother's death and now the board is trying to replace you."

"You think someone killed my mother to take over the foundation and now that same person's targeting me? That's ridiculous." Wasn't it?

Jerry began shaking his head even before she finished speaking. "It's too early to speculate. Mal's going to ask

Grace to test your mother's prescription. That should tell us whether someone tampered with her medication."

Jerry appeared to think his words would comfort her. They didn't.

Symone's skin burned as anger simmered in her blood. Had someone murdered her mother? She couldn't believe it. She didn't want to consider it. But if it was true, she swore to herself she'd bring the killer to justice—no matter what it took.

"Who would most benefit if you were to step down as chair of your foundation?" Celeste's image was projected through the laptop monitor Jerry and Symone were sharing.

Jerry felt Symone's tension as he sat beside her at the safe house's dinette table late Friday afternoon. They were on a videoconference with Zeke, Mal and Celeste. Zeke and Mal appeared in one screen as they joined from Touré Security Group's conference room. Celeste seemed to be at her desk at Jarrett & Nichols Investigations.

Hours earlier, Paul had declined their invitation to join the meeting. He'd insisted he didn't want anything to do with the investigation. The blood had drained from Symone's face when they'd read his reply. She looked as though she'd been slapped. Jerry had wanted to wrap her in his arms and assure her they'd figure this out together. Before he could speak, Symone had launched from her chair and muttered an excuse before marching from the room.

"I'm concerned about the investigation's focus on the foundation." Symone crossed her right leg over her left. She sat straight on her chair and linked her fingers over her right thigh. "I agree there's a compelling argument for it, but Paul's belief that these threats could be connected to his lawsuits deserves consideration."

Zeke's attention shifted from Jerry to Symone. "We'll look at both scenarios. Let's start with the foundation."

Jerry nodded his silent agreement. "So, to Celeste's question, who'd benefit the most if you were removed as foundation chair?"

Irritation simmered in Symone's brown eyes. "Members of the board and administration. They're eligible to be elected chair."

"People in administration?" Jerry remembered something he'd read on the foundation's website. "Paul's in administration."

"That's right." Symone nodded. "He's vice chair. As our administrative assistant, Ellie's also eligible."

Jerry shook his head. Things weren't looking good for Paul. "We need to look into both of them and your board members."

"You consider Paul a suspect?" Symone's eyes widened with disbelief. "The threats were directed at him."

Jerry searched her eyes, trying to read her mind. "You still think those threats were meant for Paul?" Was she serious? "If that's true, why didn't he agree to let us protect him? Why isn't he with us now, helping to find the person responsible for them? *Your* car was bombed, not his."

Symone crossed her arms. "My mother loved Paul very much. They'd been together for years. I can't imagine him having anything to do with these threats, especially since they put *him* in danger."

Mal's voice shattered the tense silence. "Symone, let's clear Paul's name and remove any suspicions that he could be involved."

Jerry was impressed—and relieved. Trust Mal to find a diplomatic solution for the conflict. He'd been diffusing tensions between him and Zeke for decades. But Symone seemed to need more convincing.

Her eyes stabbed him. "Am *I* going on your suspect list?"

"It's *our* list." Jerry watched the sparks flicker in her eyes behind her glasses. Mesmerizing. "And we might've added you if *Paul's* car had been bombed instead of yours."

Symone's frown deepened. "Ellie's been with the foundation for almost a year, working closely with me, my mother and Paul. We would've sensed if she was plotting something."

"Not necessarily." In some ways, the case Jerry, his brothers and Grace had just solved was similar to this one. "Sometimes people show you what you want to see."

"And you think I'd be foolish enough to fall for it?" Symone looked from Jerry to the images of Zeke, Mal and Celeste on the laptop.

Jerry shrugged. "Sometimes we see what we want to see."

Symone's full lips thinned. "There's one problem with your premise. Our foundation works with an agency to do background checks on all our applicants before we hire them or appoint them to our board. Remember?"

"That agency isn't TSG." Jerry took pride in his family's business and the quality of the services they offered: personal, corporate and computer security. The thought of walking away from his parents' legacy hurt him. He drew a breath to ease the pain, drawing in Symone's soap-and-wildflowers scent.

Symone adjusted her glasses. "None of our board members would want to hurt Paul or me. Most of them have been with us for years."

Celeste interrupted. "Symone, you just said *most* of your

board members have been with you for years. We should start with the newest ones. Who are they?"

Symone drew a deep breath, which lifted her shoulders. The action seemed to relieve some of her tension. "We have two. Xander Fence. The board member he replaced recommended him." She narrowed her eyes as though searching her memory. "He's been with us about three months." She turned those chocolate eyes back to Jerry. "You met him after we toured the foundation's offices."

"I remember." Jerry brought to mind an image of the man who'd interrupted them. "Why didn't you introduce us? He seemed curious about me or maybe about my presence with you."

"Did he?" Symone's tone was noncommittal.

Jerry's eyes narrowed. What was she hiding? "Is he interested in you?"

"Of course not." Her voice was abrupt as though his question had surprised her.

Her reaction made him even more suspicious. Surely, she knew she was an attractive woman. It went deeper than her looks, which were distracting enough. She was compassionate, taking decisive action to protect her stepfather when she believed he was being threatened. She was courageous, fighting for her family's legacy even though it could be the reason her life was in danger. And she was intelligent, although her courage and compassion were blinding her to the facts and doubts about the case and the people involved.

He tried another educated guess. "Do you trust him?"

Her hesitation was telling. "I don't have a reason not to trust him. Our screening agency vetted him and the longtime board member he replaced recommended him."

Jerry chuckled. "That's not an answer."

Mal interrupted, putting their discussion back on track. "Who's the other new member?"

Symone slid Jerry a disgruntled look beneath her winged dark brown eyebrows. "Wesley Bragg. Paul's known him for years. He's a lawyer with his own practice. He's representing Paul in his lawsuits against my mother's doctor and the pharmaceutical company that manufactures her medication."

Celeste pointed her pen toward her laptop monitor. "If Paul's somehow involved in this, they could be working together. We should prioritize background checks into Bragg, Fence and Kayple."

Jerry liked the way Celeste's mind worked. Based on the glint of admiration that sparked in Zeke's eyes, his older brother was a fan, too.

Symone's frown deepened. "I'll have the agency send you their background reports on the board, Paul and Ellie."

"That's fine." Mal nodded. "I'd like to see them, but we'll also do our own investigations. Your life's in danger. I'm not going to depend on someone else's work to identify the person behind the threats."

"Very well." Symone touched the sides of her glasses. "And you'll follow up with Paul and Wesley regarding a connection between these threats and their lawsuits?"

"Of course." Zeke leaned into the glass-and-sterling-silver conference table, bringing him closer to the computer's camera.

Symone turned her attention from the laptop back to Jerry. "If you don't need anything more from me, I'm going to my room to get some foundation work done."

"Thank you, Symone." Mal was distracted as though he'd already started on the background checks of their suspects.

"Have a good evening." Celeste tossed out the cheery farewell.

"Thank you for your time, Symone," Zeke said. "We'll be in touch."

Jerry followed her movements. He didn't need to be psychic to know she was ticked off. "I'll see you later."

"Hmm." She didn't look back as she strode from the dining area and mounted the stairs.

Celeste lowered her voice. "She's not happy that we're questioning her judgment."

Jerry frowned. "That's not what we're doing. We're questioning the character of the people on her foundation."

"And who hired those people?" Celeste's laughter was warm and friendly. "Exactly. Good luck with that. In the meantime, let's divvy up the list. The background checks will go faster."

Mal interrupted. "First, Jerry, put on your earbuds."

Curious, Jerry pulled his earbuds from his laptop case. He plugged them into his computer, then placed them into his ears. "What's going on?"

Mal expelled a tense breath. "I didn't want to deliver this news while Symone was with us. I just got an email from Grace. She's completed the tests on Odette Bishop's medication. Your instincts were right. The pills had been tampered with."

"Oh, no." Celeste gasped.

Zeke rubbed his left hand across his eyes. "I'm so sorry."

Ice filled Jerry's chest. Even though he'd thought something could be off with Odette's medicine, he didn't want to believe she'd been murdered. He looked at his brothers and saw the same pain in their expressions that he was feeling inside. He knew what they were thinking without having to ask. He had the same thoughts. A parent's death was hard enough. Learning someone had taken your parent from you before their time would be a crushing pain from which you may never recover.

Jerry struggled to clear his thoughts. "Is she sure?"

Mal nodded. The movement was jerky. "She tested it three times. Odette's pills were tainted with tetrahydrozoline. When it's ingested, tetrahydrozoline can cause heart failure."

Zeke briefly closed his eyes. "And Symone's mother already had a heart condition."

Celeste spread her arms. "How many people knew she was taking medication and who had access to her pills?"

"Paul." The name burst from Jerry's lips before he realized he was going to say it. "But there are probably others. I'll ask Symone."

Crap. He wasn't looking forward to that conversation.

Mal's eyes searched his features as though trying to read his mind. "Are you comfortable doing that? Do you want me to ask Grace to call her? She could explain her testing process to Symone."

Jerry shook his head. "I'm supposed to be watching over her." He glanced toward the staircase in the great room. "I'm her primary contact for this case. I should break the news to her. If she wants more details, she can call Grace. And she'll probably want to speak with Paul."

He wrapped up the videoconference with the rest of the team, then started toward the stairs. Every step felt heavy as though he was moving against resistance bands. Symone had been through so much already today, this year. She'd buried her mother and barely had time to grieve before someone began threatening her and her stepfather. This morning, her car had been bombed. This afternoon, she'd had to pack up and move into a safe house with someone she'd just met. She'd learned her employees and board were suspected of threatening her life.

But this news was the worst of all. He really wasn't looking forward to being the bearer of it.

Chapter 6

"My mother was murdered?" Symone didn't understand what those words meant. It felt as though she was struggling to translate a foreign language. "That's impossible. You must be mistaken."

Jerry stood just inside Symone's bedroom in the safe house Friday evening. He'd announced his arrival minutes ago with a tentative knock on her half-opened door. That was her first indication the confident, rash personal security expert was out of his comfort zone. The pain in his deep voice, tension in his midnight eyes and strain on his chiseled features were subsequent clues. He'd asked her to sit down. She was glad she had—otherwise, he'd be picking her up from the floor.

"There's no mistake." His voice was gentle, comforting. "Grace ran her tests three times."

Symone still couldn't wrap her mind around what he was saying. She wasn't getting the translation right. "Who would want to hurt my mother? Who would want her dead?" She wanted to rise from the bed to pace the room, but she wasn't confident her legs would hold her.

Jerry stepped closer. "That's what we'll need your help to find out."

Symone began to shake. *Someone had killed my mother!*

The thought screamed across her brain. Her bewilderment cleared. Her numbness thawed. Heat flooded her cheeks as rage filled her body.

Symone surged to her feet. She marched across the room to the dressing table. Her body felt stiff, brittle. "Someone plotted to kill my mother—and they succeeded. Right under my nose. I want to know who, how, when and why. They're *not* getting away with this." She clenched her fists, fighting the urge to throw back her head and scream.

"No, they won't." Behind her, Jerry's tone was hard with determination.

Symone turned to pace to the opposite wall. She pushed her words through clenched teeth. "What did Grace say? Tell me everything."

"I didn't speak with Grace." Jerry's voice came from closer inside the room. "Mal told me. He said Grace had tested the pills in the container three times. Each time, the results were the same. The pills in your mother's prescription bottle were tainted with tetrahydrozoline. We could call Grace now and ask her to walk us through her tests."

A moan escaped Symone's lips. She pressed her fist against her mouth to trap the others inside. Her eyes stung from the salt of unshed tears. She stumbled to the nightstand and pulled several tissues from the box she found there. Confusion had morphed into rage, which was shifting into soul-crushing sorrow. As her knees began to buckle, firm hands caught her elbows and held her upright.

"Why?" Her voice was muffled as she pressed the tissues against her face. "Why would someone kill my mother? Why would they take her from me?"

"I don't know, sweetheart." Jerry turned her into his arms, pressing her cheek against his chest. His voice and his heartbeat echoed in her ear.

"She's never, ever hurt anyone. She's only helped people with the foundation and the groups she volunteered with."

"I understand." Jerry's words were low.

"When they killed my mother, they took everything from me." Her voice was raw. Her tears streamed in earnest now. "My mother. My business partner. My best friend. They took everything from me and left me alone. Why? Why did they do it? They took everything."

Jerry was undone. Symone's sobs, raw with agony, ripped his heart out. He couldn't bear to see anyone in pain, physically, mentally or emotionally. Her words tore him apart. They described how he'd felt when his mother had died, as though he'd lost everything. He still had his brothers, but no one could replace his mother. Symone literally didn't have anyone, not even Paul. Her stepfather had basically disappeared from her life at the third sign of danger.

His protective instincts engaged. He tightened his arms around her. She felt fragile in his embrace. Her slight frame was battered by powerful emotions. She was so different from the woman who'd sat beside him during the video-conference. There were times he'd suspected that, if she weren't determined to maintain her decorum, she would've punched him.

Her voice grew more and more strained. She seemed lost in her misery, oblivious to their surroundings or even his presence. Through her tears, Jerry caught broken phrases, expressing her thoughts and emotions.

"It hurts…"

"They took her…"

"Why…?"

The ache he felt for what she was going through boiled his blood from equal parts anger and anguish. Jerry lifted

Symone into his arms. Two steps carried them to her bed. He laid her gently on the mattress. Taking off his shoes, he stretched out beside her. Her sobs were softer now, but still shook her slender body. Slipping his right arm beneath her, he drew Symone against him. Her head rested on his chest. After a few moments, her sobs quieted. Jerry sensed Symone slowly drifting off to sleep. As he lay beside her, he stared at the bedroom ceiling and imagined all the ways he'd like to inflict pain on the person who'd broken her heart.

Symone shifted as she slowly surfaced from sleep. The muscled arm around her waist tightened as though in reflex, bringing her closer to the hard, warm body beside her. She gasped and the scents of clean soap and fresh mint filled her head. The unfamiliar arm relaxed and dropped to the mattress. Symone pushed herself free of the broad, hard torso. She tipped her head back and looked up. Jerry smiled sleepily from the pillow beside hers.

What the...?

Her eyes dived to her white blouse—which wasn't as crisp as it had been when she'd dressed this morning—pencil-slim, knee-length gray skirt, and gray pumps.

She pinned Jerry with a suspicious glare. "What's happened?"

He arched an eyebrow. "What are you implying, Ms. Bishop? We're both completely dressed. Well, I took my shoes off."

Her face burned with embarrassment. "How did we end up in bed together?"

"You were upset." His voice was low. "I wanted to comfort you."

The memory of unbearable pain and suffocating grief

flooded back to her. Symone took a moment to catch her breath. Her eyes stung with tears at the kindness of this stranger. She blinked them back. When her mother had died, there wasn't anyone to hold her. Today, after learning her mother had been murdered, he hadn't let her go.

"Thank you." Her voice was thick.

"You're welcome." Jerry pulled his arm out from under her. He abruptly sat up, swinging his long legs over the side of the bed. He turned to face her. "My job is to keep you safe. To do that, I need you to trust me. I know that's asking a lot. We met for the first time less than ten hours ago, yet we're going to be alone in an isolated cabin for I don't know how many days. I'm going to use that time to earn your trust, which means I'm not going to take advantage of you. You have my word. Your safety depends on that. My family's reputation depends on that. Do you have any questions for me?"

Symone searched his wide, midnight eyes beneath his thick black eyebrows. He was so earnest as he waited for her response, as though her answer was vitally important to him. Her muscles relaxed. She hadn't realized how knotted they'd been. Her eyes moved over his sharp sienna features. She could trust him.

She didn't have any doubts about his capabilities or experience. When her car had exploded, he'd shielded her with his body. He'd gotten her and Ellie to safety before she'd taken her next breath. He'd directed Ellie to reassure her staff that everyone was safe, and the authorities had been contacted before she'd collected her thoughts. He'd called the detectives and updated his brothers. Yes, Jerry may be a reckless slob with no regard for a well-developed plan, but Symone was confident he could keep her safe.

She shook her head. "I don't have any questions for you right now, but I'll let you know if anything comes to me."

Jerry gave a decisive nod as he straightened his clothes. "That's fair. In the meantime, I'll get started on dinner."

Symone chided herself for watching him tuck his shirt into his waistband. She climbed out of the bed on the other side and dragged her eyes up to his. "But you cooked lunch. It's not fair to you that you do all the cooking."

"You're welcome to cook if you'd like." He bent to collect his shoes.

"I'm afraid I'm not much of a cook." Understatement. "Perhaps we could order something? My treat."

"We can't risk having strangers come to the safe house." Jerry's crooked smile made her toes curl in her pumps. He crossed to the door. "I don't mind cooking. I'll make chicken and salad."

Symone locked her knees as she watched his loose-limbed stride. "Sounds wonderful. Thank you. I'll be down in a moment to set the table."

He tossed a smile over his shoulder. "You've got a deal."

Symone watched Jerry disappear beyond the door. She exhaled as she allowed herself to drop onto the bed, letting her torso fall back onto the mattress. Closing her eyes, Symone let her mind return to the moment she'd awakened beside Jerry. Her body hummed. A sigh rose from her chest and escaped through her parted lips.

He'd given her his word he wouldn't take advantage of her. She believed him. She didn't want to be taken advantage of. But she wouldn't mind waking up in his arms again.

"That was a wonderful meal, Jerry. Thank you." Symone looked at the remains of her blackened chicken breast and salad Friday evening. She rose from her chair at the dinette table and added his plate and silverware to hers. "This time, relax while I clean up." She crossed into the bright tan and warm brown kitchenette.

"I'm fine lending a hand." Jerry's voice came from close behind her.

Symone swallowed a sigh. The scents of peppers lingered in the kitchen. "Well, I can't force you to sit still."

"You wouldn't be the first one to try, though." He watched her rinse the dishes before packing them into the dishwasher. "You don't have to prewash the dishes."

Symone shrugged. "I don't mind."

"All right." The laughter drained from his voice. He set their glasses in the sink and spoke gently. "Symone, about your mother's prescription. The fact someone tampered with it strengthens the argument that the foundation is the motive behind the threats against you. I believe someone killed your mother to get one step closer to the foundation's accounts. Now the killer's targeting you for the same reason."

"I know." Symone kept her attention on the dishwasher as though it was the only safe port in the storm.

"Tell me about your mother." He collected the pan from the stovetop and brought it to the sink.

Symone nudged him away from the counter and took his place. As she scrubbed the pan, she brought her mother to mind. "My mother's … She was a good person, and that's not a biased daughter's opinion. *Everyone* said as much. She was brilliant. Great with facts and numbers. And she had a strong personality, which was fortunate. My father was larger than life." Her lips curved with amusement at the memory. "If she'd been an introvert, he would've overshadowed her. Since they were both extroverts, they were a perfect match."

Jerry chuckled. The sound was as warm as a seductive summer evening. "Your mother and mine would've been friends."

"Your mother was an extrovert also?"

"Yes, she was. But Paul seems like an introvert." Jerry made the words a statement rather than a question. "How did they meet?"

Symone rinsed the pan. "Paul was a senior partner with Docent, Kayple and Sarchie Accounting. It's the firm that certifies the foundation's accounts. He retired in 2019. He and Mom started dating in 2020, three years after Dad died. He started proposing about seven months later. Mom said yes in 2023." She turned off the water and rested the pan on the drain board.

Jerry reached for the dish towel on the peg beside the sink and started drying the pan. "The killer would've had to have known about your mother's medication. That narrows our list of suspects. Besides you and Paul, who else knew about your mother's heart condition?"

Symone ignored that Jerry was drying the pan. Another example of his inability to sit still. She couldn't fault him. "My mother was a very private person. She wouldn't have told anyone else, not even close friends."

"Paul may have told Wesley Bragg. We have to consider that." Jerry squatted to put the pan in one of the bottom cupboards. His pants tightened across his thighs.

Symone jerked her eyes away. She wouldn't argue with Jerry about their suspect list any longer. Someone had killed her mother. As far as Symone was concerned, they could interview everyone her mother had ever known.

"We should probably also consider Ellie." She wandered

out of the kitchenette as her mind raced ahead with memories of her mother working with Ellie. "She'd been my mother's administrative assistant before she became mine. My mother wouldn't have told her about her prescription. I'll never believe that. But Ellie may have overheard her talking with her pharmacy or her physician."

Jerry hummed thoughtfully behind her. The sound sent shivers down her spine. "Would Ellie have mentioned it to someone?"

Symone stopped beside the dinette table and turned to him. "This morning, I would've said no, definitely not. But now, I don't know who to trust, or if I can trust anyone. The person who tampered with my mother's prescription would have to have been able to get close to her. My mother knew a lot of people but only a few of us would've been able to get that close—me, Paul and perhaps Ellie."

Jerry hummed again. He paced the great room as he ran his hand over his dark curls. His hair was styled in a low fade. "I believe the stalker and the killer are the same person."

"I agree."

Jerry nodded a silent acknowledgment of Symone's interruption. "The stalker was tracking you. That explains how they knew when you were home and which restaurant you'd gone to. Maybe they'd also bugged your mother's phone. That could've been how they'd known about her medication and when she'd picked up her last prescription."

"Perhaps." Symone shivered.

She was chilled to the bone. She wrapped her arms around her waist, hoping to warm herself. She was in the middle of a waking nightmare. The situation was so much worse than she'd imagined when she'd first contacted the Touré Security Group.

Jerry looked her over. His brow furrowed with concern. "Would you like some tea?" He started toward the kitchenette. "It'll make you feel better."

Symone held up her hand to stop him. "Thank you, but I can make it. I admit I can't cook, but I can boil water. Would you like some?"

"Yeah. Thanks." Jerry trailed her into the kitchenette. "I'll ask Mal to prioritize Paul, Wesley, Ellie and Xander."

"Why Xander?" Symone filled the kettle from the kitchenette's faucet. "He's new to the board and barely knew my mother." She crossed to the stove and set the water to boil.

"I can't explain it." Jerry opened one cupboard and picked out two tea bags. "There's something about him that makes me suspicious. He seemed a little too interested in my presence at the foundation."

Symone frowned at him over her shoulder. "Is this another example of you following your instincts?"

Jerry opened another cupboard for the mugs. "Yeah, you could say that."

Symone searched the nearby drawers for teaspoons. She could only hope his instincts didn't slow down their investigation. The cabin was comfortable, and their surroundings were lovely, but the homicidal stalker was an unwelcomed distraction. They needed to solve this case and secure the foundation as quickly as possible. Symone took a calming breath.

The heat from the burner beneath the kettle warmed her. "I want to be there when you question the suspects."

Jerry placed the tea bags into the two mugs. "No."

Symone blinked. His blunt refusal surprised her. "Why not?"

Jerry gave her a dubious look beneath a thick dark eyebrow. "Your mother was murdered. Someone's stalking you. A bomb was planted on your car. You'll be safer here."

Symone watched him measure honey into the mugs. "You're going to be there, interviewing the suspects. You can keep me safe."

The kettle whistled. She turned off the burner and took the mugs from Jerry.

"Yes, I could." Jerry leaned against the counter and watched her fill each mug with the hot water. "But that would defeat the purpose of what we're doing here. Why go to the trouble of settling you into a safe house for your protection only to turn around and put you in front of the people who are trying to kill you?"

Jerry had a valid point, but Symone had a compelling argument.

She handed Jerry his tea, then held his eyes. "I want a bigger role in this investigation, Jerry. Someone killed my mother. They took her from me way too soon." She blinked to ease the sting of tears in her eyes. "I'm not hiding in this cabin while you confront the suspects. I want to look them in the eye when they try to explain why they couldn't be the killer."

Jerry returned her steady stare for several silent moments. Finally, he spoke. "The answer's still no, but I'm willing to compromise. I'll record the interviews and you can listen to them in their entirety when I get back." The rigid set of his jaw was a nonverbal invitation to "take it or leave it."

"That's not good enough, Jerry. I think you can do better."

"Your safety is my priority, Symone."

She liked the way he said her name. "My priority is finding my mother's killer."

Jerry's eyes shifted from her to scan the room as though he was considering locking her in it. Could he really do that?

He sighed. "Let's be clear, *I* have the final say in this mission."

Symone arched an eyebrow. She'd let that pass—for now. But make no mistake. At the end of this impasse, one of them would be disappointed—and it would not be her.

Chapter 7

"Don't come any closer." Jerry extended his right arm, palm outward. "I probably smell pretty ripe."

He was dripping sweat as he stood behind the black vinyl, freestanding, heavy punching bag in the middle of the safe house's basement early Saturday morning. He wasn't wrong. In fact, the entire space was swollen with the sharp, salty smell of perspiration. Jerry wore a wet, smoke gray wicking T-shirt, black knee-length biker shorts, white ankle-length socks, black-and-white running shoes and silver boxing gloves. A small rotating fan helped alleviate some of the scent.

Symone had caught a whiff of the odor and heard the faint rhythmic snaps of his workout as soon as she'd opened the basement door. Curiosity had pushed her down the staircase. She wanted to know what he was doing and to see what was causing the noise. She'd only caught a few of his moves before he spied her standing on the second-to-last step.

"You really do." Shallow breaths. She softened the criticism with a smile. "How long have you been down here?" Her eyes moved over the old-fashioned weight bench, yoga mats and treadmill.

"What time is it?" Jerry used his right forearm to wipe the sweat from his brow.

Symone checked the burner cell in her right hand. "A couple of minutes before six."

"About an hour." His T-shirt had molded itself to his chest.

Symone pinched off the growing feeling of envy. "And I thought my workouts were hard." She nodded toward the heavy bag. "Perhaps you could show me a few self-defense moves while we're here? If nothing else, this experience has taught me that I have to learn how to protect myself."

"That's a good idea." Jerry removed his gloves. "Once I get cleaned up, I'll show you a few maneuvers that will help you get free in case someone tries to grab you."

"Why not show me now?" Symone stepped forward. She spread her arms, drawing attention to her outfit. "I'm dressed for it."

Jerry's eyes moved over her heather cropped yoga tank and matching midthigh shorts. Her feet were covered by white ankle-length athletic socks. His attention was like a physical caress moving over her.

Symone sensed a shift in the atmosphere, like time had stopped. Jerry's body was unusually still as though he was frozen in place. Tension leaped from him and wrapped itself around her. His eyes slowly lifted to her face. They were dark and intense. Symone reminded herself to breathe.

Jerry took a large step back and turned away from her. He set his gloves on the table in front of him. "How well can you see without your glasses?"

How anticlimactic.

Symone touched the thin black rims of her glasses. "Well enough."

Nodding, Jerry squared his shoulders and faced her again. "Maybe you should remove them. I don't want to risk knocking them off during our practice."

Symone removed her glasses and set them and her cell on one of the shelves on the other side of the room. Her vision wasn't as sharp as it was with her glasses, but they were meant mainly for reading and driving.

She turned back to Jerry—and froze. He stood about three feet from her. But his body was so still as he met her eyes. Was he planning a surprise? She wasn't ready.

Symone backpedaled. She raised her arms, palms out. "Shouldn't you demonstrate the defensive technique first?"

Jerry frowned, shaking his head. "What?"

Symone exhaled and dropped her arms. She pressed her right hand to her stuttering heart. "Oh. I thought you were going to come at me. That your teaching technique was going to be a full immersive experience."

"No." He gave her his sexy, crooked grin. "I prefer baby steps."

A relieved smile parted her lips and lifted her cheeks. Symone closed the gap between them. "Have you given other clients self-defense lessons?"

"A few." Jerry turned her around so her back was to him. "Now the key is remembering not to hurt the trainer."

Symone's chuckle sounded nervous to her ears. "Promise."

"I'm going to pretend to abduct you." Jerry's large hands rested lightly on her mostly bare shoulders. "Imagine you were working late at the office. You've finally wrapped up for the day. You're leaving the building, which doesn't have any security guards. You're walking to the parking lot, which doesn't have any security cameras—"

"All right. All right." Her laughter was much more relaxed. "I'll email the management company about providing security for the building."

Jerry squeezed her shoulders and her heart leaped into her throat.

Focus! Focus!

"Don't forget to use the laptop Mal gave you. Secure channels only." His voice was muffled under the sound of her racing pulse.

Symone nodded. "I promise." Did he notice she sounded breathless?

He squeezed her shoulders before releasing her. Symone smothered a groan of disappointment.

"You're walking to your car." Jerry started over. "Abductor comes up behind you. Grabs you around the waist to restrain you. Presses a hand over your mouth to keep you quiet. Are you ready?"

"No, but we can get started." Symone stepped forward.

Jerry came up behind her. He wrapped his right arm around her waist, pulling her back against his torso, then positioned his palm over her mouth. Even knowing what Jerry was about to do, Symone experienced a jolt of fear. It made her catch her breath and stiffen her spine. Then she remembered she was with Jerry. He would keep her safe. She relaxed back against him. His body was still warm and damp from his workout. Her skin tingled with excitement.

"Your turn. Grab me the same way I held you." Jerry released her, then turned, waiting for Symone to get into position. She'd placed one arm around his waist and covered his mouth with her hand. He removed her hand before continuing. "I'll pretend to be you. First, drive your elbow back into the abductor's solar plexus as hard as you can." He moved in slow motion to demonstrate. He tapped his elbow into the spot between the bottom of her chest and the top of her stomach. "This'll knock the wind out of them. While they're gasping for air, quickly crush their instep with your heel. The pain will cause the abductor to bend forward." Again, he mimicked the action, gently stepping on her sock-clad foot. "Next, jab your elbow this time into their face, aiming for their nose. Along with the eyes, this is the most vulnerable part of a person's face." He demonstrated the move in slow motion, stopping before he made contact with Symone's nose. "And finally, punch the abductor in the groin." Jerry didn't reenact that move. "Then run like hell."

Symone released Jerry and stepped back. Her eyebrows knitted. Her smile was uncertain. "Solar plexus? Instep? Nose? Groin? S-I-N-G. Sing. Like in the movie *Miss Congeniality* with Sandra Bullock and Benjamin Bratt?"

Jerry grinned over his shoulder. "It's a real self-defense technique." He turned to face her. "Now you try it. But remember, don't hurt the trainer."

"Promise." She tossed him a smile, then turned her back to him and waited for his arm to pull her back against him. She took a moment—just a moment—to enjoy the feeling. Then she sprang into action, pulling her punches. "Solar plexus." Jerry pretended to react, leaning forward and loosening his hold on her. "Instep." Jerry responded by releasing her. "Nose." She had to stretch for that move since Jerry was at least five inches taller than her. "Groin. SING." She spun to him on her toes. Her smile was wide and triumphant.

"Good job." He grinned his approval. "Keep practicing those moves. You could use the heavy bag. Remember, force and speed are important."

"Thank you." It was amazing how much learning those few moves boosted her confidence.

"My pleasure." He glanced at his black watch. "I should

leave so you can get your workout in before our video-conference."

The thought of the upcoming meeting to discuss their suspects' backgrounds pressed a heavy weight back onto her shoulders. "I realize we have to interview everyone who could've been involved in my mother's murder, but I just can't believe Paul could be the killer."

Jerry searched her features as though looking for clues. "How's your relationship with him?"

Symone's shrug was restless. She hesitated to speak ill of her mother's widower. "I got along with him because my mother married him, but I think you can tell we aren't close."

"I'm sorry." Jerry didn't pretend not to know what she was talking about. For that, Symone was grateful. "No one wants to believe their mother would marry a killer. If Paul's innocent, we'll clear him and it'll put your mind at rest."

Symone nodded her agreement. "I want to be there when you interview him."

Jerry sighed, rubbing the back of his neck. "Symone, we've discussed this."

She held up her right index finger. "We've had *a* discussion. Jerry, I'll be safe with you and Celeste. You and I will be together the whole time."

"No one can guarantee that." His tone was inflexible.

"I'll arrive to the interview location with you and return to the safe house with you." Symone threw up her arms. "What's the difference whether I'm with you or you're on your own?"

Jerry crossed his arms. "The difference is, if we show up together, people will know you're with me. If you stay out of sight, they won't."

Symone considered him. His T-shirt was still damp,

clinging to the muscles in his chest and abdomen. He looked so certain he was going to get his way. Poor guy. "I want to be safe, but I don't want to hide."

Jerry shook his head. "This isn't a buffet. You can't choose one or the other. It's a package deal. If you want to be safe, you'll have to stay hidden. I'm sorry."

Symone watched him stride away and jog up the stairs from the basement. She was sorry, too. Sorry he was going to be disappointed when he realized she was never giving up.

Poor guy.

"Good work as usual, Mal." Three hours later, Jerry sat beside Symone at the dinette table during their team videoconference.

He was still struggling to clear the image of her in her yoga outfit from what was left of his brain. He'd seen other women in similar outfits, but they'd never struck him speechless. Never. His mind had gone blank, and his muscles had frozen. She'd looked so different from the cool, untouchable corporate executive. This morning she'd been a warm, friendly charmer.

Symone Bishop was a collection of contrasts, and each one fascinated him.

Symone sat back. "I agree. Your reports were incredibly thorough. I wish I'd contacted you before my mother remarried."

"Thank you, both." Mal spoke from his seat beside Zeke in the Touré Security Group conference room Saturday morning. Celeste's image appeared in the box beside them. "Those are the highlights from the background checks on Paul and Wesley. The full reports have more details, of course. I'm researching Ellie now."

"And Xander." Jerry tapped the computer keys that would send Paul's report to the printer in the safe house's office upstairs. "We need to look into him, too."

Symone shifted toward him on her matching cedar chair. "I thought, for now, we were focusing on the suspects who most likely knew about my mother's prescription?"

"We should include Xander in this phase as well." Jerry hit the computer keys to print Wesley's report. His skin warmed where Symone's eyes touched the side of his face.

"Why?" she asked.

Because I didn't like the way he looked at me as though I were a threat. Am I a threat to his getting rid of you— or being with you?

But if he said that, he'd sound insane. "I told you I have a feeling about him."

Her chocolate eyes clouded with confusion. Jerry sensed her trying to decide how best to respond to his claim.

Zeke offered his insight. "Jerry's instincts are correct 99 percent of the time."

Jerry rolled his eyes. "I'd argue 100 percent."

Mal's voice was dry. "We'll give you ninety-nine-point-five."

Symone shook her head. A smile ghosted her lush lips. "All right. But I want to prioritize Paul, Wesley and Ellie. They're the ones most likely to know about my mother's heart condition. I'm anxious to find my mother's murderer."

"Of course." Celeste seemed to be behind her desk at her agency. Her camera framed her wearing a black, button-downed, short-sleeved blouse. "We understand. As Mal said, we have enough here to start with Paul and Wesley. Great work, Mal. And he's already started on Ellie's report. We won't lose focus."

Symone relaxed beside him. "Thank you."

Celeste's tone was brisk. "The killer wants to replace you as chair, presumably so they'd have total control of the foundation's funds."

Symone interrupted. "Not total control. Our bylaws mandate that our accounts are audited annually. They also allow board members to request additional audits under specific conditions."

"There are ways around that." Celeste waved a dismissive hand. "Bribes. Dummy accounts. Duplicate books."

Zeke jumped in. "I see where you're going, Celeste. If the killer's motive is money, Paul isn't our strongest suspect. He's not carrying much debt and his finances are strong."

"But his behavior's suspicious." Jerry sat back, crossing his arms over his chest. "Why doesn't he want protection? Why isn't he helping us find Odette's killer?"

These points alone put Paul at the top of Jerry's suspect list. However, he and his brothers had assigned two agents to guard him from a distance. They weren't comfortable leaving him unprotected if there was even the slightest chance his life was in danger.

"*That's* where I was going." Celeste gestured toward Jerry through the monitor. "Paul seems like our strongest suspect. No offense, Symone."

"None taken," Symone said.

Celeste counted off the strikes against Paul on her long, slender fingers. "He knew about Odette's heart condition. He had access to her prescription, and he's a member of the administration. But he doesn't appear to have a financial incentive. When we question him later today, we need to keep in mind that money may not be the motive—or at least not the only one."

Jerry nodded. "Good point."

Symone sat forward, resting her forearms on the table in front of her. "I want to be there when you speak with Paul."

"No," Jerry repeated.

"Of course," Celeste responded at the same time. She frowned at Jerry. "Why not?"

"I can't believe this." Jerry scrubbed his hands over his face. "What's the point of bringing her to the safe house if we're going to parade her in front of people who may want to kill her?"

Celeste blinked at Jerry. "To get her feedback and insights in real time. Jerry, you and I don't know these people. Symone has known Paul for years and she's worked with Wesley and Ellie for months. She can read their body language and fact-check their responses on the spot. Having her with us will make this investigation go a lot faster."

Jerry hadn't considered the points Celeste was making. They were good ones. Still, Symone was his responsibility. Her safety was his priority. And the best way to keep her safe was to make sure she was hidden away and her location a secret. He couldn't allow another one of his charges to be placed in danger. Not ever again.

He exchanged a look with her. He couldn't read her expression. Her emotions were under wraps. But he sensed her confidence growing. She thought Celeste's words would change his mind. He hated to disappoint her. He'd hate getting her killed even more.

Jerry switched his attention to his brothers. "Will you guys back me up?"

Zeke hesitated. "Celeste makes a good point. We need to identify the threat as quickly as possible. Having Symone at the interviews could help us do that."

"I agree," Mal said. "Grace helped with the interviews

while we were protecting her. You and Celeste will keep Symone safe."

Jerry read the signs of his defeat. He turned to Symone. "All right. You're coming with Celeste and me when we interview Paul later. But if I sense any danger, if there are any signs someone's following us, we're leaving you behind in the future. Got it?"

Symone's eyes glowed with satisfaction. "I've got it."

He could get lost in those brown eyes—but he would not let his attraction for her get in the way of keeping her safe.

Symone flinched when they walked into Paul's house early Saturday afternoon. Jerry followed her line of sight to the taped boxes stacked in a corner of the family room. What hurt her more, losing this last connection to her mother? Or confirmation that the final member of her family was walking away from her at a time when she needed her family most?

"Thank you for agreeing to see us, Paul." Jerry stepped aside for Symone and Celeste.

Symone was dressed in a cream shell blouse and powder pink skirt suit with matching stilettos. She'd accessorized with her pearl earrings and matching necklace. In contrast, Celeste had tucked a black, button-down, short-sleeved cotton blouse into the waistband of her slim black jeans. She wore black sneakers. Sterling silver stud earrings were mostly hidden by her cascade of wavy, ebony hair.

Jerry scanned the half-dozen boxes arranged two to a stack as he walked past them. The large brown cardboard containers looked new. They were labeled by item—clothes, linen, books. Paul must've spent most of the previous day packing, but it looked like he still had a lot to do.

Symone's stepfather led them to the dining room and sat on the carved dark wood seat at the head of the table. "I tried to call you last night, Symone. Did you get my message?"

"I sent an agency-wide email explaining my cell's turned off." Symone rounded the table to take the seat opposite her stepfather. Jerry held her chair, then sat to her left. "I'm using a secure phone until the stalker is caught."

Paul looked from Symone to Jerry and back. "And where are you staying?"

Symone's expression was unreadable. "Somewhere safe."

Jerry smiled to himself. Excellent. It was nice having a client who took her safety as seriously as he did. He once again shook off memories of the immature pop star and his high-maintenance father.

Paul's frown was disapproving. "I was expecting you to call me back."

"Was there something you needed?" Symone's voice was polished and solicitous. Had she gone to some expensive finishing school where people were taught to speak like that?

"Yes." Paul stacked his hands on the table. "When will you be able to remove your mother's things? I want to put the house on the market as soon as possible."

Jerry's fists clenched. Did Paul realize how cruel and thoughtless he sounded? He felt the impact of the other man's comment like a physical blow. He glanced at Symone to gauge her reaction. Her expression was frozen as though she didn't know how to respond. He turned back to Paul, intending to check the older man, but Celeste spoke first.

"Wow. That was harsh." The private investigator had taken the seat to Symone's right.

Paul's head swiveled toward Celeste. His lips parted. "I beg your pardon?"

Celeste jerked her thumb toward Symone. "She's a little busy right now. Someone's trying to kill her. Remember?"

"How dare you!" Paul's face flushed a deep red. "Is that how you speak to a client?"

Celeste jerked her head toward Jerry. "I don't work for you. I work for TSG."

Symone caught her stepfather's eyes. "You're not the client, Paul. I am." Her voice was cold enough to give Jerry frostbite.

He ignored Paul's simmering anger. "I see you've started packing. When are you leaving?" Jerry made a mental note to alert Eriq and Taylor that their prime suspect in Odette Bishop's homicide was making plans to leave town.

Paul drew his attention from Symone and turned to Jerry. "As soon as my brother returns from his vacation. It should be another week or so." He glanced at Symone. "In the meantime, I'm tendering my formal resignation from the foundation."

Surprise and some other emotion—grief?—swept across Symone's face. "Paul, I understand your wanting to leave the company but…can you wait until after the board votes? I need your support to keep my position with the foundation."

Jerry heard the tension in her voice. It made him even more suspicious of the older man's motives. What was behind the timing of his leaving? If it was fear for his safety, why wouldn't he accept the protection Touré Security Group offered? Or was he hoping to vanish before they connected him to Odette's murder?

"You don't need me." Paul's voice was gentle. "I know

you don't want to hear this, Symone, but maybe you should consider leaving, too. You have to take these threats more seriously. Your parents wouldn't want you to put your life at risk for the foundation."

Symone paused. She seemed to be considering both the message and the messenger. "Paul, Mom didn't die from natural causes. She was murdered."

Blood drained from Paul's round face. His dark eyes widened. His soft jaw dropped. "What? No. How?"

Symone's throat muscles flexed as she swallowed. "I'm afraid it's true. Someone altered Mom's prescription. The pills in her last bottle were tainted with tetrahydrozoline. If ingested, the drug can affect blood pressure, causing it to speed up at first, then slow down."

"This can't be happening. Who would have done such a thing?" Paul's words were barely audible. He collapsed back against his seat. His expression was blank as though the news had stunned him. His eyes landed on Symone, but Jerry didn't think he saw her.

Celeste's eyes fastened onto Paul. "How was your relationship with your wife?"

"What?" Paul's eyes wandered toward Celeste. He seemed to be coming out of a trance. "I... Wait, are you suggesting *I* switched my wife's medication? I would *never.*"

Jerry considered the older man. He appeared shocked to learn his wife had been murdered—or maybe he'd been surprised that the tetrahydrozoline had been discovered. He seemed angry to have been accused of tampering with Odette's pills, but perhaps he was a good actor.

"Tell us about your relationship with Odette, please, Paul." Jerry made it sound like an invitation. "Were you happy?"

Paul turned to Symone. His eyes were cloudy with confusion. "She never told you?"

Symone's winged eyebrows knitted. "Told me what?"

Paul straightened on his seat. He set his chin at a defensive angle. "Odette had filed for a divorce."

Jerry's eyebrows leaped up his forehead. That was unexpected. He looked at Symone for her reaction.

Symone's eyes stretched wide. Her lips parted. "When?"

Paul shifted on his seat. His throat worked as he swallowed. "Three days before she died."

"She never told me." Symone shook her head. "What happened?"

Paul's shrug was restless. His shoulders were slumped. He stared at the wall behind Symone as though he wasn't able to meet her eyes. "I couldn't compete with Langston Bishop's memory. Your father was larger than life. I knew that when I married Odette. But I'd loved her so much for so long. I thought the strength of my love would be enough." He shrugged again. "It wasn't."

Symone frowned. "Why didn't she tell me?"

The pain and confusion in her voice made Jerry's arms ache with the need to comfort her. He folded his arms across his chest to suppress the feeling.

"I thought she had." Paul finally met Symone's eyes. "You can't seriously believe I would have had anything to do with your mother's death. I loved her. I was suing her doctor and the pharmaceutical company for malpractice. Why would I do that if I'd been the one to poison her pills?"

Symone didn't blink. "We had to ask, Paul, so we could clear you as a suspect. This isn't just about the threats against us anymore. I have to get justice for my mother."

"That's right." Celeste gave Symone an approving nod

before turning back to Paul. "So, Paul, do you have any serious thoughts on who might've wanted to kill Odette and why?"

Paul cocked his head as he appeared to consider Celeste's question. "Odette was a wealthy and powerful woman. She carried a lot of influence in the health care industry, at least in the Midwest. But she wasn't feared. She was respected and very well liked. She was kind and intelligent. I can't think of a motive for anyone to want to hurt her, much less kill her."

Jerry heard Paul's love for his deceased wife. But again, he could be acting. "We think whoever killed Odette is now targeting Symone. The obvious link between them is the foundation."

Paul gestured toward Symone. "That's another reason for you to leave the foundation. Someone's already committed murder because of it, which makes it more likely they'll kill you, too. You could stay with my brother and me in North Carolina at least until your mother's killer's been found."

Symone squared her shoulders. "I'm staying to help find her killer."

A glint of what looked like admiration shone briefly in Paul's eyes. "You are your father's daughter."

Jerry wished he'd known Langston Bishop. He must have been an impressive person to have earned Odette's and Symone's devotion, and the respect of an entire industry.

He shook off the regret and refocused on the case. "Can you think of anyone who'd want to take over the foundation? Someone on the board, perhaps?"

Paul was shaking his head before Jerry finished speaking. "No, no. Of course not. All our employees go through extensive screening. So do the applicants for our board. Most of them have been with the foundation for years. Wes and Xander are the most recent members. I've known Wes for years. And the member Xander replaced recommended him."

Symone arched an eyebrow at Jerry. He read the I-Told-You-So message in her eyes. He wasn't ready to make concessions, though. Paul's endorsement of the board members didn't carry any weight since, in Jerry's opinion, Paul was still under suspicion. A lot of it. He wasn't prepared to clear the vendor who did the background checks for The Bishop Foundation, either, since it appears it had approved a killer's board application.

He glanced between Celeste and Symone. "Do you have any other questions?"

Celeste tilted her head. "One last question, Paul. Did you tell anyone about Odette's heart condition?"

Paul shrugged and lowered his eyes. "I may have mentioned it in passing to Wes. But I don't recall exactly."

Symone frowned. "I wish you hadn't done that, Paul. You know Mom was a very private person."

Paul nodded. "I'm sorry. I wasn't thinking."

Jerry sent a text to the Touré Security Group agent stationed outside. "Clear?"

The reply came back. "Clear."

Still looking at Paul, Symone continued. "Call me before you leave Columbus. I don't want you to go without saying goodbye."

"Be careful, Symone." Paul stood. "I want to help find Odette's killer, too. If I think of anything else, I'll email you."

"Thanks." Jerry straightened from his chair. "And if we have any other questions, we'll call."

Paul led them to the front door. Jerry stepped out first, using his body to shield Symone. He looked up and down the broad newly paved asphalt street. A row of large, old maple trees bordered it on both sides. Everything seemed quiet in this suburban community. Two of the three cars parked at the nearby curb were empty. The third belonged to one of the agency's personal security consultants.

Jerry nodded at Paul, then looked at Celeste and Symone. "We're good to go."

They moved quickly to get Symone into Jerry's car before Celeste jumped into her own dark gray sedan.

As Jerry pointed the car in the direction of U.S. 33 East, he checked the rearview mirror and both side mirrors. No one appeared to be following them. Yet.

He glanced at Symone. She sat stiff and quiet on the passenger seat. "Are you all right?"

"I thought my mother and I told each other everything." She kept her eyes on the windshield. "Why hadn't she told me she was divorcing Paul?"

Jerry met her clouded brown eyes before returning his attention to the late afternoon traffic. "Maybe she didn't want to worry or upset you." He felt Symone's eyes on him.

"What other information did she withhold to avoid upsetting me?" Her voice was tight. "Had she known she was in danger?"

Jerry's eyebrows knitted. "That's a very good question."

Chapter 8

"**P**aul's not off the hook." Jerry caught the displeased look Symone sent from under her thick eyelashes. She wasn't happy with his decision. Fortunately, his job wasn't to make her happy. It was to keep her safe. "The interview left me with more questions than answers."

They'd logged onto the videoconference from the safe house's dining area late Saturday afternoon. Jerry could still smell the garlic, cumin, paprika, cheese and onions from the chili he'd made for lunch.

He and Symone were updating Zeke and Mal on their meeting with Paul earlier in the day. Both brothers wore crisp white shirts and jewel-toned ties, but they had taken off their suit jackets. Celeste had joined the videoconference from her office.

"I agree." Zeke's words came slowly as though he was processing the information Jerry, Symone and Celeste had shared with him. It was a lot. "I'm sure he believes he loved her. But there are numerous cases of spouses who'd professed to still be in love with the partners they killed."

Harsh but true.

Symone leaned forward, bringing her and her wildflower scent closer to Jerry. "Paul genuinely loved my mother. I don't have any doubt of that."

"Then I believe you." Celeste shrugged her shoulders. "Maybe it was a case of If-I-Can't-Have-Her-No-One-Can."

Symone spread her hands. "What does that have to do with the foundation?"

Celeste drummed her fingers against her desk. "I guess nothing, at least not on the surface. We need to know how long it would take someone who isn't on their heart medication to have an episode."

Mal broke his silence. "I asked Grace about that. She said the speed at which Odette's heart reacted to being off her heart medication would've depended on several factors, including her overall health and her body's response to the medication. But if she had to guess, Grace thought Odette's withdrawal from her prescription could've triggered a heart attack in a relatively short period of time, perhaps a week or two."

Symone drew a shaky breath. "And by the time we got her to the hospital, it was already too late."

Jerry squeezed her hand as it rested on the table beside his. "We're agreed that we'll keep Paul on the list."

Symone tilted her head. "No, we're not agreed. He had access and opportunity, but he didn't have motive. He has his own income separate from the foundation and it's quite comfortable. Now he's taking his wealth to North Carolina."

Jerry arched his eyebrows in surprise. He hadn't expected a high-society figure like Symone Bishop to paraphrase future NBA Hall of Famer LeBron James's 2010 quote about leaving the Cleveland Cavaliers and taking his talents to the Miami Heat. This was an unexpected side of the heiress.

"Let's compromise." Mal's words brought Jerry back to the meeting. "We'll keep Paul on the list but move him down. Have you scheduled your interview with Wesley Bragg?"

"Tomorrow at ten." Celeste looked up from her smartphone. "I'll meet you both at his house."

Jerry nodded. "One of our personal security consultants will again scout the area while we're meeting with Wesley. It's another layer of security."

Zeke inclined his head. "Good idea."

"Yes, good idea." Mal flipped through a multipage printout beside him. "Bragg has an interesting background. He's carrying a lot of personal debt."

Celeste raised her straight, ebony eyebrow. "I wonder why that would be."

Jerry was curious, too. "I look forward to asking him tomorrow."

Symone couldn't concentrate. She blamed that on the murder investigation hanging over her head. The varied schemes revealed over the past two days had sent her thoughts racing in half a dozen directions. Someone had killed her mother. That same person was most likely now threatening her. The board had scheduled a no-confidence vote against her—which made them suspects in her mother's murder. Her mother's husband also was a viable suspect, at least that's what Jerry kept saying. Her mother had filed for divorce from Paul—but hadn't told her.

In the meantime, she was hiding in an idyllic cabin in a lush, secluded woodland resort with an incredibly attractive bodyguard who cooked like a five-star chef.

What did it say about her lifestyle that she'd have to be in danger to get a date? Fate could be so cruel.

Her burner phone chirped, notifying Symone of an incoming call. She recognized Ellie's work cell phone number.

"Hello?" She rose from the desk in her bedroom.

"Oh, thank goodness!" Her admin's greeting rushed out on a relieved sigh.

"Ellie?" Symone crossed the room to sit on a corner of her bed. "What's the matter? Why are you calling me on a Saturday evening?"

Foundation employees may sometimes have to work long hours during the week, but her parents had prided themselves on ensuring their staff and board always spent holidays and weekends with their families.

"What?" Ellie's voice rose several octaves. "Symone, how could you ask me that? Someone's trying to kill you and I haven't heard from you since yesterday morning. I've been worried sick."

It wasn't completely true that her assistant hadn't heard from her in more than twenty-four hours. Symone had sent an email to staff and board members, explaining she would be working remotely and they could reach her via email or through a new phone number. Ellie must have read that email. How else would she have known the number for her secure phone?

Symone chose not to point that out. "I'm sorry you were worried."

"I'm not just your admin, Symone. We've worked closely together for almost a year now. I consider us to be friends." Ellie drew a deep breath as though trying to make herself relax. "I can't wait until this is over."

"That makes two of us." Three, counting Jerry.

Symone's eyes drifted toward their shared wall. He was probably looking forward to sleeping in his own bed. What was he doing right now? After the videoconference with Celeste, Zeke and Mal, they'd gone to their rooms.

She was supposed to be revising her report for the board. He'd mentioned some work he had to take care of as well.

"How are you?" Ellie's voice startled her.

Symone had almost forgotten she'd been on a call with her admin. "I'm fine, all things considered."

She rose, turning her back to the wall she shared with Jerry. Symone wandered to her secure laptop, which waited for her on the small cedarwood desk positioned between two large windows.

"Are you sleeping okay? How's your appetite?" Ellie's questions kept coming.

Symone smiled at her admin's fussing. "I'm getting some sleep."

"Are you there by yourself or is someone there with you? Where are you?" Frustration was seeping into Ellie's words.

Symone could understand. She was frustrated, too. It had only been two days, but already she was anxious for her life to return to normal. She could only pray they found the stalker/killer soon.

"I'm sorry, Ellie." Symone sat behind her desk and logged on to her email account. "I understand you're concerned, and I appreciate it. I really do. But the fewer people who know where I am, the better."

"What should I say if the board asks about you?" Her voice was tentative.

Symone shut her eyes. This situation couldn't have come at a worse time. Or maybe that was the point. If someone on the board wanted to ensure she was voted out as chair, then forcing her into hiding for her protection and thereby limiting her access to the board was an excellent way of achieving their goal.

Symone sighed, opening her eyes again. "I'm safe. That's all the board needs to know."

"What about Paul? Is he there with you?"

"We're both safe." Symone scanned her email inbox and noticed a message from Dr. Grace Blackwell. What was that about?

Ellie's sigh carried through the phone. "Good. I'm glad. That's what's important. Let's hope you both stay that way."

"Absolutely." Symone sat up, anxious to open Grace's email. "Ellie, I'm sorry. I should get going. Thank you for calling."

"Of course, but one last thing before I go." Her voice sped up. "Did you get my email with the new report numbers?"

"Yes, I see it here." The message had come in late Friday, about the time she'd fallen asleep in Jerry's arms. Symone shook her head to get rid of that thought. "Thank you so much for all of your hard work."

"You're very welcome, Symone. Stay safe."

"Thank you. You as well." Symone disconnected the call, then launched Grace's email.

Dear Symone,

Mal said it would be all right for me to send this email as long as you open it on either the secure laptop or the secure smartphone he provided to you.

I'm so very sorry to learn of your mother's passing and that her death appears to have been premeditated. I didn't have much interaction with your mother, but she impressed me during our brief conversations. I wish I'd gotten to know her better. She was a great champion for the health care industry.

Please know that I'm thinking of you during this difficult time. I'm giving you my phone number in case you need to talk. I'm here to listen. Just please remember to

only use the secure cell Mal gave you. Your safety is everyone's first priority.
With deepest condolences,
Grace

Symone blinked away tears. She was so grateful to Grace for reaching out to her. The other woman's simple, heartfelt message stated everything she needed to read to know she wasn't alone. She'd been feeling alone and lonely ever since her mother's death. Her mother had been her last blood relative. She'd been her business partner and her best friend. With Odette gone, Symone didn't have anyone to talk with, to confide in.

She read the phone number in Grace's email and tapped it into the secure cell phone.

Grace answered on the second ring. "Hello?"

Symone took a breath. "This is Symone Bishop. Is this Grace?"

There was a smile in the other woman's voice. "I'm so glad you called."

Symone's neck and shoulders relaxed. "Thank you for your email. Is this a good time to talk?"

Symone relaxed back against the warm brown, overstuffed sofa after dinner Saturday evening. Jerry sat on the sofa's other end. They'd been hidden in this safe house for a little more than a day and had found a routine that worked well, at least for their meals. He cooked while she set the table. They both cleaned the kitchen afterward. Then they wandered into the great room to relax and unwind for an hour or so.

Jerry shifted on the sofa cushion. "I've checked the

security system. Everything's fine. The video shows no one's approached the cabin. I'll check again before bed."

Symone's muscles eased, releasing the tension she hadn't known had settled in her neck and shoulders. "Thank you. I'm very grateful to you for monitoring the security system so diligently." Her eyes circled the spacious pine-and-cedar room with its fluffy tan sofa and armchairs. "If my car hadn't been bombed, I could pretend I was on vacation."

"You're right, although for you it would be a working vacation. How's your report for the board coming?" Jerry's interest surprised her.

Symone searched his dark eyes. Was he making polite conversation, or did he really want to know? She shrugged off her hesitation. It would be nice to talk about it with someone. "It's coming along slowly. Right now, all I have is an outline for the revisions. I have some ideas for changes to the application criteria. And Ellie's just forwarded the new figures from our investment firm."

Jerry shifted toward her on the sofa. "What exactly does the board want you to do?"

They want us to change the very essence of the foundation's mission statement.

Symone reeled in her aggravation and gathered her thoughts. "The board believes the foundation has been too conservative with our recent investment strategies and with the applications we've awarded. Members want us to increase the return on our investments and to approve more grant applications for broader-based health programs and products."

Jerry paused for several long seconds. Symone could feel his thoughts churning. She forced herself to remain still and return his intense regard.

Finally, he broke his silence. "What's in it for the members?"

Symone looked away. Stress and aggravation pressed down on her like unbearable weights. "The board wants more investments. The increased revenue would allow the foundation to provide more grants and to invest in additional projects."

It sounded like a reasonable proposal. Was her resistance to it unreasonable?

"But you think more money means more problems." Jerry made it a statement rather than a question.

Symone sent him a quick look before returning to her distracted study of the wall across the room. "Something like that. My grandfather created the foundation because so many of his loved ones had died from cancer, diabetes and heart conditions. He was devastated but determined to do something about it. He made it the foundation's mission to support medical research focused to preventing these diseases. He also was committed to finding cures and ensuring quality of life for people living with these illnesses."

"I read about your grandfather and the foundation's origin story on your website. Hearing it from you, though, makes the foundation's mission even more powerful because it's personal. Your grandfather sounds like a really impressive individual."

A slight smile curved Symone's lips. "I always thought he must have been larger than life. I'm sorry I never knew him. He died before I was born. He had pancreatic cancer."

"I'm so sorry." Jerry paused before continuing. "You don't seem sold on changing the foundation's investment or application strategies."

"I'm not." Symone pushed off the sofa to pace the room. After their meeting with Paul, she'd changed into powder blue shorts, white cotton T-shirt and taupe slipper socks. "It's risky. But maybe it's worth the risk? I don't know." She paused, staring down at the cold fireplace. "It breaks my heart that the diseases my grandfather was fighting to end took him and both of my parents from me. My father also died of pancreatic cancer. My mother died of heart disease. Yes, the board's strategy could provide more money to support research to treat and hopefully cure these diseases—or we could lose everything."

"There's a mission statement on the foundation's website."

Symone looked at Jerry over her shoulder. "Yes, my grandfather developed it."

Jerry stood, shoving his hands into the front pockets of his black pants. "Your grandfather's mission statement reads like a map for the foundation. You should use it to help you decide whether this next step that the board wants to take makes sense in terms of your grandfather's vision."

"My parents and I have always depended on my grandfather's mission statement to guide the foundation's decisions. That's been its touchstone for more than 40 years." Symone paced toward the bay window that overlooked the south side of the cabin.

"What's changed?" Jerry's tone suggested he already knew the answer.

The tint covering the windowpanes allowed her to enjoy the view while preventing anyone from seeing inside. Symone's attention lingered on the cabin's gray-stone-graveled walkway that led to a dirt path that disappeared into a forest of tall, stately, ancient maple and oak trees. From this angle, she couldn't see the river that ran along the resort ground's perimeter. Would she get a chance to walk beside it once this ordeal was over? She hoped so.

Symone turned to Jerry. He stood less than two yards from her. "The board changed. I realize that's significant for our investigation. But it also makes me wonder if it's time for the foundation to change."

"I know the foundation's important to you, of course. It's your family's legacy. But let's table the report for a sec." It was Jerry's turn to pace the spacious great room. Long, loose-legged strides brought him to the fireplace. "The board members aren't as committed to the foundation's mission statement anymore. So what's changed about the board? It has two new members, Wes Bragg, who we're meeting with tomorrow, and Xander Fence. Mal's doing a background check on him now."

Symone interrupted. "Our vendor already did a thorough background check on all of our members *and* both Wes and Xander have personal recommendations from people associated with the foundation."

Jerry slid a skeptical look in her direction as he crossed to the wall beside the bay window where Symone stood. "We're looking into their references as well."

Symone wanted to roll her eyes. With great effort, she did not. "You've already checked Wes's personal reference. It was from Paul."

"And Mal's doing a background check on Ellie." Jerry turned to pace in the opposite direction.

Symone was torn between defending her board, her staff and her vendor, and supporting Touré Security Group's efforts to keep her safe. The bottom line was her mother was dead because someone had tampered with her medication. Did she have confidence in the Touré brothers'— and Celeste Jarrett's—ability to help bring her mother's killer to justice?

Absolutely! She trusted them with her life. The matter

was resolved. She'd follow Touré Security Group's and Jarrett & Nichols Investigations's lead.

"Paul resigned from the foundation today. What does that mean for the board's vote in a couple of weeks?"

Symone took a moment to consider his question as she watched him walk past the fireplace. He was like a jaguar on the prowl—silent, unpredictable, dangerous. "For the vote itself, nothing would change. The board would still need a supermajority of the foundation's remaining eight voting members—seven on the board and one in administration— to remove me as chair. However, there would be one fewer person to speak on my behalf."

"Having fewer people in your corner is a concern, but at least it doesn't affect the vote count. They'd still need six on their side." Jerry turned to travel back across the room. "Who are the six members you think might vote against you?"

Symone shook her head, spreading her arms. "I really couldn't say. If you'd asked me three months ago, I wouldn't have thought anyone would vote against having a member of my family lead the foundation."

"But as you said, the board's changed." Jerry stopped in front of her. "So who do you think would vote against you now?"

Symone went back to her memories of the last board meeting and the discussion of the no-confidence vote. It wasn't hard to recall each member's reaction and what they said. "If I had to guess, I'd say Tina Gardner, the board president, then Julie Parke, Aaron Menéndez and Xander would support replacing me."

"That's four members." Jerry frowned. "Do you think the vote to replace you would be that close?" His voice was tight.

Symone felt his concern and drew strength and comfort from it. "I'm only guessing based on members' reactions during the last meeting. I hope Ellie and Wes will support me. Judging by their reactions, I think Keisha Lord and Kitty Lymon also will."

Jerry ran a hand over his thick, tight curls. A deep sigh expanded his muscled chest and lifted his broad shoulders. Symone sensed his thoughts racing. "What would happen if the vote ends in a tie?"

Symone spoke over her shoulder as she wandered back to the fireplace. "I'd remain the chair of my family's foundation."

"Then our side would have two chances to win, a simple majority of five votes in your favor or a tie." Jerry gave her a crooked smile.

Symone's breath lodged in her throat. "Uh-huh." She drew a breath. "I hadn't thought about that, but you're right. I still wish Paul would reconsider his resignation, at least until after the vote, as selfish as that might seem." She sighed as the other revelation from their earlier discussion with her stepfather returned to the forefront of her mind. "Why hadn't my mother told me she and Paul had discussed getting a divorce? Why hadn't I realized she'd been so unhappy with him?"

Jerry stepped forward, closing the distance between them. His voice was a gentle caress over her open emotional wounds. "I think the answer to both of those questions is she didn't want you to know."

"But why not?" She searched his kind, midnight eyes. His face was blurry through her unshed tears. "I'm her daughter. I thought we told each other everything."

Jerry reached out, cupping his right hand around her left upper arm. The warmth of his palm seeped into her muscles, soothing her. "There're probably so many reasons your mother hadn't had a chance to tell you she'd filed for divorce before she died. I'm sure she wanted to. She just didn't realize she was running out of time."

Lowering her eyes, Symone nodded. She rubbed tears from her eyes before looking up. "Thank you again for looking after me. I know I'm paying you and your brothers for your security services, but I feel so much safer knowing you guys and Celeste are involved in this case with me."

"You're wrong, Symone." Jerry dropped his hand to his side. "My brothers and I could've assigned your case to one of our security teams. We're each working on this case personally because we want to. I wanted to be here."

Jerry's words were like a dozen long-stemmed red roses. He and his brothers were standing by her because they cared. She really wasn't alone. She wanted to throw her arms around his neck and hold him close.

Instead, she forced herself to take a step back. "Thank you, Jerry. I'm going to work on that report for a couple of hours before turning in. Good night."

Jerry's well-wishes for the night followed her from the room. Symone concentrated on convincing her legs to carry her upstairs. She needed to identify her mother's killer/her stalker as soon as possible. It wasn't only her life that was in danger. As long as they were standing by her, the Touré brothers and Celeste also were targets.

Chapter 9

"**Y**ou're Symone's bodyguards?" Wesley Bragg, one of the two new members of The Bishop Foundation Board of Directors, took Jerry's and Celeste's measure as they joined Symone and their host in Wes's living room Sunday morning.

They were meeting with Paul's lawyer at his home. The Cape Cod-style house was spacious with wide rooms and high ceilings. The living room's heavy, silver-and-black furnishings tempered the spill of natural light from the long, narrow front windows. The air carried the hint of lemon wax from the highly polished dark wood flooring.

Jerry returned Wes's regard. "Celeste Jarrett and I are working with the police to find the person behind the threats against Symone and Paul. Paul thinks the threats are connected to his lawsuits. He said you're handling that matter for him."

"That's right. It was my idea to sue Odette's doctor and the pharmaceutical company that manufactured her heart medicine." Wes managed to sound boastful and altruistic at the same time.

Symone interrupted him. "Paul told me you'd approached him with the idea the day after my mother's funeral."

Jerry couldn't tell whether Wes caught the hint of disapproval that chilled her words. He looked at Symone sitting politely between him and Celeste on the long, black leather sofa. She wore a modest blush, scoop-necked blouse and slim tan skirt suit with matching three-inch pumps. She'd once again accessorized with pearl earrings and a matching pearl necklace. The overall impression was cool and professional, but Jerry sensed it was a disguise masking a volcanic temper.

"Of course." Wes had the matching leather armchair to himself. "We needed to file the suit as soon as possible."

Celeste crossed her jean-clad legs. This pair was dark blue. She wore it with a square-necked black shell blouse. "Why were you so intent on suing them?"

Wes's expression was somber as he met Celeste's eyes. His thin lips were unsmiling. "You didn't see Paul when Odette died." He shifted his attention to Jerry. "He'd been in love with Odette for years, but he loved her more than Odette loved him." He looked at Symone. "Don't get me wrong, Odette liked Paul and enjoyed his company, but he knew she was still in love with your father. Did you know he'd proposed to her at least twice before she'd finally agreed to marry him?"

Symone nodded. "Yes, she told me."

Jerry could believe it. Symone said Langston Bishop had been larger than life. Like his parents. Her father be a tough act for anyone to follow, especially an introvert like Paul Kayple.

Wes shook his head. "At first, Paul had accepted that Odette would never love him as much as she'd loved your father but over time, it wore him down. When she died less than two years into their marriage, he was devastated."

"I know." Symone leaned back against the sofa. "We all were."

Wes's eyes widened as though he'd realized that as Paul was grieving the death of his wife, Symone was also grieving the death of her mother. "Of course. And that's the reason I offered to represent Paul in his lawsuits."

Celeste arched a straight eyebrow. She gave Wes a once-over. "Because he was heartbroken over Odette's death?"

Wes inclined his head. "That's right. I thought justice for Odette would bring him comfort and that was all I could offer him. Odette had contacted her doctor twice about her symptoms before her heart attack. Their first contact, he'd brushed her off. When she'd called the second time, he'd scheduled an appointment almost two weeks out. His lack of action shows he didn't take her concerns seriously. He should have urged her to come into his office immediately."

Jerry glanced at Symone. She was silent and still. Her temper showed in her thin lips and tight jaw. Underneath that subdued anger, he sensed her devastation. He searched Wes's innocent expression and replayed his altruistic words. He didn't buy the lawyer's act. He was capitalizing off Odette's death to make money to pay his debts.

Jerry gave the other man a curious look. "Are you sure your motivation for encouraging Paul to file these lawsuits wasn't the potential payday you'd get from suing a medical doctor and a large pharmaceutical company?"

Surprise wiped all expression from Wes's face. His lips parted and his eyes widened. "What do you mean?"

Jerry cocked his head. "We know you're in debt up to your eyeballs, Wes."

Celeste leaned forward, bracing her elbows on her thighs. "You're making child support and alimony payments to multiple ex-wives."

"Three of them." Jerry held up the index, middle and ring fingers of his right hand.

Celeste gestured around the room. "You also have mortgage payments. Your solo practice isn't doing well. Cases are slow. I get it. I run a business, too."

Jerry considered the older man. "Are you sure your financial situation isn't the real reason you convinced Paul to file the lawsuits?"

Wes's frown transformed from confusion to surprise. His eyes swept from Celeste and Jerry to settle on Symone. "You're checking up on me? Did Paul say something to you? Is he complaining about me?"

"What would he have to complain about?" Symone asked.

"Nothing." Wes's voice rose.

"Watch the tone, Wes." Jerry frowned over Wes's rudeness toward Symone. She didn't deserve that. He sensed her eyes on him.

"I'm sorry." Wes directed his apology to Symone, then divided a look between Jerry and Celeste. "You're right. I convinced Paul to sue because I need money. Business has been slow for a while. The few clients I've had are even slower to pay. Paul thought the extra money from my position on the board would help and he's right. It did help, but not enough. My mortgage payments and office rent alone wouldn't be so bad. It's the alimony and child support that are crushing me."

Symone crossed her right leg over her left and folded her arms below her chest. "We had my mother's medication tested. Her pills had been tainted with tetrahydrozoline."

Wes's bushy brown eyebrows knitted. "What are you saying?"

Symone pinned the other man with a hard look. "Someone poisoned my mother."

Wes's jaw dropped. "Symone, I'm so very sorry. But why would someone want to harm Odette? Everyone loved her."

Jerry turned his attention from Symone back to Wes. "That's what we're wondering. It would have to be someone who knew about Odette's prescription. Paul told us he'd mentioned Odette's heart condition to you."

Wes straightened on his chair. "You think *I* had something to do with Odette's death? I *absolutely* did *not*."

Jerry was tempted to believe his righteous outrage, but he knew the emotion could be faked. "As a member of the board, you'd be eligible to replace Symone as chair of the foundation if the board votes her out."

Wes's face flushed an angry red. "You think I'd kill Odette to take over the foundation?"

"Would you?" Celeste asked.

Wes leaned forward on his chair. "*No*, I would *not*. I don't have any interest in taking over the foundation. I have a law practice to run."

Jerry nodded. "You said yourself your practice isn't doing so well. You admitted you need cash for alimony and child support payments."

Wes's nostrils flared. "It'll turn around. The problem with the foundation is that the chair doesn't have control of the foundation. Not really. The way the bylaws are written, the chair's answerable to the board. No offense, Symone, but I don't envy you and I wouldn't want your job."

Celeste snorted. "You expect us to believe you?"

"It's the truth." Wes's voice was rough. "I'd rather pull out my fingernails than report to the narcissists on the foundation's board."

Symone gave a soft sigh. "I believe you."

Jerry's head jerked in her direction. "You do?"

"Yes." Symone nodded. "Because some days, I feel the same way."

Jerry turned back to Wes. Based on the board's plan to oust Symone, he could understand why she'd feel that way, but was that enough to dissuade Wes from taking Symone's job—especially if he needed the money?

Jerry read the skepticism in Celeste's eyes. He agreed with the private investigator. Wes was staying on the list.

He retrieved his cell phone from his front pants pocket. "Clear?" He sent the text to the security consultant stationed in a nondescript car across the street and down the block from Wes's house. The Touré Security Group agent was watching for suspicious cars, pedestrians and activities while he, Symone and Celeste interviewed Wes.

His phone chimed, alerting him to the consultant's reply. "Clear."

Jerry stood, returning his cell to his pants pocket. "Thanks for meeting with us, Wes. If we have any other questions, we'll be in touch." He waited for Symone and Celeste to stand before falling into step behind them.

"Of course." Wes escorted them to the front door. "Whatever I can do to help." He paused with his hand on the dark wood door's ancient bronze doorknob. He met Symone's eyes. "Paul really loved Odette even though he knew he might not have much time with her because of her heart condition. I think it made him even more anxious to marry her. He wanted as much time with her as possible."

Symone frowned as though unsure how to respond. "Thanks for your time, Wes."

Jerry was confused, too. Had Paul been anxious to marry Odette because he wanted as much time as he could get with her? Or had he married her for access to the foundation's money upon her demise? Paul's friend had just given them more evidence against him.

"Wes didn't kill my mother." Symone stared through the windshield as Jerry sped down U.S. 33 East late Sunday morning. Their safe house was about an hour south of Columbus.

Safe house. The term sounded more romantic than ominous. Was that because of her companion? Symone glanced at Jerry's clean, classically handsome profile as he sat behind the steering wheel of the rented smoke gray sedan. A sexy, pensive frown wrinkled his brow. He had a way of making the cramped interior seem cozy. The air held a hint of soap and mint. Symone took a quick breath to test it. Her body hummed restlessly.

She jerked her attention back to the scene outside. A gentle breeze nudged the few fluffy white clouds that dotted the bright cerulean blue sky. The thought of spending the rest of this beautiful, early summer day inside caused her stomach muscles to twist with regret.

"What makes you so sure he didn't kill her?" Jerry checked his rear and side mirrors before switching into the far-left lane.

He was switching lanes a lot. Was he an impatient driver? Or was he making sure they weren't being followed? Probably both. She'd noticed him scanning both sides of the street when they'd entered Wes's home and when they'd left. He'd done the same thing when they'd met with Paul the day before.

Symone returned her attention to the windshield. "You heard the way Wes talked about Paul's feelings for my mother. Wes and Paul have been close for years. He wouldn't kill his friend's wife."

The vehicle's interior vibrated with Jerry's skepticism. "Give someone a strong enough motive and they'll do anything. Money's a very strong motive."

"You want my opinion based on my experience with our suspects. With what I know about Wes and his relationship with Paul, I don't believe he's a threat." Symone's shrug was restless as she tried to put her feelings into words. "I've known Wes since before he joined the board. He's been to dinner with my mother and me. He was always talking about how proud he was of his children and things he was doing to bring in clients. I just can't imagine that person plotting to kill my mother."

Jerry maneuvered his way back to the far-right lane as they closed in on the exit to Ohio State Route 180 West. "He's been to your mother's house?"

"Yes." She frowned at his sharp tone.

"Was he there the month before your mother died?"

Symone made a quick calculation. "Yes. The four of us tried to get together for dinner at Mom and Paul's house the first Friday of the month. We all couldn't always make it, but we did that last Friday."

Jerry's intense eyes caught hers before returning to the traffic. "If he was in the house, he could've slipped away to replace your mother's prescription with the fake pills."

Symone was shaking her head before Jerry finished speaking. "I don't recall Wes disappearing. At least not for a lengthy period of time and not without an explanation."

"An explanation?"

Symone shifted on her seat to face him. "He may have excused himself to go to the bathroom or get something from his car."

Jerry flipped his right hand before returning it to the

steering wheel. "Either one of those excuses would've given him enough time to plant the pills."

Symone spread her hands. "How would he have known where my mother kept her medication?"

Jerry shrugged. "Most people keep their prescriptions in their nightstands."

That was true. "You heard him, though. He doesn't want to be chair. He said he'd rather pull out his fingernails than answer to the 'narcissistic' board. Even though I grew up with the foundation, I still get frustrated with the board. If someone doesn't have the same connection to the foundation that I have, the members can be a bit much."

Jerry checked his blind spot before exiting the state route. "Symone, I get that the idea that someone you know and thought you could trust would want to hurt you or especially your mother would be hard to deal with. But you have to remember this isn't about either of you. It's not personal. It's about the money."

Impatience made her skin crawl. "I understand that but when are we going to start removing people from our list so we can focus on viable suspects? I want to find my mother's killer, not continually debate the pros and cons of each candidate."

Jerry glanced at her before returning his attention to the traffic. "Wes *is* a viable suspect. He had motive, money. He had opportunity during the dinners. And for method, it wouldn't be hard for someone to get tetrahydrozoline." He turned right onto the main road that would take them back to the cabin resort.

How could she argue with that? He'd explained his reasoning so clearly and succinctly. And, even more frustrating, he'd made sense. Symone expelled a breath. Maybe she should ask him to explain the foundation's mission statement to the board.

Symone turned on her seat to face the windshield. "All right. I'll concede you've made some good points. Maybe we should keep Wes on the list, at least a little while longer. But I want to go on record that I don't believe he killed my mother. Call it a gut instinct."

Jerry sent her his wicked grin, the one that made her toes curl. "There's nothing wrong with following your gut. I do it all the time." He shrugged. "This time, our guts are on different sides of this issue."

"So we have Paul and Wes." Symone unclenched her teeth and shook her head. "It really bothers me that the two people with whom my mother and I were closest are the top suspects on this list."

"It bothers me, too." Jerry's voice was somber.

Symone blinked. "Thank you."

His empathy helped ease her wounded spirit. She didn't know what she'd expected from her first—and hopefully last—personal security consultant but Jerry was more than she could've imagined. They'd only known each other three days, but she trusted and respected him more than most of the people she'd known for years. It was the way he protected her with such single-mindedness. And the way he listened to her, paying attention to her voice and her body language. She even enjoyed their debates.

I wanted to be here.

Don't read into his words, Symone. It wasn't personal. It was about the assignment.

The sooner they found her mother's killer, the better. And then she and Jerry would part ways, never to see each other again. Disappointment felt like an elephant sitting on her lap.

* * *

Jerry's cell phone rang as he and Symone entered the safe house Sunday afternoon. They'd entered the cabin via the attached garage. The rented sedan's tinted windows and the garage provided cover in case someone was watching for them.

"What's up?" Jerry answered on the second ring, locking the breezeway door behind them.

Symone smiled at his casual greeting. He must've recognized the caller. She started to turn away to give him privacy, but he caught her hand.

"It's Mal and Zeke. They want me to put them on speaker." He tapped the screen without releasing her hand. "Okay. Go ahead."

"We have a problem." Mal's grim voice rose from the smartphone. Coming from the calmest Touré, the warning carried additional weight. "I can't find Dorothy Wiggans."

Symone's fingers tightened around Jerry's big, warm hand. *Oh, no.*

Jerry frowned. "The board member who'd recommended Xander Fence as her replacement?"

Dorothy "Dottie" Wiggans had served five full terms, the maximum amount of time, with the board. She was the last member to have worked with Langston Bishop. Symone pictured the woman. Dottie was a cross between Mary Poppins and Mrs. Santa Claus. The silver-haired septuagenarian was petite with laughing cornflower blue eyes and a riot of silver curls framing a pixie face.

Symone leaned closer to the cell phone. "Mal, what do you mean you 'can't find' her?"

"Someone filed a missing persons report for Dorothy Wiggans three months ago." Papers rustled just beneath Mal's words. Symone imagined the computer expert sifting through mountains of papers. "There hasn't been any activity on her credit cards or bank accounts since April. Her utilities have been shut off due to unpaid bills."

"April?" Jerry's eyes sharpened on Symone's face. "That's the same time your mother died."

He voiced the thought that had flashed across Symone's mind. What was happening? Was Dottie's disappearance somehow connected to her mother's murder? Symone's knees shook. Jerry helped her across the room to the soft, tan love seat. She dropped onto the left cushion.

Jerry settled beside her. "Are you okay?"

Symone nodded. "I'm fine. Thank you."

Zeke's voice came through the speaker. "Celeste's on her way to interview the neighbor who filed the police report. We've left messages for Eriq and Taylor."

"I've already reviewed the foundation's file on Xander." Mal jumped in. "I'm going over it again. And we've asked the foundation's background-check vendor for Dottie's file. In the meantime, what can you tell us about her?"

Symone's mind spun with the steps the brothers had already taken to find out what had happened to Dottie. "She was born and raised in Australia. Melbourne, I think. She'd immigrated to the United States in her twenties. She'd joined the board when my father was chair. She'd been a pathologist before she retired about five years ago. She'd never married. She didn't have any children, and she was the only member of her family in the United States. She'd told my father she was lonely and had a lot of time on her hands." Symone smiled. "She'd also been an amateur actor. She starred in musicals with a local community theater group. Even after she retired, she remained on the board. She would've been termed out this month. Board members are only allowed to serve five consecutive terms, which would be fifteen years."

Jerry shifted to face her. Their knees were inches apart. "Why did Dottie decide to leave before her term was up?"

"I was surprised by that, too." Symone spread her hands. "She told Paul she wanted to slow down. She was also going to visit her twin sister in Australia. Her sister was her only surviving relative after their older brother had died of cancer. They'd been estranged for years. Mom and I were thrilled that they were trying to reconcile."

"When and how did you receive her recommendation for Xander?" Mal asked.

Symone narrowed her eyes as she brought to mind the time frame. "It was late March, I think. A few weeks before Mom died. That's when Dottie called Paul. Paul was the foundation's board liaison at the time. She'd emailed her recommendation to him."

"Paul was the last person to speak with her?" Jerry's question was devoid of inflection.

Symone gave him a sharp look. She felt his suspicion toward her stepfather building. "My mother spoke with her also. She said Dottie sounded tired, so she didn't keep her very long."

Now Symone wished she'd followed up with Dottie. Both she and her mother had thought Dottie's abrupt departure had been uncharacteristic. She should've done more to learn what had been behind her decision. But she'd ignored her instincts and now she was learning Dottie had been missing for at least three months.

Zeke broke the brief silence. "What's your impression of Xander Fence?"

Symone shook her head although Zeke couldn't see her. "He doesn't say much during the board meetings. Neither does Wes. I thought that was because they're the newest members. They're still getting a feel for the organization and the board."

Jerry ran a hand over his hair. "We're going to have to step up our time frame for speaking with him."

Symone met his eyes. "I agree."

Zeke's sigh carried through the internet connection. "We'll contact you again as soon as we hear back from Celeste, Eriq and Taylor."

"Stay alert." Mal's voice was firm. "And, Symone, remember not to turn on your personal devices. The more we uncover in this case, the more certain I am that you were being tracked."

A chill flashed through her system. "I'll be careful."

Once Jerry had ended the call, Symone rose and looked down at him. "You were right to include Xander on our suspect list. I apologize for doubting you."

Jerry stood. "No apology necessary. I get it. You've known these people a lot longer than you've known me."

Then why do I trust you more?

Symone turned and walked toward the kitchenette. She needed a mug of tea to help settle her nerves. She felt trapped in a nightmare by unanswered questions that kept her from waking up. What had happened to Dottie? What role, if any, had Xander played in her disappearance? Did Paul have anything to do with this?

She clenched her fists. And the most terrifying question of all: Who else was involved?

Chapter 10

Jerry froze in the basement of the safe house early Monday morning. Symone stood in profile on a mauve yoga mat five or six yards from where he stood in the shadows of the staircase. She was clothed in a powder blue yoga tank and mid-thigh shorts that hugged her lean muscles and traced her firm curves. Surrounded by silence, she raised her slender arms above her head. Slowly, she bent forward from her waist and lowered her forehead to her thighs and her fingertips to the mat. She extended her legs behind her, first one, then the other, to form a plank. Her back was straight and her chin was lifted.

He was familiar with the yoga poses she was performing—sun salutation, cobra, planks. But it was the strength, grace and flexibility she exhibited that mesmerized him. She worked out in silence, but there was music to her movements. It was like watching a dance. Her stretches were long, well-balanced and fluid. Time stood still.

Jerry waited for Symone to finish before stepping forward out of the shadows. "That was impressive."

She must've jumped half a foot into the air. Her breath left her in a whoosh. She pressed her right hand against her heart as though trying to keep it from leaping out of her chest. "I didn't realize you were there." Breathless, nervous laughter escaped her parted lips.

"I'm so sorry." Jerry chuckled. "I didn't mean to startle you. I wanted to compliment you. That was an amazing workout."

Symone grinned up at him. Her chocolate eyes twinkled with good humor. "After seeing *your* workouts, I realize that's quite a compliment coming from you. Thank you."

She'd enjoyed watching him work out? Jerry hoped his grin wasn't as goofy as it felt.

Sweat slid over Symone's slender shoulders and trailed her toned arms. She squatted to roll her yoga mat. She was leaving. He wanted her to stay, at least a little while longer.

"Have you been practicing the self-defense moves we reviewed?"

Symone stood, carrying the mat to the far-left corner of the room where she'd left her matching yoga bag.

"Yes. I pantomime the steps a few times before my regular workout." She shoved her mat into the bag, zipped it, then leaned it against the corner before stepping forward to demonstrate the moves. "Solar plexus." She braced her legs, then drove her elbow into an imaginary solar plexus. "Instep." She ground her heel into a nonexistent instep. "Nose." She made a fist with her right hand, then punched backward over her shoulder. "Groin." She punched down with the same fist.

Jerry winced, imagining the impact. "Good. Now practice on me." He held out his left arm, palm out. "We're going for a real-world simulation but remember—pull your punches. You don't want to injure your personal security consultant."

Symone tossed him a cocky smile. "I'll be gentle."

Jerry chuckled. He hadn't met this Symone before. She was confident, in control. Even sexier. He liked this side of her. A lot.

She strode to him. When she was about an arm's length away, she turned her back to him and pretended to scroll through an imaginary cell phone. Nice touch.

Jerry came up from behind her. He wrapped his right arm around her lithe waist and clamped his left palm over her lush lips. Apparently startled, Symone flinched. The shift in her weight threw them both off-balance and they started to fall. Jerry snatched her to his chest and twisted his torso so Symone would land on top of him. Holding her close, he absorbed their impact as he landed on the padded flooring.

"Oh my gosh! Oh my gosh!" Symone rolled over on top of him. "Are you okay?" Her eyes had darkened with guilt and worry.

Jerry shook with laughter, causing Symone to bounce on his torso. His arms were loose around her waist. "I'm fine. How are you?"

"I'm so sorry." Her wide eyes searched his head and face as though she thought he was lying about being okay.

"As a self-defense technique, that maneuver needs a bit of work." He grinned up at her.

Symone's eyes met his. Amusement nudged away guilt and worry. "I hadn't expected you to grab me so aggressively."

"It was a *real-world* simulation. I had to sell it."

"You sold it a bit too well." Symone chuckled and her body moved against his.

Jerry knew the exact moment Symone realized she was lying on top of him. It was the millisecond after he became aware of her soft, warm body against his. Humor evaporated. Their bodies stilled. Their eyes locked. Air drained from the room as electricity arced around and between them.

Jerry was afraid to move, afraid the desire whispering in his ears would seep into his muscles and take control of him. It taunted him with commands he knew he couldn't obey.

Touch her.

Hold her.

Taste her.

His pulse raced. Jerry strained to ignore his body's orders. Sanity was a fading echo in the back of his mind.

She's out of your league.

She has to be able to trust you.

She's a client!

Jerry set his hands at her waist. He wanted to help her to her feet. He needed distance between them. He had to clear his mind.

His palms burned where they touched her skin. "Symone, I—"

She lowered her head and pressed her lips against his. Heat exploded in his gut like a shot from a cannon. His muscles stiffened in surprise, then relaxed in welcome.

Her lips were so soft and so warm. Her taste was sweet and spicy. Seemingly of its own accord, Jerry's right arm circled her waist to hold her closer to him. His left hand cupped the back of her head. Symone's palms slid over his chest to grip his shoulders. She shifted higher on his torso and angled her head to deepen their kiss. Jerry parted his lips. She accepted his invitation, sweeping her tongue inside his mouth to explore him. Symone moaned. He echoed the sound.

Sanity was once again shouting to be heard from somewhere far, far away. Its cautions were barely audible above the blood rushing in his head. *What are you doing? She's your client. You're betraying her trust. You come from different worlds.*

Those statements were true—but she felt so right in his arms.

Jerry drew Symone's tongue deeper into his mouth. His hands traced the lines of her firm, warm figure.

"Symone, you feel so good." He whispered the words against her lips.

"So do you." She tipped her head back and he trailed kisses along the length of her throat. "I want—"

Without warning, Symone scrambled off him. "Oh my gosh! Oh my gosh!" She surged to her feet. "I'm—I—Oh!" She rushed from the room.

What just happened?

Craning his neck, Jerry followed her flight until she disappeared up the stairs. Gritting his teeth, he dropped back against the padded flooring. He pressed his left forearm across his eyes and pounded his right fist against the ground. "Idiot! What have you done?"

"I'm sorry to say we found Dorothy Wiggans's body." Eriq's voice was heavy with grief. He and Taylor had joined the early morning videoconference. They appeared to be using a laptop in one of the police precinct's interrogation rooms. "She'd been a Jane Doe at the county morgue. The killer had suffocated her, probably with a pillow, then moved her body to a construction site on the far west side. Someone on the crew discovered her the next day."

"Oh, no." Symone's voice was muffled behind her palms. The temperature in the room felt as though it had dropped ten degrees. She shivered in reaction.

Taylor continued their report on Dottie. "Her neighbor identified Ms. Wiggans from the coroner's photos. Her body's already been cremated. The county has to either bury or cremate unclaimed bodies after sixty days."

Symone rubbed her arms, trying to get warm again. "I should've followed my instincts. I knew something was wrong. She wouldn't have stepped down before the end of her term. She's—she was—the kind of person who always completed a task. She was compulsive that way."

From his seat on her right, Jerry put his hand on her shoulder. His dark eyes were soft with empathy. "Don't blame yourself. You aren't the one who harmed her."

Symone's face burned with discomfort. She looked away. Jerry was distracting in an emerald polo shirt and black slacks. His midnight eyes were even more hypnotic since their kiss earlier that morning. What had she been thinking? That was the problem. She hadn't been. She'd acted on impulse, giving in to her feelings, to the moment. To the madness. But she hadn't been sorry. That's why she hadn't apologized. She would have been lying.

Breakfast had been awkward, to say the least. Jerry had made an effort to put her at ease. It was another example of his kindness and empathy. She'd been grateful to him, but her responses had still felt stilted and embarrassed.

"Jerry's right." Celeste swung back and forth on the black executive chair in her office. Her hazel brown eyes gleamed with anger. She wore another black T-shirt. This one was a V neck. "I'm sure her death is connected to this case. We'll find her killer."

"Thank you." Symone liked the other woman's confidence. Her certainty that they'd get justice for Dottie helped Symone refocus on their case. She drew a deep breath, catching the aroma of the coffee coming from the nearby kitchenette. And just beneath it, Jerry's soap-and-mint scent.

Celeste gave a curt nod, acknowledging Symone's words. "And we'll get started later this morning. Xander agreed to meet you, Jerry and me at the foundation."

"Keep us posted, CJ." Eriq's expression was still grim. The older detective wore a pale blue shirt beneath a black jacket. He'd complemented his outfit with his customary bolo tie. The silver slide clip was shaped like a white bass. "I want to close this cold case."

"Be careful." Zeke's tone betrayed a hint of concern. He looked professional in a white shirt and bronze tie. "Xander's now our top suspect. If he is the killer, we don't know how he'll react if he realizes we're onto him."

Celeste smirked. "This isn't my first barbecue, Zeke. Remember I was on the force with Eriq."

Zeke arched an eyebrow but otherwise remained silent. Symone wondered about their exchange and made a mental note to follow up with Jerry about it later.

"Thanks, Number One." Jerry's voice bounced with poorly masked amusement. "We'll be careful."

Symone still felt weighed down by grief. "I want to speak with Paul again."

"Why?" Celeste shrugged. "We just spoke with him Saturday."

Symone adjusted her glasses. "That was before we realized he and my mother were the last people from the foundation to speak with Dottie. He might be able to tell us something about her demeanor."

Jerry nodded his approval. "That's a good point. We'll circle back to Paul."

"Do you like him for these murders?" Taylor's crimson blouse made her large jade eyes pop. She'd gathered her wealth of honey blond hair into a ponytail that trailed down her back.

"It's hard to tell." Jerry dragged a hand over his tight dark curls. "As far as opportunity, Paul had access to Odette's medicine. But we believe the killer's motive is control of the foundation's money. Paul has his own wealth."

Celeste snorted. "Does anyone ever think they have enough money?"

Zeke gestured toward his monitor. "True, but Wes Bragg has a stronger motive. He actually needs money. And he knew about Odette's heart condition. As Jerry's pointed out, Wes could easily have tampered with her prescription during their last group dinner."

Mal turned his attention to Symone. Like Zeke, he wore a white shirt, but he'd paired it with a copper tie. "What do you think, Symone?"

She moved her shoulders restlessly. "I don't know what to think. I don't want to believe my mother had married a killer when she'd married Paul. I don't want to think she'd welcomed a murderer into her home each month when she invited Wes to dinner, either."

"No, there are no good options there." Celeste rubbed a pen between her palms. Her expression was thoughtful. "You know, they could be working together."

Symone had considered that idea herself. It made her feel sick. She wouldn't have stood by cluelessly while her mother had been surrounded by murderers. Would she? She would've known somehow that her mother had been in danger. Wouldn't she?

"We have two other suspects to interview, Xander and Ellie." Mal flipped through a short stack of printouts in front of him. "I'm almost done with Ellie's report. I should have it by tomorrow."

"Thanks, Mal." Jerry turned to Symone beside him. "Do you have any other questions or concerns?"

She shook her head. "No, thank you."

Jerry checked his watch. "If there's nothing else, I think we're done here. Celeste, Symone and I'll meet you at the foundation at ten. I've asked a couple of our consultants to stake out the area as added protection. They'll text me if they see anything suspicious."

Celeste nodded. "Good. I'll see you then." She left the videoconference without another word.

After wrapping up the meeting, Jerry quit the software application, logged off his system and closed the laptop. His movements seemed pensive and deliberate. He stood from the table and turned to Symone.

The skin on the back of her neck tingled. *Oh, boy.* Symone sensed an awkward encounter in her immediate future. She wasn't ready for it.

She popped off the cedar dining chair. "I'll get my purse."

His voice, deep and soft, stopped her. "May I have a moment of your time, please? We need to talk about our kiss."

No, we don't.

Symone briefly squeezed her eyes shut. Jerry stood between her and the staircase. Bummer. She took a breath and locked her knees.

"I'm sorry if I made you uncomfortable." Her hand on the table steadied her.

Jerry raised an eyebrow. "Did I seem uncomfortable?"

She hesitated. "I don't suppose you did."

Actually, he'd seemed very engaged. The memory of his responsiveness woke the butterflies in her stomach. It also made her feel powerful and confident.

Jerry sighed. He seemed as uneasy with this conversation as she was. That was small comfort. "Symone, you're a very beautiful woman. You're also my client. It's my job to keep you safe. It wouldn't be a good idea for us to become distracted by a personal relationship. This situation is too dangerous and we're already taking more risks than I think we should."

Symone cleared her throat and adjusted her glasses. "You're right. We should keep things between us strictly professional. Thank you for that."

She managed a smile as she strode past him on her way to the staircase. As she mounted the steps, one statement played on a loop in her mind, *Jerry Touré thinks I'm beautiful—very beautiful.*

"Symone, it's so good to see you." Ellie hurried across the foundation office's main room toward the entrance doors late Monday morning. Symone, Jerry and Celeste had just arrived.

Ellie's straight auburn tresses swung like a bell behind her slender shoulders. Her four-inch black stilettos were silent against the powder blue carpeting.

She came to a stop in front of Symone and searched her face with wide, dark blue eyes almost the exact shade as her knee-length coatdress. "How are you?"

Jerry could feel the excited vibrations radiating from the administrative assistant. Ellie must've really missed her boss. He half expected the older woman to pull Symone into a bone-crushing embrace.

"I'm fine, Ellie. Thank you. How are you?" In her understated cream skirt suit and matching pumps—how many pairs of shoes did she have?—Symone was several inches shorter than Ellie. Symone's poise and elegance made her stand out regardless of what she wore. At least, that was Jerry's opinion.

Ellie blew out a breath. "I've been a nervous wreck, worrying about you. But I'm so glad to see you looking

so well. Your bodyguard's taking excellent care of you."
She turned to Jerry and her sapphire earrings, a perfect
match to her necklace, swung from her earlobes. Her eyes
were warm with gratitude. "Thank you."

Jerry inclined his head. He appreciated her kind words
as well as her concern for her boss. What he really wanted,
though, was a lead to Symone's stalker. The sooner they
solved this case, the safer Symone would be. And then
she'd walk out of his life. He ignored the twisting pain of
regret in his chest and checked his watch. Xander should
be here in a couple of minutes.

Symone's smile was poise and elegance, as well as
warmth. "I don't know where you've found the time to
worry about me. You've been so busy with Paul *and* me
out of the office."

Ellie flashed a grin as her eyes took in the area. "It's a
good busy, if there's such a thing. And it makes the day
go faster."

"Yes, it does." Symone chuckled. "You're doing a wonderful job, Ellie. I appreciate all your efforts."

"I'm happy to do it." Ellie's expression grew somber.
"We were all sorry to learn that Paul's stepping down.
Thank you for sending that email. It was very thoughtful.
How do you feel about his leaving?"

Symone adjusted her glasses. "Of course I don't want him
to leave, but I understand his decision. With my mother's
death, he lost his only tangible connection to the foundation."

"That's a good point. I hadn't thought of that. Well,
you know I'll do everything I can to help make this transition easier for you." Ellie flicked looks at Jerry and Celeste before giving Symone an apologetic look. "Xander
called, Symone. He asked me to give you his regrets and

to explain something's come up. He's hoping the two of you can reschedule."

"*Something* came up?" Celeste wore gray jeans with her black cotton T-shirt and black jacket. Her lips were parted with surprise. Her eyes were wide with incredulity. "What was it?"

Ellie stepped back. Her brown eyebrows sprang up her pale cream forehead. "I don't know. He didn't tell me."

"It's all right, Ellie. Thank you." Symone gestured between Ellie and Celeste. "Eleanor Press, my administrative assistant. Celeste Jarrett of Jarrett and Nichols Private Investigations."

Ellie gaped at Symone. She lowered her voice. "A bodyguard *and* a private investigator? Symone, what's going on? Has something else happened?"

Symone's slender shoulders rose and fell with a sigh. She glanced at Jerry before responding. "Let's talk in the conference room."

"Sure, Symone." Ellie sounded uncertain, but she turned to lead the way back across the main room.

Symone followed her. Jerry came up the rear beside Celeste. Were they doing the right thing by interviewing Ellie now? They didn't have Mal's background report on her. He didn't like going in unprepared. They'd have to depend even more on Celeste's interview experience, and on Symone's familiarity with Ellie to determine whether the admin was being honest or whether she was withholding information. The problem was Symone had tunnel vision when it came to people she cared about. And she seemed to care a great deal about Ellie.

Once again, at almost every cubicle and workstation they passed, employees hailed Symone, eager to find out how she was, when she'd return full-time to the office and to update her on personal developments in their lives.

"For Pete's sake. Is it always like this?" Celeste's question snapped with impatience. "I feel like I'm at a political rally and Symone Bishop is the presumptive nominee."

"Really?" Jerry shrugged. "I think they're more like red carpet events for awards shows or movie premieres." Her staff adored her, and he could understand why. His chest felt close to bursting with pride.

Celeste grumbled as they stopped at another workstation. "Has the board seen these encounters? Because I seriously doubt they'd vote her out if they had. Her staff would mutiny."

"Good point." Another confirmation that the no-confidence vote was more about the foundation's money than its mission.

The conference room was quite small—and windowless. The cream walls displayed framed images of the foundation's logo, which looked like a bishop's chess piece with wings, and covers of its five most recent annual reports. The room held a hint of lavender, probably from the plug-in outlet device beside the walnut wood credenza in the back. Four sterling-silver-and-powder-blue-cushioned chairs surrounded the circular midsized walnut wood conversation table that dominated the space.

Jerry waited until Ellie, Celeste and Symone were seated before taking the last chair. Its back was to the door. From the perspective of a personal security consultant, Jerry acknowledged the arrangement wasn't his first choice, but it seemed unchivalrous to ask Ellie to switch with him.

"My mother didn't die of a heart attack, Ellie." Symone shifted to face her assistant. Ellie sat across the table from Jerry. "Someone tampered with her prescription."

Celeste had taken the chair to Jerry's left. "How well do you know Xander Fence?"

Ellie's eyes widened with surprise. "You think Xander did something to Odette's medicine?"

Celeste repeated her question. "How well do you know him?"

Ellie glanced back at Symone before returning her attention to Celeste. "Not well at all. I only know him through the board, but I heard he'd been highly recommended."

The admin seemed shaken. Was it because she'd just learned Odette had been murdered? Or was Celeste making her nervous? Celeste could be a little scary. Jerry would give Ellie that.

He sat back against his chair. "The former board member who'd recommended Xander was murdered shortly after the foundation received her referral."

"What?" Blood drained from Ellie's face.

Jerry pushed. "The timing of her death calls into question the validity of Xander's referral. We're doing another background check on him. That's one of the reasons we wanted to meet with him today. Are you sure there's nothing more you can tell us about the reason he canceled our meeting?"

Ellie's eyes stretched wide. "No, there's nothing. I told you what he told me."

"How did he sound when he called?" Jerry asked.

Ellie frowned as though trying to remember. "Like his normal self. Maybe distracted, busy. I don't know."

"You knew Odette had a heart condition, didn't you?" Celeste's question was abrupt.

"What?" Ellie gasped. "No, I didn't. I didn't know until Odette had already passed and Symone told me." She turned to her boss. Her voice was a whisper. Jerry strained to hear her words. "Symone, are you accusing me of killing your mother?"

Symone didn't flinch. "I'm trying to clear your name, Ellie. Jerry and Celeste are working with the police to find my mother's murderer."

Jerry didn't outwardly react to hearing Symone repeat the reason he gave her for keeping Paul's name on the suspect list. Inside, he was impressed. She was a quick study.

Ellie didn't look 100 percent convinced. She scowled at Celeste. "Well, I couldn't tamper with a prescription I didn't know existed, could I? So that blows a hole in your theory."

Not quite. "You've worked for the company for about nine months." Jerry remembered Symone mentioning that when he'd convinced her to give him an information dump on everyone on their suspect list.

Ellie turned her irritated attention to him. "That's right. Odette hired me and now I report to Symone."

He continued. "So you're in a position to replace Symone as the foundation chair, if the board votes her out."

Ellie's jaw dropped. Her eyes skated from Jerry to Symone and back. "That's absurd. And furthermore, you're wrong. Yes, I'm a voting member of the administration, but I wouldn't be the top candidate for foundation chair. I don't have the background, experience or enough time in my current position. And besides, I'm helping Symone with the report that's supposed to persuade the board to continue supporting her as chair. Why would I do that if I wanted her job?"

"To sabotage her so you could get her job." Celeste's response was dry.

Symone leaned forward to squeeze her assistant's shoulder. "Thank you for your time, Ellie. I'm sorry we've upset you, but I hope you understand our goal is to find my mother's killer." Symone rose from her chair. Jerry stood with her.

Ellie was shaky getting to her feet. "Of course. I do understand. And I'm so sorry your mother's death wasn't from natural causes. I hope her killer's brought to justice quickly."

"So do I." Symone glanced at Jerry, who'd stepped back so she could pass him. "Thank you."

Jerry and Celeste said goodbye to Ellie, then followed Symone from the room.

He pulled his cell phone from his front pants pocket. "Clear?" Jerry sent the text to one of the TSG guards on surveillance.

Her response came back. "Clear."

Jerry texted back. "Thanks." He smiled when he received her thumbs-up emoji. When they arrived at the suite's entrance, Jerry reached forward to open the door for Symone and Celeste.

Celeste grinned at him from over her shoulder. "You Touré brothers are living proof that chivalry's not dead." She pressed the elevator button before turning to Symone. "So? What does your gut tell you?"

Symone crossed her arms. "I don't think Ellie substituted my mother's pills."

Celeste looked crestfallen. Her bright eyes dimmed with disappointment. "I was sure we were on a roll with that one."

Jerry replayed parts of their interview in his head. "She couldn't be considered to replace Symone anyway. She hasn't been with the foundation long enough."

Symone looked up at him. "That part's not true."

"Really?" Hope flickered in Celeste's eyes.

The elevator doors opened. Symone dropped her arms and led them onboard. She pressed the button for the lobby. "If there are multiple new members on the board, you could request to be considered despite not having a year of leadership service. There are two new board members."

"Wes and Xander." Jerry's neck and shoulder muscles tightened with tension. "Too many things are happening at just the right time to threaten your position with the foundation. They can't all be coincidental."

"Hold on." Celeste held up her hands. "Is Ellie aware of the exception clause?"

Symone shrugged. "She is if she read the bylaws. But as she said, she doesn't have the qualifications. The board wouldn't vote her in."

"Unless she has another play to get control of the foundation's finances." The elevator doors opened onto the lobby. Jerry held them as Symone and Celeste walked off.

"Like what?" Celeste asked over her shoulder.

Jerry ran his hand over his hair. "Like bringing in a partner who does have the qualifications."

Chapter 11

"I promise I'll be vigilant." Symone led Jerry into the great room after dinner Monday evening, the end of their fourth day together.

Jerry had made chicken fajitas for dinner. The scents of the peppers, onions, olive oil and cheeses had followed them from the kitchen after he'd helped her clean up.

They'd gotten into the habit of spending an hour or so unwinding before turning in for the night. Symone enjoyed this time of the day. Even though they talked only about the case and foundation, she was getting to know Jerry through his questions, what he said and what he didn't say.

She settled onto the far end of the fluffy, brown sofa, expecting Jerry to take his customary position at the other end. She was disappointed when he chose the armchair closest to the dining area instead. Was the change in seating arrangements due to this morning's kiss?

"This is about more than 'vigilance,' Symone." Jerry held her eyes. "Xander is a strong suspect in your mother's murder. And there's a good chance he knows we're onto him."

"I'm sure that's the real reason he didn't show up to our meeting this morning." Symone was restless with anxiety. She doubted she'd be able to sleep tonight.

"Exactly." Jerry propped his right ankle on his left knee.

"If we question him, we don't know what he'll try. I'm also afraid he's not working alone."

A chill raced through Symone's system. "What makes you think that?" She was definitely not sleeping tonight.

"Like I said earlier, there are too many things happening at the same time for all of this to be a coincidence. And they all impact your tenure as foundation chair." Jerry counted off on his fingers. "Your mother's murdered. Dorothy Wiggans's murdered. Wes and Xander joined the board. One person can't pull all that off by themselves."

"That would require a lot of coordination for one person." Symone shook her head. "Switching my mother's pills. Hiding Dorothy's body. Stewarding Wes's and Xander's background checks."

"If Xander was involved, he must've had a partner, which means we're protecting you against two people."

"I understand." Symone shifted on the sofa to face Jerry, folding her left leg under her. "I promise to be careful when we go out and to pay attention to our surroundings during the rest of this investigation—just as I'm doing now."

Jerry considered her in silence for several moments. Was he questioning her integrity? The idea hurt.

"Eriq and Taylor should interview Xander without us. I'd be putting you in danger if we met with him. His partner could be nearby, waiting to kidnap you or worse."

Fear scattered Symone's thoughts. She struggled to sweep them back together. At least he wasn't questioning her honesty. Small victory. "You've had TSG guards surveilling the area while we interviewed the other suspects. They could do the same thing this time."

Jerry was shaking his head even while she spoke. "I'm sorry, Symone. It's too risky."

She winced from the stinging betrayal. Jerry knew how

important it was for her to confront her mother's killer. She wanted them to know she'd had an active role in getting justice for her mother. She wanted to look them in the eye and see the moment they realized they were going to be punished for what they did to her family.

"You're going back on your word. You agreed to let me participate in the interviews."

Jerry held up his hand. "I agreed with having you present as long as I was there. I'm not going to interview Xander, either. I'm going to be with you."

I'm going to be with you. Why were those six words so distracting?

Symone searched her mind for another solution. "You've taught me some self-defense techniques. I won't be completely helpless."

"Xander's partner—or partners—could have weapons, Symone." Jerry's eyes darkened with concern and regret. "I don't want to risk your life. Please try to understand. I don't want to deliver you to the people we think want to kill you."

Symone couldn't think of any other arguments that might persuade Jerry to her side—yet. "All right. Will Celeste be with Eriq and Taylor when they bring Xander in for questioning?"

"I'll ask them to invite her." Jerry's demeanor relaxed. The idea of her being in danger must have caused him more stress than she'd realized. "Thanks, Symone. I know backing off isn't easy for you. I appreciate your making this concession."

"You're welcome." She almost felt guilty for continuing to look for ways to change his mind.

Almost.

"How's your report coming?" Jerry's question broke

her concentration. It also changed the subject. Very clever of him.

She sighed. "It's moving a lot more slowly than I'd intended. The board wants me to be bold and to take risks, but that's not me. My whole life, I've been risk averse. I've always worked from a plan. My plans have plans. I don't know how to take risks."

Jerry chuckled. "You have to learn to trust your instincts."

Symone jerked her chin toward him. "You mean like you do? I've been meaning to ask how you knew someone had tampered with my mother's medication."

"I didn't." A slow smile curved his lips and flipped her stomach. "I was acting on instinct."

Symone swallowed to ease her dry throat. "My abilities aren't as finely honed as yours appear to be."

"I disagree." Jerry smiled into her eyes. "You have very good instincts."

Was he pulling her leg? "What makes you say that?"

Jerry arched a thick eyebrow. His expression was almost chastising. "You have impeccable manners, as though your parents sent you to a finishing school. Yet when you gave me a tour of the foundation, you never introduced me to anyone. I think that's because you instinctively knew you couldn't trust everyone in your organization."

"It was as though a little voice was whispering in my ear to be careful." Symone had been so tense that day. But now that she knew Jerry was on her side, she wasn't as anxious.

"Trust that little voice." He nodded his approval. "Just like today when you decided to interview Ellie in the conference room instead of your office. That was a good call. Your office could be bugged. My brothers and I haven't swept it."

Symone leaned back against the soft sofa cushions. "You make it sound so easy. 'Trust the little voice.'"

Jerry chuckled again. "It doesn't have to be hard."

"But that voice doesn't always want to talk to me."

"Or maybe you're not listening."

Symone rolled her eyes. "Okay, smart guy, share your secrets with me. How are you so comfortable taking risks?"

Jerry shrugged. "I don't know. It comes naturally to me. Risk is like a reflex to me. I've always trusted my gut—or at least I used to."

His smile faded. All at once, he seemed distant and cool, as though he'd been pulled back to a time and place she couldn't follow. His eyes drifted away from her. The restless energy that powered him seemed drained.

"What happened?" Symone's voice was a whisper. She was loath to intrude but desperate to know what had caused this change in him. "Why don't you trust your gut anymore?"

Jerry drew his eyes back to hers. The dark orbs seemed haunted. "Because I put my client in danger."

Jerry's mind recoiled from the memory and its paralyzing pain. He hated reliving that experience, which was the reason he avoided any mention of it at all costs.

Then why in the world had he brought it up with Symone? She was his client. Not his sister—thank goodness—his friend or his confessor. What had prompted him to share something so personal and damaging with her, something he hadn't even told his brothers?

His eyes moved over her tousled, golden brown tresses. They floated just above her slender shoulders, her round face, winged eyebrows, wide chocolate eyes and lush, pink lips.

What was it about her that made him want to unburden himself even more?

"What happened, Jerry?" Her voice was soft but insistent. "What's caused you not to trust yourself anymore?"

He stood and crossed to the fireplace. It took several deep breaths to calm the pulse pounding in his skull. It was July. The fireplace was cold. His mind projected the events of his past against its stone-and-wood surface like a movie trailer. "Nine months ago, my brothers and I accepted a contract to protect a pop star who was coming to Columbus. He was doing a concert here, one night only. But he was going to be in town for six nights." Six very long nights. "His father wanted round-the-clock security to protect his teenaged son from overzealous fans. Zeke, Mal and I didn't think it would be a complicated assignment. Our company's protected executives of billion-dollar industries and their families, state and federal politicians and their families, even international officials and their families. I thought one teenager—even with a legion of fans— shouldn't be more complicated than those assignments."

I'd been wrong.

"Did you treat the singer the same way you treated a visiting head of state?" Symone sounded puzzled.

"We use the same safety protocols whether you're the British prime minister or a D-list actor." Jerry spoke over his shoulder, though he still couldn't meet Symone's eyes. "It had been our parents' policy and it works."

"It's a good policy."

His restlessness pushed him to pace the room in front of the fireplace. "Yes, it is, and it would've worked this time except our client's son seemed to think our security services were a challenge he needed to beat. His first day, he tried to duck them at every opportunity—leaving the hotel, returning to the hotel, before and after concert rehearsals, at promotional stops, you name it."

"Oh, no." Symone's tone was thick with disappointment and disgust.

"Exactly." Jerry paced to the bay window. He paused to look out at the view from the side of the cabin. All he saw was the pop star's smug expression. "Our consultants are good, but he was treating his safety like a game."

"What did his father think?" Her voice was sharp with temper.

"He thought we should be able to control his son." Jerry turned from the window and paced past the fireplace to the dining area that separated the main room from the kitchenette and the rear entrance. "After the second day with the same crap, my brothers and I agreed to change the details. Instead of four two-person teams made up of younger agents who could relate to the charge, we assigned more seasoned agents who wouldn't put up with his pranks. I was with the overnight team, midnight to seven. I also checked in more frequently during the day."

"It's incredible that one kid caused so much havoc and his father—your client—didn't even care. He'd wanted a babysitter as much as a bodyguard. Did you consider canceling the contract?"

"No." Jerry dragged a hand over his hair. "We were contracted to provide a service. Our first reaction was to find a better way to deliver that service. But in retrospect, maybe we should've canceled the contract and returned our client's money. Because things went from bad to worse."

Symone groaned. "I'm afraid to ask."

Jerry slid his eyes her way. She looked interested and attentive. He didn't detect any judgment from her one way or the other. Her reaction was more than he'd hoped for.

He turned to continue pacing. "During my first shift, which was his third night here, I caught him climbing down his hotel room's balcony. Keep in mind, his room was on the fifth floor. To make it to the parking lot, he had to climb down four other balconies."

Symone interrupted. "Fortunately, you were waiting for him when he made it to the ground."

Jerry snorted. "With emergency services on speed dial in case he fell and broke his neck."

"Did his father at last step in?" She unfolded her leg from under her and sat forward.

"No, he just congratulated us on returning his son to his room." Jerry unclenched his teeth. "I was sure we were being pranked."

"I could understand why." Symone's winged eyebrows disappeared beneath her bangs. "Didn't your client share the hotel room with his son?"

Jerry nodded. "They had a suite with separate rooms and didn't spend a lot of time together."

She crossed her arms beneath her breasts. "Unbelievable."

Jerry's eyes locked with Symone's. He still didn't detect any judgment in her words, her voice or her body language. Nor did he feel any of the anguish, shame or guilt he'd carried for the past nine months.

"What is it?" Symone asked.

Jerry shook his head. "Nothing. I... Nothing." He shoved his hands into the front pockets of his dark gray cargo shorts.

"Is the singer's Spider-Man impersonation the reason you think you almost got him killed?"

"I wish it was." Jerry's eyes dropped to the main room's cedar flooring. "The next night, I got to the hotel early for the shift change. Our charge had already disappeared."

Symone's hand flew to her mouth. "Oh my goodness." Her words were muffled behind her palm.

Jerry's reaction at the time had been similar although not the same. "We calculated he had at least a twenty-minute head start on us. Of course, his father was furious—"

"What a hypocrite."

"I left my partner at the hotel room and took off to look for him. The client insisted on joining me—"

"Oh, *now* he wants to get involved."

Symone's constant interruptions were amusing—and reassuring. In an effort to be fair to his former client, Jerry was doing his best to leave out the types of editorial comments Symone was injecting. His charge's father had been a pain in his backside during their entire association. And his charge had been a spoiled, disrespectful, childish brat.

Jerry continued, trying not to smile. "As the client and I drove to the west side, I called Zeke and Mal to give them an update."

Symone's eyes widened with amazement. "How did you even know where to look for him?"

"The night I'd caught him climbing out of the hotel, I'd asked Mal to check the singer's computer to try to find out if he'd had a destination in mind."

Symone gave him a cheeky smile. "Was that your gut talking?"

Jerry chuckled. "Yes, it was. We weren't sure, but it seemed he was looking for illegal gambling clubs."

"You've *got* to be kidding me." Symone shook her head.

"I'm afraid not." But he wished he was. "Zeke and Mal met me and the client at the location. Luckily, we caught up with the charge before he entered the club."

"Oh, thank goodness." Symone exhaled. "Good job."

Jerry frowned. "Good job? He should never have been

able to slip past the guards. He should never have made it to that club. Anything could have happened to him. He was a kid. Those clubs are dangerous and attract dangerous people. At the very least, he could've been arrested."

Symone shook her head. "You're being too hard on yourself."

"No, I'm not. I knew he'd been looking for illegal gambling clubs. I withheld that information from the teams. All I told them was that he'd climbed down the balconies to the parking lot."

Symone threw up her hands. "Frankly, Jerry, that should have been enough to put everyone on high alert. But at the end of the day, the blame lays solely and squarely with your client and his bratty son. What did his father say when you found him?"

Jerry blew a breath. "He fired us on the spot."

Symone blinked. Her eyes stretched wide. "Unbelievable." She drew out the five syllables.

"I know." Jerry scrubbed his face with his palms. "That case was the first time in TSG's history that we've ever been fired. I can't risk putting my brothers and our company in that position ever again. My brothers don't blame me, but I blame myself. That's why I'm leaving our company."

"Jerry, no." Symone popped off the sofa. "Your charge put himself in that situation. You're not to blame."

He shrugged. "We could debate where to place the blame, but the bottom line is my charge could've been hurt because of me. That fact has shaken my self-confidence. Now, I'm second-guessing my every move."

Symone crossed to where he stood in front of the fireplace. She rested her hand on his upper arm and captured his eyes. "You couldn't be more wrong about your instincts. Yes, your client's son *could have been* hurt, but because of you, he *wasn't.* Your gut didn't fail you, Jerry. Because you trusted your instincts, you were able to prevent your charge from getting into trouble."

Tension Jerry hadn't realized had settled over him eased, releasing the muscles in his neck, shoulders and back. Symone's words were healing his self-inflicted wounds from the pop singer's case. They were cleansing his soul. She was looking at him as though he was some kind of hero. He wasn't. But she was making him feel like one.

Jerry struggled to clear his head. He was a professional. He needed to keep his distance from her. He couldn't become personally involved with a client. But in this moment, Symone wasn't his client. In this moment, she was the balm he desperately needed to become whole again. He knew he should take a step back. He should take several steps back. Instead, he stepped forward and covered her lips with his.

Symone had hoped she'd end up here again, kissing Jerry. She sighed and let her eyes drift closed. His scent, clean soap and fresh mint, surrounded her. It intoxicated her. She breathed deeply, filling her senses with it. His scent was an aphrodisiac, making her ache.

His tongue swept across her lips. She parted them, welcoming him in. Her arms eased up his torso. His hard muscles beneath her fingertips thrilled her. Her palms slid over his shoulders. She linked her fingers behind his neck. Symone pressed her body against his and deepened their kiss.

Jerry's arms wrapped around her waist, lifting her up on her toes and holding her even tighter against him. Her breasts were crushed against his chest. His hips were hard against hers. Symone moaned. Jerry's tongue caressed hers, encouraging her to taste him. She sucked him deeper into her mouth. Stroking his tongue, caressing his teeth. Every taste of him fueled the heat building inside her.

Symone couldn't be still. Her pulse was beating at the base of her throat. Her breath sped up. She pulled Jerry even closer to her. She whimpered when he broke their kiss, then sighed as his lips trailed down her neck. She tipped her head back to give him better access. His large hands cupped her hips against him. Symone gasped and trembled in his arms.

And then his warmth was gone.

Symone blinked her eyes open, trying to bring her surroundings back into focus. "What…?"

Jerry stepped back. "I apologize, Symone."

His voice was deep and rough. The sound did nothing to cool the desire building in her.

She was so confused. "Why? I…"

He shook his head. "As I told you this morning, you're my client. My job is to keep you safe. I'd never forgive myself if my distraction in any way jeopardized your well-being."

"But…"

"I'm sorry. I give you my word this won't happen again." Jerry turned and mounted the staircase.

Symone watched him disappear upstairs. What had just happened?

I give you my word this won't happen again.

That was depressing. And how dare he take all the credit for that kiss. She may be a bit out of practice in the dating scene, but she was fairly certain his reaction meant they wanted the same thing.

With her eyes still on the staircase, Symone squared

her shoulders. Being around Jerry was making her want to take risks. Good ones. Jerry could deny their attraction, if it made him feel better, but she was determined that they would indeed kiss again. And again.

Chapter 12

"**X**ander Fence is missing." Eriq made the announcement during their videoconference late Tuesday morning. The detective adjusted his bolo tie against his wine-red shirt. This tie had a copper slide clip shaped like a walleye.

Eriq and Taylor had joined the meeting from a police interrogation room again. It looked like the same room. The stains were familiar. Celeste was with them. Zeke and Mal sat at the conversation table in Zeke's office. Jerry was with Symone at the dinette table.

He still felt awkward around her after their kiss last night. His behavior had been inappropriate, unprofessional and inexcusable. Symone was beautiful, smart, funny and kind. But her attractive qualities didn't give him permission to make a pass at her, especially since she was a woman alone in a secluded cabin with a virtual stranger. That fact was an additional incentive to keep his hands to himself.

This morning, he'd gotten up earlier than usual to work out. Then he'd made sure he was out of the basement and back in his room before Symone arrived. This was his best option. He had to keep unnecessary contact with her to a minimum. Even now, the scent of her perfume was a distraction.

"He's missing?" Zeke glanced at Mal before returning his attention to his monitor. "When was he last seen?"

Frustrated, Jerry leaned into the table. Celeste, Eriq and Taylor were supposed to have interrogated Xander this morning. Identifying him as a strong suspect in Odette's murder and the threats against Symone was a big break for their investigation. Jerry had been counting on wrapping up the case today. He needed Symone to be safe.

Symone sat straighter on her chair. Confusion furrowed her brow. "Ellie said he'd called her yesterday morning."

"He could've been calling from anywhere." Mal frowned. He wore a dark gray shirt and black tie.

Celeste's black cotton T-shirt almost blended into the room's dark walls. Her hair fell in waves over her slim shoulders. "According to the file we received from the service that does the foundation's background checks, he works for GWI Investments. We went to the company. No one's heard of him."

"What?" Symone narrowed her eyes in thought. "But our vendor confirmed he worked there when they did a background check on him."

Jerry turned to Symone. "You need to have a conversation with your service. Remember, Mal found a bunch of red flags on Xander. Something seems off."

"My family has used them for decades." Clouds of concern and confusion swirled in Symone's dark eyes.

Jerry wanted to move heaven and earth to take her troubles away. "It may be time to consider a change."

"There's no *maybe* or *consider* about it." Celeste was abrupt. Her tone was irritated. "You need a company you can trust with something as important as background checks. It wasn't that Xander *no longer* worked there. He'd *never* worked there. Your vendor should've told you that."

Symone took off her glasses and rubbed her eyes. Jerry felt her confusion. "There must be a reason for these mistakes in Xander's file. Why would the service deliberately mislead us about Xander?" She put her glasses back on.

"You're right. We shouldn't jump to conclusions." Jerry was livid that a vendor Symone trusted may have been so dangerously sloppy, but he needed to be fair and not judge them before confronting them with these errors. "Let's discuss their report with them first."

"But for now, get ready for more bad news." Taylor wore a blue-green button-down blouse. "After we struck out at the investment company, Eriq, Celeste and I went to his condo. The property manager let us in. It looked as though he'd packed in a hurry and his car was gone."

Celeste drummed her fingers on the interrogation room's table. The sound was a low steady roll. "The place looked like a tornado had swept through it."

Zeke looked disgusted. He crossed his arms over his tan shirt, which he wore with a brown tie. "What did the manager say about him?"

"The usual." Eriq shrugged. "Good tenant. Quiet. Kept to himself. Rarely saw him."

Mal was doing his best sphinx impersonation. "How long had he lived there?"

Taylor took that question. "Six months."

Mal nodded. "And he'd been on the board for three."

Symone took a sharp breath. Her eyes flew to Jerry's, then back to the monitor. "Do you think he relocated to Columbus just to take the foundation away from my family?"

Mal paused as though considering Symone's question and his answer. "I don't know. He may have lived somewhere else first. But the speed of his disappearance makes me think he'd been prepared to run."

Symone's eyes dropped to her hands. They were clasped so tightly on her lap. "This is a nightmare."

Her words were a whisper. Jerry didn't think she'd meant anyone to hear her. But he had and he didn't have the strength to keep his distance.

He placed his right hand on her clenched fists and squeezed them gently before letting her go. "You're not going through this alone."

Symone straightened her back and returned her attention to the meeting. "What's our next move?"

Eriq's voice was kind. "We've put a BOLO on Xander and his car."

Celeste interrupted. "The property manager gave us the make, model, color, year and license plate number she had on file."

"Perfect." Zeke's attention seemed to linger on Celeste. "Let's hope he hasn't switched vehicles."

"We still need to find his partner." Jerry balanced his forearm on the table. "I'm convinced he's not working alone. Especially now that we know someone fabricated his background report."

"Agreed," Mal said.

Zeke, Celeste, Eriq and Taylor echoed his response.

His eldest brother sat forward. His tone was somber. "It goes without saying you and Symone need to be even more vigilant. Xander knows we've identified him. He's desperate, and we don't know where he is."

Jerry gestured toward the monitor, encompassing everyone in the meeting. "You all need to be careful, too. We don't have any idea how much he knows about our investigation and who's involved."

Once the meeting was over, Jerry turned to Symone. "Are you okay?"

Symone looked up at him. Her shoulders were slumped. Her eyes were dark with grief. "If Xander is the killer, he's killed my mother and a dear family friend, convinced my vendor to issue a false background check and tried to kill me. And he's apparently working with someone else at my family's foundation. How deep does this scheme go?"

"I promise we'll find out." It was a promise he was determined to keep, but it didn't feel like enough.

"Thank you." Symone pushed herself to her feet. She stopped halfway to the staircase. "You and your brothers are really good at what you do. And you work well together. Don't let doubts left over from your case with the pop singer push you out of your family's business. Talk with your brothers. Let them know how you feel. If you leave, you'll regret it, probably for the rest of your life."

She turned and left the room, not giving Jerry a chance to respond. He didn't need to. Symone was right, but it was a conversation he wasn't looking forward to.

Jerry was still avoiding her. Symone stood from the desk in her room Wednesday evening where she'd been trying to work on her revised report for the board. It was difficult to concentrate, though. After two days, they still hadn't located Xander. They hadn't made any progress identifying his partner, either.

So they were going to be stuck in this safe house/romantic cabin in the woods a while longer. Should she be concerned that she wasn't more upset about that? She'd had her reservations about being secluded with Jerry at first. At the top of the list was the fact he was a slob. She would never get over the condition of his office. While at the cabin, though, he was making an effort to be tidy, proving there was hope for him.

Symone sighed and checked the time. It was a few minutes past seven. She couldn't focus on the board's report. In part because she and Jerry had already been in the cabin for six days.

And it had been two days since she and Jerry had kissed. Twice. Now he didn't seem to want to be in the same room with her. Symone wandered to the dressing table. She traced her fingers along the cool cedar frame of the rectangular mirror on top of it before strolling away.

Last night and tonight, Jerry had gone to his room after dinner instead of lingering to talk with her as they'd gotten into the habit of doing. It was hard not to take that personally. In fact, his repeated rejections of her attempts to spend time with him were chipping away at her self-esteem. He'd kissed her before. Why was he pushing her away now? She understood he wanted to be professional. How could she make it even clearer to him that she *wanted* his attention?

Should I put it in a memo?

Symone glanced toward the small desk tucked between the two long narrow bedroom windows where she'd set up the clean laptop Mal had given her as well as stacks of grant applications. She shook her head, dismissing the memorandum idea.

She'd enjoyed talking with Jerry not just because he was handsome, interesting, intelligent, funny and kind. It was also because she didn't have anyone else to talk with. Her parents had been her best friends. She'd spent most of her time with them. She had a couple of good friends but most were friendly acquaintances. It didn't matter, though. Symone couldn't call one of them up to chat. What would she say if they asked to get together with her at the end of the week or the weekend?

Sorry, I can't commit to a date. I'm in protective cus-

tody. Someone's trying to kill me to gain control of my family foundation's money.

That would be awkward.

Symone strolled to the bed on the other side of the room. She smoothed her hand over the soft tan cotton coverlet. There *was* one person she could call. Grace Blackwell was a friendly acquaintance. Symone admired her and her dedication to finding a cure for diabetes. As an added bonus, Grace had been through a similar situation and had worked with the Touré Security Group. She would have at least some idea of how Symone was feeling.

She pulled out the safe phone Mal had given her. She selected Grace's number from the list of recent calls. The other woman answered on the second ring.

"Hi, Grace. It's Symone. Are you free to talk?"

"Of course, Symone." There was a smile in Grace's voice. "How're you holding up?"

"I'm okay." She positioned a pillow against the headboard and half sat, half reclined on the left side of the bed. "But it's stressful, as I'm sure you remember."

"Oh, I remember." Grace sounded grim. There was a pinging sound in the background like metal hitting porcelain. The other woman must be making coffee or tea. "We shouldn't talk about the case, though. I recognized your number from the last time you called. I'm sure the phone's safe, but I don't want to take any chances. What else should we talk about?"

"Actually, I have some questions about Jerry." Symone's cheeks burned with embarrassment. She struggled to sound casual. "What's your impression of him?"

"Oh, no. Are you and Jerry getting along all right?" The scrape of a chair against hardwood flooring meant Grace was either shifting to stand up or sit down.

"Everything's fine." Her eyes strayed to the closed bedroom door. What was Jerry doing now? "He's very diligent about my safety. He, Celeste and his brothers are working hard on the investigation. I'm just curious about what he's like when he's not working a case."

Symone winced. Could she be any more obvious about her personal interest in her bodyguard?

"Ah. Yes, the Tourés are very attractive." Grace chuckled. Apparently, the answer to Symone's question was no, she couldn't be more obvious. "I don't know Jerry or Zeke well, but if you spend any time at all with them, you realize they have very distinct personalities. Mal hates being the center of attention. He'd rather sit back, ask questions and observe."

Symone nodded. She'd noticed that during their initial meeting. And Mal had been the same way during their videoconferences. He rarely spoke.

Grace continued. "Jerry's the exact opposite. He usually jumps in to fill the silences."

Symone laughed. "He does like to talk." But when it was just the two of them, he often listened. "What about Zeke?"

"Well, he talks more than Mal and he listens more than Jerry." Grace hummed. "He's the hardest one to read. He's more focused on his brothers and their company. But one thing the three of them have in common is that they're protective of and loyal to the people they love. They'd rather take the punch than have someone they care about get hurt."

"I know what you're saying." Symone had experienced that with Jerry. Literally. He'd used his body to shield her and Ellie when her car had exploded. And when she'd caused them to stumble during her last self-defense training, he'd twisted his body so she'd landed on him.

"Jerry's a natural charmer. He can't help himself. When

his protection detail with my grandmother ended, he broke a lot of hearts at the senior retirement community where she lives. Grandma's still talking about that." Grace and Symone laughed at the anecdote. "But he's first and foremost a professional. He's not going to start a relationship with his charge."

Symone sighed as disappointment weighed on her shoulders. "I know. He told me."

Why would the stars align for her to meet such a fascinating, exciting and attractive man when her life was in danger? What was Fate trying to tell her?

"Really?" Grace's voice dripped with curiosity. "How far have things progressed? No, don't answer that. I'm sorry for prying. Listen, if you want my advice—"

Symone jumped at Grace's offer. "I do. I've never felt this way before. This isn't about adrenaline or fear because of this situation. It's him. When I wake up in the morning, I can't wait to see him. I love listening to him and I love the way he listens to me."

Did she sound as goofy as she felt? Symone forced herself to stop talking.

Grace's soft sigh traveled their phone connection. "I know how you feel. My advice is to go after what you want. But, Symone, make sure it really is what you want. A lot of feelings will be involved. And if Jerry gives up his personal code to have a relationship with his charge, I'd hate for him to have his heart broken."

Symone heard the gentle warning in Grace's words. "Thank you, Grace. And I promise I won't break his heart."

She hoped hers wouldn't be broken, either.

Jerry activated his wireless headset Wednesday evening before choosing Mal's number in his cell phone. He planned to do a three-way conference call with his brothers. He would be more comfortable without video for the conversation he was about to have with them. He propped two pillows behind his back to half sit and half recline on his queen-size bed as he waited for the connection to go through.

He shared the wall behind him with Symone. Low murmurs and bursts of laughter carried through the drywall. Whom was she speaking with? Whoever it was had a great sense of humor. More merry laughter bounced into the room. It seeped into his chest, warming him. Jerry smiled. He loved her laugh. It was so carefree, like childhood memories of running through the lawn sprinklers with his brothers on a hot summer day.

"What's up?" Mal's voice came on the line. Jerry heard tapping in the background as though he'd caught the second Touré in the middle of a project, probably an internet search.

"Hey, Mal. Hold on. Let me get Zeke." Jerry selected his eldest brother's number.

Zeke picked up on the second ring. "Hi, Jer. Is everything okay?"

"It's all good, Number One. I've got Mal on the line with us. Listen, there's something I wanted to talk with you about."

"Okay." Mal's tapping stopped.

"What is it?" Zeke's words were shaded with concern.

Jerry took a breath. He could hear Symone's words again as though she was whispering in his ear. *Talk with your brothers. Let them know how you feel. If you leave, you'll regret it, probably for the rest of your life.*

Leaving his cell on the mattress, Jerry rose and crossed to one of the two long bedroom windows. It was still bright and sunny at seven o'clock on a July evening. The wide-open field of lush green grass ringed by maple, oak and birch trees beckoned him out. He'd accept the invitation—if he and Symone weren't hiding for their lives.

"I hadn't been considering leaving TSG because I wanted to start my own business. I was using that as a cover story because I didn't want to admit the truth, at least not out loud. I was going to leave because I didn't want to screw up TSG any more than I already have."

"What are you talking about?" Zeke's tone was incredulous.

"Wait. What?" Mal responded at the same time.

Jerry turned away from the window and sat on the edge of the bed. "I really messed up with that pop star c—"

Mal interrupted him. His tone was firm, boarding on harsh. "No, you did not."

"Mal's right, Jer. That kid didn't know what he was getting into with that crowd at the illegal gambling casino. If it wasn't for you, he would've ended up in jail or worse."

Jerry stared blindly at the hardwood flooring. He held his head in both hands. "That's why I should've acted sooner to make sure he didn't slip out of that hotel a second time."

"What were we supposed to do, Jer? Handcuff him to a chair?" Zeke sighed. "We took every ethical precaution open to us. At some point, the kid had to take responsibility for his own safety."

Mal interrupted. "Not climbing over hotel balconies or visiting underground casinos would've been good starts."

Zeke continued. "But he wasn't willing to do that, and his parent wasn't holding him accountable for his behavior."

Jerry stared at his cell phone where it lay on the coverlet. He imagined his brothers sitting on either side of it, discussing the pop star case fiasco with him. He appreciated everything they'd said. But then they'd never, ever blamed him for the botched assignment. So what had he expected them to say today?

"What bothers me most about that case is that I got us fired." He stood again, walking away from his phone to tour the cozy room. "For the first time in the history of TSG, our client fired us because I couldn't handle the job." His bark of laughter was hollow.

"Jer, why are you beating yourself up like this?" Zeke sounded as upset as Jerry felt. He sensed his older brother shaking his head. "We knew you were more upset about this case than you let on."

"Why didn't you talk with us sooner?" Mal asked.

Jerry stiffened. Setting his hands on his hips, he drew a deep breath. "I was embarrassed."

"What?" Mal exclaimed.

Zeke bit off a curse. "Come on, Jerry. We're your brothers."

"I know. I know. But, I mean, think about it." Jerry marched across the room. His voice sped up. "It's the first time ever in the history of our family-owned business that a client fires us and it's because of me. How would you have felt if it had been because of you?"

"You tell us." Mal made it sound like a challenge. "Pretend Zeke had been the one assigned to protect an immature, self-centered narcissist masquerading as a pop star. Imagine he'd gone through everything you went through. And in the end, instead of thanking Zeke for saving his son from the terrible ramifications of his very bad decisions, our client fires us. Think about it. Would you blame Zeke for what happened?"

Jerry had never played role reversal with this situation.

He'd been too busy running from the memory to make the effort. But to satisfy Mal, he considered the event from the perspective of someone else going through the experience.

It made a difference. "No, I wouldn't. Our client had been unreasonable."

"That's right," Zeke said. "And remember, after we refunded his money, his son gave the other security company the slip, went to the illegal gambling casino and got arrested. It hit the national news."

Mal snorted. "Damaged his record sales and his career."

Jerry shook his head as he returned to the bed. He would never wish bad luck on anyone, but he hoped father and son had learned a valuable lesson from that experience.

"What made you finally decide to discuss your concerns about that case with us?" Zeke asked.

Jerry paused, staring at the shared wall between him and Symone. "Not what, who. Symone encouraged me to confide in you. She said if I didn't, I'd regret it for the rest of my life."

"Good advice." Mal sounded impressed. "I'm glad you took it. You usually don't."

Zeke chuckled. "I'm glad, too. So does this mean you're staying with the company?"

Jerry grinned. He felt lighter, freer than he'd felt in months. "Yes, that's exactly what I mean. You're stuck with me."

"Yes!" Zeke and Mal responded at the same time.

Jerry's eyes lingered on the wall. He was overwhelmed thinking about what Symone had done for him. She'd cared enough to push him out of his comfort zone to prevent him from making the worst mistake of his life, leaving his family's company. No one outside of his family had ever shown such concern for him. Jerry dropped onto the mattress as his legs began to shake.

There was no longer any doubt in his mind. When this assignment was over, he wasn't going to be able to walk away from Symone. She'd become more than a client. She was a necessity.

Chapter 13

"I thought you might like some tea." Jerry's voice coming from her bedroom doorway Wednesday night startled Symone.

She jerked upright on the cedarwood chair and swung to face the threshold. After ending her conversation with Grace about an hour earlier, Symone had opened the door. She'd heard Jerry's laughter through the wall her bedroom shared with his. The sound had made her smile. It was so full and alive, reminding her of that feeling she had as a little girl when her father would push her swing until she'd swung so high, she'd thought she could touch the sky.

"Thank you." Symone stood and walked toward him. "Would you like to come in?" *Please say yes.*

Jerry stepped forward, offering her one of the cream porcelain mugs. "Sure. Thanks. What're you working on?"

Symone returned to her chair. "I'm reviewing proposals for health care programs and products looking for foundation grants. Again."

As she'd intended, Jerry smiled at her dry tone. "Are you looking for—what was it?—cutting-edge, innovative proposals for the board's approval?"

Symone nodded. "That's right."

"How's that coming?"

With her free hand, Symone took off her glasses, set them on the table behind her and rubbed her eyes. "Not well. When we went through this exercise the first time three months ago, my mother and I had identified proposals that were cutting-edge, innovative *and* reflected our mission statement." She gestured toward the papers stacked on the right side of her desk. "Very few of these proposals are cutting-edge or innovative, and none of them align with our mission."

Jerry nodded toward the proposals. Without her glasses, he was slightly out of focus. "That's a huge pile of papers. It sounds like you're wasting your time."

"It feels like I'm wasting my time." Symone sipped her tea.

"I don't understand." Jerry leaned his hips back against the dressing table. "If it's your family's foundation, why does the board get to call all the shots?"

Good question. "When my grandfather created the foundation, he wanted to make sure his descendants would be good stewards of the organization. He was afraid the chair, acting alone, could lose sight of the foundation's purpose. So he set up the board with oversight authority to make sure the foundation remained focused on its mission."

Jerry frowned. "But it's the board that's derailing the foundation."

"Is it? Or is it trying to respond to the next generation of health care needs?" She shrugged. "I'm not sure."

"It's derailing the foundation." Jerry's tone was unequivocal. He straightened from the table and faced her. "I spoke with my brothers a little while ago."

Symone blinked. His sudden segue confused her. "Is everything all right?" She put her half-empty mug on the table.

"Everything's fine." He drank his tea. "I took your advice and told them how I felt about the botched assignment."

Symone stilled, waiting for him to continue. When he didn't, she prompted him. "It must have gone well. I heard you laughing."

Jerry smiled as though remembering those parts of their conversation. "It went…very well. They don't blame me at all, and they helped me to stop blaming myself."

"I knew they wouldn't blame you." Symone sprang from her seat. Her breath left her in a whoosh. "That's wonderful. So are you staying with the company?"

Jerry nodded. "I am. And I want to thank you for convincing me to tell them how I felt. I'm so glad I took your advice."

"That's wonderful news." Symone hurried across the room to hug him. She wrapped her arms around his waist and pressed her left cheek to his chest. His warm, hard body made her restless. With her ear against his chest, Symone heard his heart skip, then speed up to a strong, steady rhythm.

Jerry's arms wrapped around her slowly. He pulled her closer. Symone snuggled into him, breathing his scent. A soft sigh escaped her. Here. Like this. She wished she could stop time to be here in Jerry's arms like this for just a moment or two. A day or two. Forever.

He pressed his face to the curve of her neck. Symone leaned her head back and arched into his body. Jerry moaned and tightened his arms around her.

She turned her head and whispered against his ear. "You and I know we're going to make love. What does it matter whether it happens next week—or now?"

Jerry pressed his hips against her. Symone gasped at the feel of his arousal.

* * *

Symone's words were like gasoline poured over the embers burning inside Jerry. Desire, all consuming, ignited inside him. His body's response was swift. His lips parted, covering hers. He swallowed her gasp of surprise. He swept his tongue inside her mouth in search of the sweetness he'd tasted before. He stroked, caressed and suckled her, feasting on her reactions. Symone moaned and his movements grew bolder. She gasped and he demanded even more. She was restless in his arms, fueling his need.

Jerry tightened his arms around her, drawing her closer to him. His breath caught in his throat as he felt her heat. His arousal swelled at her response to him. He stroked her waist, and she pressed her breasts against him. He cupped her hips, and she arched her body into his. Her arms wrapped around him and moved up his back. Her fingers traced his spine. Her palms curved around his hips. Every touch, every caress made him crave her.

Symone pulled his shirt from him and pressed him back onto the bed. Holding his eyes, she unbuttoned her blouse, revealing a nude demi-cup bra. Jerry's throat went dry. He swallowed. Symone dropped her blouse to the floor. Still holding his eyes, she shed her tan shorts. Her matching underpants were a wisp of material that hugged her slim hips and dipped low to frame her navel. Jerry's heart raced as his eyes traveled over her. Her limbs were long and toned. Her breasts were full, waist tight and stomach flat. Jerry's muscles tightened with a sweet ache.

"You're like a fantasy." His voice was raw. He was torn between staring at her forever and kissing her all over.

Symone smiled. A blush warmed her chest and rose up into her cheeks. "So are you," she whispered back.

She climbed onto the bed, straddled him and leaned forward for his kiss. Jerry opened his mouth to join his tongue with hers. He stroked into her. She took him deeper. His muscles shook. His pulse raced. His breath was ragged.

He felt her fingers at his hips as she unfastened his shorts. Jerry pulled his wallet from his pocket and tossed it beside him on the bed. Symone freed his mouth to pull the rest of his clothes off, dropping them to the floor with hers. She kissed and licked her way up his legs. When she reached his hips, Jerry gripped the coverlet. He watched her draw him into her mouth. His hips surged up. He squeezed his eyes shut. She traced his length with her tongue. He groaned deep in his throat. His mind went blank. Pleasure, warm and sweet, spread throughout his body. Symone's hands caressed his hips, waist and torso. Her fingers traced his thighs, his erection. Her nails skimmed across his abdomen. As the pressure tightened inside him, Jerry gripped her shoulders.

"Stop." His voice was a shaky whisper. He rolled over, tucking her under him. He managed a smile. "My turn."

Symone's reply was a moan. He drank the sound, sliding his hands beneath her to release her bra. He leaned back, bringing the scrap of clothing with him. "Beautiful."

Her nipples tightened before his eyes. He leaned forward and took one into his mouth.

Symone's lips parted on a soundless scream. Her skin heated. She pressed Jerry's head to her breast and arched closer to him. His tongue licked her skin. His teeth teased her nipples. With his left hand, Jerry fondled her other breast, cupping it and stroking the tip with his palm.

"Jerry. Jerry."

"Symone," he whispered in her ear.

She shivered beneath him. Jerry slid down her body, caressing every inch of her skin. A stroke. A lick. A nibble. A kiss. He stripped off her underpants. She spread her legs.

He paused, moving his eyes over her limbs, hips, breasts and face. "You are so beautiful."

"So are you." She lost her breath as she looked at him, standing at the foot of the bed. He was broad shoulders, slim hips and long, muscled thighs.

Holding her eyes, Jerry returned to the mattress. He lay between her legs and lifted her hips to his tongue.

"What?" Startled, Symone widened her eyes, then squeezed them shut as he touched her.

She pressed her head against the pillow and fisted the coverlet in her hands. Her hips pumped against Jerry's lips as he kissed and caressed her. Her nipples puckered. Her muscles tightened as she raced toward her climax. Symone stiffened, then trembled as wave after wave after wave of pleasure broke over her. She tossed against the mattress, pumping her hips.

Jerry lowered her. As echoes of her climax trembled between her legs, Symone watched Jerry pull a condom from his wallet and make quick work of putting it on. Positioning himself on top of her, Jerry kissed her deeply as he entered her with one strong stroke. His erection moved inside her, deep and full. Symone gasped as she felt her passion building again. Her nipples tightened. Her muscles strained. Her hips matched his rhythm. She pressed her fingers against his shoulders and wrapped her legs around his hips as she tensed against him.

"Jerry." She whispered his name against his neck.

"I'm here." He worked his hand between them. "I'm with you." He lowered his head to her breast. He drew her nipple into his mouth as he touched her.

Symone shattered. Her body bucked and trembled as

a second orgasm rocked her. Jerry's body stiffened in response. She held on tight as his hips arched into her. Then he relaxed.

Gathering Symone into his arms, Jerry rolled over, positioning her on top of him, and brought her lips to his for a kiss.

Chapter 14

Symone woke early Thursday morning to find Jerry lying on his side and smiling sleepily beside her. She could get used to that. "Were you watching me sleep?"

His smile widened. "Good morning to you, too." His morning voice was deep and gruff. Sexy.

"Good morning." She tilted her head back on her pillow to look at him. Her eyes traced his mouth. Her body warmed as she remembered all the things those wonderful lips had done to her last night.

"Do you always smile in your sleep?"

She chuckled. "Are you trying to get me to say I was dreaming of you?"

"Were you?"

She laughed. "What an ego."

Symone took in his lean, sienna features. Except for his morning stubble and his slightly unkempt hair, he looked just as wonderful first thing in the morning as he did during the day. Her eyes dropped to his bare torso. Maybe better.

She felt alive. Her body hummed with energy. It had been months since she'd slept so well. Jerry's loving had helped her to forget the board, the conspiracy, the murders and the threats—at least for a while.

Beneath the covers, she rolled onto her back and

stretched her arms and legs. That's when she remembered they'd slept naked. It had seemed like a great idea last night. This morning, not so much. She was much more modest with the sunrise.

Symone's eyes swept the room. Her glasses were on the desk several feet away on her left. Her clothes were on the floor at the foot of the bed. Her robe was in the closet on the other side of Jerry on her right. And she was naked.

"Jerry?" She rolled her head on her pillow to look at him again.

"Symone?"

She heard the humor in his voice. He was in a good mood today. So was she. It had been a very good night.

Her skin heated with a blush. "Could you close your eyes?"

Confusion quickly cleared with realization. Jerry feigned surprise, widening his eyes and gasping. "Are you naked under there?"

Symone fought not to laugh. "You know that I am. Will you please close your eyes?"

"All right, but you have to promise to do the same when I get out of bed." He stole a kiss, then rolled onto his stomach and closed his eyes.

Symone hesitated as she traced his broad, hard back with her eyes. Her fingers itched to touch him. Instead, she pressed a kiss to his spine. His muscles rippled. She heard his sharp intake of breath. Symone smiled as she leaped out of bed and hurried to the closet for her powder pink satin robe. She shrugged into the garment, then tied the band around her waist. The wide sleeves hung over her wrists, but the hem ended midthigh.

"Okay, I'm decent."

Jerry rolled over and opened his eyes, folding his arms

behind his head. His midnight eyes caressed her. "You're much better than decent."

Symone liked the way he looked at her. He made her feel strong, desirable and wanted. She smiled. She didn't think she could stop smiling. "Do you want me to look away so you can get out of bed?"

Jerry stretched. The muscles in his arms flexed as he raised them above his head. The sheet slipped down his waist. Symone watched, mesmerized, as his pecs contracted.

He flashed a grin. "Do you want to look away?"

Before she could answer, he tossed the sheet aside and climbed out on the other side of the bed. Symone couldn't stop her eyes from feasting on him. Jerry was unapologetic physical excellence. Broad shoulders, narrowing to a trim waist and slim hips. Long, powerful thighs and calves. Flat stomach and molded chest.

"Stop. You'll make me blush." Jerry circled the bed.

Her eyes flew to his. He was looking at her with a wicked smile. Desire glinted in his eyes. Her nipples tightened in response.

Symone kept her voice light. "I doubt you're capable of blushing." She gave him a cheeky look as she turned away. "I'll race you to the exercise room."

Jerry caught her hand to stop her. "What will I get when I win?"

Symone stepped closer to him. His scent brought back a sweet ache. She lowered her voice. "What will you give me when *I* win?"

His slow smile curled his lips—and her toes. "Whatever you'd like."

She chuckled. "Then I think we'll both win."

* * *

Symone half sat, half reclined on Jerry's bed late Thursday morning reviewing the stack of rejected foundation grant applications. Jerry was at his desk across the room, searching the internet for clues that could led them to Xander or Xander's associates. The silence was deep, but comfortable.

She watched him in silence for a moment. After their exercise, he'd changed into a brick red polo shirt, black cargo shorts, tube socks and sneakers. The bold colors looked wonderful on him. As though he sensed her eyes on him, Jerry looked over his shoulder at her.

Startled and embarrassed to have been caught staring, Symone said the first thing that popped into her mind. "Any luck?"

"Not yet." Jerry shifted on the chair to face her better. His voice was tight with irritation. "And I'm having trouble finding anything about him beyond five years ago. It's as though Xander Fence didn't exist before then."

"For Pete's sake." Symone removed her glasses and rubbed her eyes. How many more discrepancies in Xander's identity were they going to find? "Our vendor who does the background checks has a lot of explaining to do. I left a message for them earlier, asking them to call me."

"Good idea." Jerry nodded his approval. "I'd like to take part in that conversation, if you don't mind. They might say something that could help us learn more about Xander, his partner and their plan to take over the foundation."

Symone suppressed a shiver. "Of course. I'd appreciate your joining me. You might think of additional questions to ask."

Hearing Jerry put it that way—*their plan to take over the foundation*—frightened Symone. It sounded sinister, but it was true. Their investigation had uncovered a complicated, multipronged plan to take control of the foundation from her family. Symone still couldn't believe longtime board members could be involved.

Jerry inclined his head toward the stack of applications on the bed beside her. "How about you? How's the application review going?"

Symone put her glasses back on. "I'd rather be training with you." She exchanged a smile with him.

"You did well today."

Hours earlier, Symone had done power yoga while Jerry lifted weights. She'd run the treadmill and he'd kickboxed. Then they'd worked on her self-defense training. This time, she didn't trip him when she'd practiced freeing herself from her would-be abductor. He'd also taught her to flip a person over her shoulder.

Then they'd made love while they'd showered. Her body still hummed with the memory.

"Thank you." Symone's smile faded. "I haven't found any winners in this pile of applications, at least not yet. Of the ones I've taken another look at so far, I would be compromising myself and the foundation if I selected any of them."

"I'm sorry, Symone." Jerry stared at the flooring with narrowed eyes. "What would happen if you didn't select a program or product from among these applications?"

Symone shrugged, shaking her head. "The board would factor that into their no-confidence vote, which means it wouldn't go well for me. They asked me to pick a different grant applicant and to revise our investment strategy for the new fiscal year. If I fail to do either or both of those things, they'll vote me out and replace me with someone who will."

Jerry frowned, gesturing toward the stack of papers beside her. "Even though these applicants don't meet the mission criteria?"

"I'm afraid so." Symone lowered her voice. "That's my greatest fear, that I'll lose The Bishop Foundation—the organization my grandfather established. You know how important family legacies are."

"Yes, I do." Jerry's voice was dry. "We don't want to be the ones who lose them."

"No, we don't." Symone heard the tension in her voice. "But the board's adamant that it wants to take more risks, with or without me." She looked at the application in her hand. "More and more, it looks like it will have to be without me. There's more than one way to lose a legacy, and that includes compromising its integrity."

Jerry broke the tense silence. "Symone, I know this is hard. There's a lot at stake. But just for a moment, stop thinking and just feel."

Symone's brow furrowed. She didn't understand. "Feel what exactly?"

Jerry leaned forward, bracing his elbows on his legs. "What do you want for the foundation?"

"What do I want? I want a new board." Symone swallowed the nervous laughter that bubbled up her throat.

Jerry spread his hands. "If that's what you want, then go for it. You're already facing the worst that could happen, losing your family's foundation."

Symone blinked. "You're serious?"

"Of course I am." Jerry shrugged. "Why not go on the offensive?"

Symone considered Jerry's expression. He really was serious—and he had a point. The worst-case scenario was already on the table. Why not go out fighting?

She slipped off the bed. "You know what? I'm going to take your advice and go for it. It's a risk, but it's a risk worth taking. I'll start by reviewing the foundation's bylaws."

Jerry stood. "Perfect. Good luck. Let me know what you find."

"I will." Symone gathered the application folders and hurried to her room. Excitement powered her muscles. She had the beginnings of a plan. Granted, it was impetuous, and she was still putting it together, but it was the start of her taking a stand.

Symone rushed into her room and made a beeline for her desk. She deposited the files beside her laptop, then pulled the burner phone from the pocket of her knee-length, pleated lavender dress. She sighed. The foundation lawyer's number was in her personal phone. She dug through her purse for her cell, turned it on, then scrolled through her contacts list until she came to Percy Jeffries's information.

The law offices of Jeffries & Henderson PLLC had represented The Bishop Foundation before the organization had opened its doors. Symone's grandfather had worked with Percy's father until the other man's retirement. The foundation had started working with Percy once he took over his father's interest in the firm more than ten years earlier. Percy had become a good friend as well as their lawyer.

She tapped his direct-dial number into her burner cell. Symone was surprised when he answered on the first ring. She'd been expecting his voice mail. "Percy, it's Symone. How are you?"

She pictured the solicitor, seated behind his desk. Percy was a few years older than her father would've been if he were still alive. He was about her height and solidly built with close-cropped, salt-and-pepper hair. The lawyer was always impeccably dressed in dark three-piece suits. Faint lines creased his brown skin across his brow and on either side of his thin lips.

"Symone." His booming voice carried through the connection. "It's so nice to hear from you. I'm fine. How are you managing?"

"I'm fine, thank you, but I'd like your help with something, please." She wandered to the window. "I'm not in my office. Could you send me a copy of the foundation's bylaws via email?"

"Of course. Is there a problem?"

She heard typing in the background as though he was dropping everything to accommodate her request. Symone smiled. That was Percy. She should've thought to call him sooner.

Symone started to turn away from the window. "I—"

"Hang up!" Jerry burst into her room. "Hang up the phone! Now!"

Symone's eyes stretched wide. "Percy, I've got to go." She hung up on his frantic questions. "What's wrong?"

"We're being tracked." Jerry grabbed her cell phone from her hand. He turned it off and pocketed it. "We've gotta go. Now."

Chapter 15

"Get your things. We're out of here in ten." Jerry's sharp warning rang in her ears.

Symone ran around her bedroom in the formerly safe house. Her heart galloped in her throat as she grabbed shoes and a suitcase. "How do you know we're being tracked?"

She shoved her feet into her white canvas shoes, then dashed back to her desk. She heard Jerry opening and closing doors and drawers, and tossing things. A zipper opened.

"I got an alert on my cell phone." His voice was tense and breathless as he shouted back. "Hurry, Symone. We're taking only what we pack in ten minutes. Everything else is left behind."

"I'm hurrying." Her hands shook as she turned off her clean computer and shoved it into its case. With sweating palms, she threw grant applications and fistfuls of underwear, bras, sock, blouses and skirts into a suitcase. She zipped it closed, then raced to meet Jerry in the hallway. Her breaths were coming too fast. "Ready."

Without a word, he grabbed her suitcase with his free hand and led her on the flight down the stairs and into the garage. She circled the rented sedan while he threw their cases into the trunk.

"Where are we going?" She settled onto the passenger

seat and connected her seat belt. Her pulse drummed in her ears.

"I don't know yet." He climbed behind the steering wheel and fastened his seat belt as he activated the automatic garage door opener.

Symone half expected to see a force of masked gunmen surrounding them in the yard.

Jerry backed the car out of the garage. His eyes made rapid sweeps of the area as he drove above the speed limit out of the resort.

"Why are we going this way?" Symone searched their surroundings through the windshield and side window.

"This exit leads to an isolated road." Jerry lifted his left hip to free an access keycard from his back shorts pocket. "There's only one way into the resort. This access lets you out, but it won't let you back in."

For the past six days, they'd been using the complex's front gates to exit and enter. Now they were traveling in the opposite direction. The condition of the trail grew worse the farther they traveled. The rental car bounced and rocked with increasing frequency. The asphalt surface had broken and deteriorated over the years. After a few miles, it disappeared, leaving behind depressions, ruts and cracks caused by water erosion. No one had been motivated to fix this section of the trail, which was strange since the rest of the resort was so well maintained. Perhaps the road's condition was a deliberate attempt to dissuade visitors from exploring this part of the resort.

A pristine wrought iron gate rose from the ground at the end of the dirt path. This seemed to confirm Symone's suspicion about the road's poor condition being a deterrent. Jerry made the briefest stop to wave his keycard in front of an electronic door lock. The gate retracted. Jerry drove through as soon as there was enough space for the car to clear. He turned the vehicle toward Ohio State Route 180, east to Columbus. They were going home. She wasn't sure how she felt about that. Home was where the danger had started. It also meant the end of their sanctuary.

Symone stole a look at Jerry in her peripheral vision. His expression was the grimmest she'd seen since they'd started this case. "It's because I turned on my cell phone, isn't it?"

"Yes." His stark response sent a chill through her. Symone wanted to kick herself. He continued. "It's my fault. I didn't do enough to emphasize the seriousness of this situation. I should've scared you more."

He was blaming himself for her mistake. Classic Jerry. That was the same thing he'd done with the uncontrollable pop star. Symone didn't want to be in the same category as that emotionally stunted child. Jerry's taking responsibility for her irresponsible act magnified Symone's guilt and shame.

"You've kept me adequately afraid." Telling her people were determined to kill her was scary enough. "I wasn't thinking. This is entirely my fault, not yours and I'm so very sorry. I can't apologize enough."

"It's my job to keep you alive. And keeping you alive is what we have to focus on."

Symone gave him a sharp look. What was he implying? Was he ending their love affair as it was starting? To her, this wasn't just about great sex. In less than a week, Jerry Touré had stolen her heart. Was he going to pretend it was something else? Was their relationship a mere breach of protocol that needed to be rectified?

She forced her attention back to the windshield and briefly closed her eyes. One problem at a time. The issue that had them running from assassins should take precedence.

"How much damage do you think I've done to our safety?" She hated that her carelessness had not only endangered her—it had also threatened Jerry.

"We won't know until we're sure we're not being followed." Jerry repeatedly checked the rearview mirror. He also scanned the cars in front of him. This part of the state route was one lane in either direction. "I'm taking us to Mal's house. His security system's even better than mine and Zeke's."

Like Jerry, Symone kept scanning their surroundings. She felt crushed with guilt over not turning off her cell phone earlier. "Will he mind?"

Jerry glanced at her. "No. He'll understand. I'll let him know once we get there. For now, I need to make sure we're not followed and that I get you there safe and sound."

Symone corrected him. "*We* need to make sure *we* arrive safe and sound." His lack of response wasn't encouraging. "I don't want to put anyone else in danger. What else can I do to keep us safe?"

Jerry paused as though thinking. "I don't know yet. I'd turned off your cell phone and left it in my room at the safe house."

Symone raised her eyebrows. "Oh. Okay. That makes sense." She'd probably never look at another cell phone the same way again.

"Once we get to Mal's, I'll hold on to your laptop. It's what I should've done with both of your devices from the beginning."

"All right." She clenched her hands together on her lap. "You have every right to be upset with me."

He cut her off. "I'm not upset with you."

Hmm. He had a strange way of showing it.

Symone let that pass. She cleared her throat. "I really am sorry for my stupid mistake. You and Mal told me repeatedly not to use my cell phone. You said someone was using it to track my location. You both told me the risk. I only meant to turn it on for a minute, but I got distracted when Percy answered the call so quickly. It was stupid and thoughtless. I truly am sorry."

Jerry shook his head. He vibrated with impatience. "Stop apologizing. It's not your fault. It's mine. I should've made sure you knew not to take any chances. I should've taken the battery out of your phone. I should've taken your phone. I was stupid to have left it with you. You're my charge, my responsibility."

Symone's heart sank. She studied the clean, sharp lines of his profile. "I'm your charge?"

Jerry kept his eyes on the road. "That's right. I shouldn't have allowed our relationship to get personal. *I'm* the professional. I should've known better."

Symone caught her breath. "All right."

She turned back to the windshield, blinking to ease the sting in her eyes. She was his *charge*, someone he was obliged to care for. Then, at the first opportunity, he would leave. Like Paul. With her mother's death, she had to get used to being on her own. It was good that she'd found out now before she fell any deeper in love with a fantasy.

Jerry pulled his rental into Mal's driveway late Thursday morning. He was tense and tired after driving an hour from the cabin resort to his brother's home in northwest Columbus, but he was certain they hadn't been followed. He turned off the engine and shifted to look at Symone on the passenger seat beside him. She'd leaned forward to study the exterior of Mal's house. It was the home in which he and his brothers had grown up. What did she think of it?

For most of their journey, she'd been quiet. What had she been thinking about? What was she thinking about now? Was she nervous about being back in Columbus and within reach of the people who were threatening her?

"We'll be safe here." Jerry waited for her to look at him before he continued. Her chocolate eyes were cool. "The resort was safer because it's farther away. But Mal's got a very secure system. It's the latest technology."

Her smile was polite. "Thank you." She went back to looking at Mal's house.

Jerry pulled out his cell phone and selected Mal's number. "I'll put Mal on speaker."

His brother answered right away. "What's up?"

"Mal, I'm with Symone. We have you on speaker. We're outside of your house. Symone's phone was on. The stalker tried to use the connection to track us."

Mal chewed a curse. "Are you both all right?"

"Yes, we're good." Jerry glanced at Symone.

She started to lean toward him, then seemed to catch herself. "I'm so sorry, Mal."

"What matters is that you're both safe," he said. "Hold on. I'll get Zeke."

Less than two minutes later, Zeke joined the call. "Are you sure you're both okay?"

Jerry sat back on the driver's seat. He heard typing in the background as though Mal had gone back to work. "We're sure but we need a new safe house."

"Use mine." Mal continued working his computer keyboard.

Jerry smiled. "I was hoping you'd say that. Thanks."

Symone pressed against the passenger seat. "Thank you, Mal. It's very kind of you."

"No problem." Mal's typing stopped. "I tried to trace the hacker, but I couldn't find the signal. They must've shut off the program."

Jerry nodded. "Thanks for trying."

"Of course." Mal paused. "And, Jerry, remember—no food in the living room."

Jerry rolled his eyes. "It was one time, Mal." He and his brothers wrapped up their conversation.

"What was that about?" Symone asked. "Why doesn't Mal want you eating in his living room?"

"Mal holds grudges." Jerry scanned their surroundings. "Let's go in. I'll get our bags after I show you around."

Mal's two-story home was an American Craftsman model with white siding and gray stone. Small holly scrubs bordered the well-tended lawn and led visitors up a winding concrete path. Three wide concrete steps carried Jerry and Symone up to the porch and to the chestnut wood door. Jerry unlocked the door and deactivated the alarm before inviting Symone in.

She looked around the open floor plan. "This is a beautiful home."

Jerry pictured Odette and Paul's house. It was spacious and stately despite Paul's horrible decorating style. He was sure Symone's family home had been just as grand. "It's a modest space compared to what you're probably used to, but we enjoyed growing up here."

Her eyes widened with excitement. "This is your family home? It's wonderful."

"Thank you." He turned toward the staircase. "I'll take you upstairs."

Jerry turned right at the top of the stairs. "You can take this guest room. I'll make up the bed after the tour."

Symone moved past him. She stood in the middle of the spacious square room. Two windows allowed plenty of natural light in. A dressing table and matching nightstands were made of teakwood. Vibrant, jewel-toned sectional rugs were laid on the polished hardwood floor around the queen-size bed.

"It's so bright and welcoming." She glanced out one of the windows, then turned to the rest of the room. "Whose room was this?"

"It was originally Zeke's. I took it over when he moved onto OSU's campus." Two years later, he'd joined his older brother at The Ohio State University, where their arguments had become legendary. Mal had wisely attended Ohio University to get away from the brothers' constant fights. "I'll be in Mal's old room across the hall."

Her eyes widened on the framed colored-pencil image beside the closet. She crossed to it. "This is beautiful. Antrim Lake." She adjusted her glasses as she leaned in to read the artist's name. "It's Zeke's work?" She looked at the other two drawings in the room. "Park of Roses. Scioto River. Did he do the paintings in your conference room?"

"Yes, he did." Jerry's chest filled with pride. He enjoyed her reaction to his brother's talent.

Symone smiled. "Your brother's a wonderful artist. I thought you'd bought those pieces from a gallery."

"The agency doesn't have that kind of money." Jerry was going to enjoy sharing Symone's comment with Zeke and especially Mal. "I'm sorry there isn't a desk in the room, but you can work in the dining room or kitchen."

Symone shrugged. "I'm used to working in bed."

"Okay." Jerry nodded. "Are you ready to see the rest of the house?"

"Yes, please." Her brown eyes gleamed with excitement. Over seeing his family home?

Jerry escorted her to Mal's office. He stopped in front of the iPad, which stood on a short, black metal file cabinet. "This device is connected to a twenty-four-hour home security system. The screen displays real-time video feeds from the six cameras stationed around the perimeter of the house. Mal and I'll watch it closely."

"Thank you." Symone's eyes swept the office, pausing on Mal's project board, computers and bookcases. "It's wonderful that you grew up in a big family. Even though your parents are no longer with you, you still have your brothers. You're not alone."

Symone's back stiffened. Her eyes widened as though she was surprised that she'd spoken the words out loud. She turned and walked out of room, stopping in front of another door.

Jerry paused beside her. He wanted to reach out to her, take her hand and assure her she wasn't alone. He wanted to wrap his arms around her until the loneliness left her eyes. He crushed those instincts. His feelings for Symone were what got them into this latest mess in the first place.

He nudged the door open. "This is the guest bathroom. I'll get us fresh towels later."

Symone assessed the turquoise decor and blue ceramic tiling. "Mal's very tidy. If I didn't know someone lived here, I'd think this was a display home."

Jerry chuckled. "I'll have to tell him you said that."

Symone spun toward him. Her lips were parted in shock. "Don't you dare."

Jerry grinned, staring into her big brown eyes before

forcing himself to turn away. He nodded toward the end of the hall. "That's Mal's bedroom. He has an adjoining bathroom, so we'll have this one to ourselves. Last stop is the basement."

He took her through the living and dining rooms, and the kitchen on their way to the basement. "Washer and dryer." He gestured toward the laundry units in the corner, then drew her attention to the treadmill, elliptical machine, old-school weight bench and black vinyl boxing bag. "Exercise equipment."

Symone's eyebrows disappeared beneath her bangs. "You Tourés really take your fitness seriously."

"We have to." Jerry shrugged. "Our clients' lives depend on it."

Symone nodded. "Thank you. And thank you so much for allowing me to stay with you and your brother. Hopefully, you won't have to put up with me much longer."

Put up with me... "What's that supposed to mean?" Jerry followed Symone up the basement stairs to the kitchen. Her steps were so fast. Was she running from him?

"I'm your client. Your charge." She didn't stop at the kitchen. She continued through the dining and living rooms, speaking over her shoulder. The flirty skirt of her lavender dress swung at him like a chiding finger. "You have a job to do and once you're done, you'll move on to the next."

"Symone, you hired my brothers and me to protect you. Your safety is our priority." Jerry appealed to her back as he followed her up the main stairs to the top floor. "We have to focus on keeping you safe. We can't risk being distracted. We need to find the people who killed your mother and who are trying to kill you."

Symone turned in the doorway of her guest room. Her

frown questioned him. "You want to put our relationship on pause until after the investigation?"

He saw the spark of hope in her brown eyes. It almost weakened him. He wanted so badly to give in to his need for her—but that was only a delay. He could never make her happy. They were just too different. "Symone, I don't think that would be a good idea."

Hurt replaced the hope in her eyes. "Why not?"

Jerry closed his eyes briefly. He didn't have the strength for this. Ending things with Symone was like cutting off his arm. "Let's stick to the case."

"No." She shook her head. "I need to understand how it's possible for you to make love with me this morning and now act like we're barely more than strangers."

He dropped his eyes to the hardwood flooring. "Symone, you and I wouldn't fit. We're from two different worlds."

"Are we?" Symone tilted her head. "I'm from Earth. Where do you think you're from?"

Jerry rolled his eyes. "You know what I mean. We're too different."

"You're going to have to do better than that, Jerry." She crossed her arms over the lavender bodice of her dress. "How are we so very different?"

He gestured between them. "For example, my family and I are struggling to keep our security business open. Your family founded a multimillion-dollar foundation to advance medical research. You're pearls and designer suits. I don't even wear a tie."

She released her arms. "Are you really that shallow?" Her eyes widened with amazement. "You're loyalty and courage, and doing what's right. You inspire *me* to be courageous. You give me hope that there are more people like you and your brothers in this world."

She was giving him that look again, as though he was some sort of hero. She made him want to live up to those expectations, so he'd actually be worthy of her regard.

Jerry ran a hand over his hair. "I'm sorry, Symone. I wish I could give you what you need, but I can't."

"Can't? Or won't?" Her eyes glowed with temper as she looked him over. "How do you do that, Jerry?"

He frowned. "Do what?"

"Turn your emotions on and off. One moment you care…the next, you really don't."

"Symone—"

"I was thinking about you on the drive over here." Her full lips twisted in a cynical smile. He didn't recognize her. "You blame yourself if your charges put themselves in danger like I did by leaving my personal cell phone on, or like that spoiled teenaged singer did by sneaking out of his hotel room to go to an illegal gambling hole. Everybody thinks you're doing that because it's your case so you're in total control. If there's any finger-pointing to be done, then by golly, they should point their fingers at you because that's where they belong."

By golly? "If I take point on a case, then yes, everything to do with that case is my responsibility. How's that a bad thing?"

Symone started shaking her head before he'd finished speaking. "But that's not the reason, Jerry. Maybe you've tricked yourself into believing it is, but it's not."

He folded his arms across his chest. "Then tell me, Symone. You know me so well. Why do I accept responsibility if things go south on my case?"

"You're not blaming yourself for everything and anything that goes wrong on a case because of some over-developed sense of responsibility." She stepped closer to him, holding his eyes. "Blaming yourself is your way of running from your emotions."

"What?" Where had that come from? "What are you—?"

Symone continued as though she hadn't heard his interruption. Her face flushed. Her body vibrated with agitation. "You treat yourself like a machine—like an android—because you don't want to feel."

"That's ridi—"

Her words sped up. "You're afraid that if you feel, you'll get hurt and that's probably the only risk in your entire life that you don't want to take."

Through her unshed tears, Jerry could see the hurt and anger in her eyes. His heart shattered in his chest.

His head spun. His ears rang. Symone's words were like a punch in the face from a heavyweight champion. "You're wrong." His voice was raw, even to his ears.

"Am I?" She stepped backward into the room. "We'll do this your way, Jerry. This is a job. I'm your charge. You're my bodyguard. When this is over—and I pray it will be soon—I'll write you a check and we'll never have to see each other again."

"Wait, Symone, I—" He didn't know what he was going to say. He only knew he didn't want their conversation to end like this.

"I have work to do. Could you bring up my bags, please? Thank you." She closed the door between them.

Jerry stared at it as thoughts, snatches of conversations and images of Symone's tear-filled eyes spun in his mind. She wasn't going to open the door. She wasn't going to hear him out. She'd made it clear she was done talking with him, at least about their personal relationship. He forced his legs to turn and walk away.

He'd made so many mistakes with this case. He should've taken Symone's personal cell phone from her. He shouldn't have gotten involved with a charge. And he never should've fallen in love with a woman who was out of his league.

Chapter 16

"Thanks again for cooking, Jer." Mal finished his spaghetti and meatballs. Seated at the head of the table, he lowered his knife and fork to the cream porcelain plate and sipped his ice water.

"It was delicious. Thank you." Symone avoided his eyes as she lowered her blue-tinted acrylic glass.

Jerry took a deep drink of water to ease his dry throat. "You're both welcome. I'm glad you enjoyed it. Dinner is the least I can do, Mal, since you're letting us stay here without any notice."

Jerry and Symone were still in the clothes they'd worn when they'd run from the safe house. Mal was wearing the business casual gray slacks, blue shirt and gray tie he'd worn to work.

Symone gave Mal a warm smile. "I can't thank you enough."

Mal waved away their words. "No problem. I'm glad you came here."

"I feel like we're putting you out." Symone dropped her eyes to her nearly empty plate. "It was *my* thoughtless actions that caused the change in plans." She stroked moisture from her water glass with the tips of her long, slender fingers.

Jerry remembered the feel of her hands on his skin. Her

touch had made his body burn. He grabbed his glass and drained the last of his water.

Mal looked from Symone to him and back. His brother had masked his expression, but Jerry could tell Mal had picked up on the tension between him and Symone. The voice in his head spewed a string of curses.

Dinner had been a comfortable experience for the most part. Symone had asked Mal about the search for Xander—nothing new to report—and their search for his possible accomplice—no leads yet. Conversation had flowed between Symone and Mal, and Jerry and Mal, but Jerry's exchanges with Symone had been stilted. Mal would've had to have been in a deep sleep to miss it. His brother never missed anything.

Mal gave Symone an empathetic smile. "There's no such thing as a perfect plan. That's why we have backups and safeguards like the alert on Jerry's phone in case we need to make changes in the middle of an investigation."

"You explained that so well, Mal." She adjusted her glasses. Her expression was thoughtful. "Instead of looking for someone to blame, your explanation acknowledges that it's humanly impossible to be in complete control all the time. Thank you."

"Sure." Mal's response was neutral. But Jerry knew his brother. On the inside, Mal was laughing at him.

For Pete's sake.

Jerry drew a calming breath, catching the scents of tomato sauce, oregano, garlic and Parmesan cheese from their meal. He forced his stiff facial muscles into a professional smile. "Bottom line—TSG believes the burden of adjusting our original plans lies with us, not our clients."

"Or your charges." Symone looked through him. Her detachment cut like a blade.

Mal coughed as though his drink had gone down the wrong pipe. He caught his breath after a moment. "Speaking of making adjustments, I'll work from home until the killer is caught. That way, I can be additional protection for you, Symone."

"Thank you. I would really like that." Her smile was like the sun coming out.

Jerry felt the burn. Did she think they'd need a buffer going forward? Thinking about the tension between them during dinner, she may be right. "Thanks, Mal."

Symone adjusted her glasses again. "I'm a little embarrassed to be causing all this trouble."

Mal shook his head. "Your safety isn't trouble, Symone. It's our priority."

Symone stood to gather her place setting. "That's what Jerry said. Several times."

Jerry stood more abruptly than he'd intended. He put his hands on Symone's dishes to stop her from clearing the table. "I'll take care of that."

Her eyes fell short of his. "That's not fair. You cooked. I'll do the cleanup."

Mal rose from the table. "Jerry's right. We've got this."

Symone hesitated. "All right, if you insist. I've got some work to do anyway. Thank you, gentlemen. I'll wish you good night now."

"Sleep well," Mal responded.

"Night." Jerry watched her disappear at the staircase. A weight pressed against his chest as he thought about all the meals they'd shared and how they'd worked in perfect sync to clean up afterward. Kitchen patrol had never been so enjoyable.

Mal carried his dishes to the sink. "What's up?"

Jerry followed him, carrying Symone's place setting. "What do you mean?"

Mal turned to him. His brother was maybe an inch taller than him. Wonder Woman had her Lasso of Truth. Mal had his direct stare. He pinned Jerry with it now. "Don't pretend, Jer. When I got home, I thought I'd set my air conditioner too low. That was before I'd seen either of you. And you made spaghetti and meatballs."

Jerry frowned. "So what?"

Mal arched a thick dark eyebrow. "It's your go-to comfort food. What did you argue about? Was it the case—or something else?"

Jerry's gaze fell. He lowered his voice, hoping Symone wouldn't hear them talking about her. "Things got personal at the cabin. Neither of us expected anything to happen, but… She's amazing. Shy and bold. Intense and funny. Super smart and kind. You should see the way her employees react to her. It's like a Beyoncé concert—or at least the way I imagine a Beyoncé concert."

Mal smiled. "She's great. I know. I've spoken with her, too. What happened?"

Jerry leaned his hips against the white-and-silver marble countertop beside the sink. He folded his arms under his chest. "I let myself get distracted. I lost my focus, and the killer almost tracked her to the safe house."

His gut filled with ice each time he thought about what could've happened if he hadn't received the alert that the killer had connected with Symone's phone.

"That's not what happened."

Jerry's eyes shot to Mal's. "Yes, it is."

Mal shook his head. "Symone made an honest mistake and you're using it to put distance between you because you think you're falling in love." He returned to the dining room to continue clearing the table.

Jerry didn't *think* he was falling in love—he was afraid he was already there. He followed Mal. "How could I be in love? We've only known each other a week."

"Mom and Dad said it was love at first sight for them. It was the same for me with Grace." Mal collected the water pitcher.

Love at first sight? Jerry almost dropped his dishes. "Symone and I are too different. She comes from generations of wealth. Mom and Dad were retired military."

Their parents had met while serving in the Marine Corps.

"This is about you and Symone, not your extended families." Mal loaded the dishwasher.

Jerry considered the back of Mal's clean-shaven head. His plain-spoken brother was always honest with him regardless of how much the truth might hurt. "Do you think I run away from my feelings because I'm afraid of getting hurt?"

"Yes." Mal spoke over his shoulder.

That stung. "I disagree."

Mal continued packing the dishwasher. "You're allowed."

"Symone and I wouldn't last. She barely uses contractions and says things like, 'Our bylaws mandate.'" Jerry put his dishes in the sink, ready for Mal to load them.

"And you're a slob." Mal straightened from the dishwasher. "Do you want to give a relationship with her a chance or not?"

Jerry thought about his time with Symone at the cabin. They were strangers to each other in an unfamiliar environment, running for their lives. Their circumstances had been unusual to say the least but the week they'd spent together had been incredible.

"Of course I do." Jerry's voice was hoarse. "But I have to face facts. The time Symone and I spent in the cabin, that wasn't real. What if she agrees to continue our relationship in the real world and then realizes I don't belong there?"

Mal shrugged. "What if she realizes you do?"

Jerry shook his head as he turned to walk away. *Only in my dreams.*

"Symone! I was worried about you. What happened?" Percy answered her call after the first ring early Friday morning.

Symone half sat, half reclined on the bed in Zeke's old room. Her thoughts raced. She couldn't tell The Bishop Foundation's lawyer and longtime family friend the truth about what happened yesterday—*The person who's trying to kill me was tracking my cell phone*—but she owed him an explanation. "I'm so sorry, Percy. I had a sudden emergency."

"It must have been a matter of life and death." His tone was dry.

"Aren't they always?" She hoped her humor sounded natural.

Percy chuckled. "Before I forget, you should call Ellie after we talk. When I didn't hear back from you yesterday, I called her to ask if she'd spoken with you. I'm afraid I scared her. She asked if I knew where you were and who you were with. Of course I didn't. But I told her whoever heard from you first should make sure to ask you to contact the other one."

Symone stared at the teakwood dressing table across the room without seeing it. She wished Percy hadn't involved

Ellie in yesterday's events. She understood why he had. She probably would have done the same. Symone would deal with Ellie, but that would have to wait until later. "I'll give her a call. Thank you."

"Wonderful." Percy sighed. "Now, how can I help you, my dear?"

Symone swung her legs off the mattress and rose from the bed. The sectional rug was soft beneath her bare feet. Like the safe house, Mal had covered all the windows in his home with one-way tinted screens. Still, the room received enough sunlight that Symone had chosen to leave the overhead lamps off.

She wandered to the wall beside the closet to study Zeke's colored-pencil framed drawing of Antrim Lake. The image was from the perspective of the dock overlooking the free-form lake. It was soothing. Zeke was incredibly talented.

A couple of hours ago, she'd risked a trip to Mal's basement to exercise. She'd hoped to arrive early enough to avoid Jerry. He seemed to have had the same hope. They'd arrived at the same time. Mal was meeting up with Zeke for their usual six-mile run around Antrim Lake. Jerry, however, remained inside. The killer knew Jerry and Symone were together. If Jerry was seen in the neighborhood, the killer would've known Symone was nearby. While exercising, Symone tried to ignore him, but it would've been easier to ignore the sun.

After cleaning up and dressing in a cream blouse and tangerine culottes, she'd made this call to Percy. "Thank you for sending me a copy of the foundation's bylaws."

"Of course. It's my pleasure." Beneath Percy's voice, the pinging sound of metal hitting porcelain was a strong hint the lawyer was enjoying a mug of coffee. "Did it provide the information you were hoping for?"

"I'm not sure." Symone returned to the bed where she'd left her printout of the bylaws. She'd marked several passages with yellow highlighter. "That's why I'm calling. Could you pull up a copy to follow along with me?"

"I can. Give me a moment." Rapid tapping broke the brief silence. "I've got it. What questions can I help you with?"

"Could you explain Article Two, Section Three? I can read a prospectus and spreadsheets, but legalese is too much for me." She waited for Percy to find the section she referenced.

"Ah, this language deals with the board." His tone was distracted as though he was skimming it in preparation for her questions. "What would you like to ask, my dear?"

"I want to be clear on the separation of powers between the board and the chair, and the specific responsibilities board members have."

Percy hesitated. "Is everything okay, Symone?"

No, everything's not okay. "I just want a better understanding of the board's responsibilities to the chair and the foundation. Section Three requires each member of the board to bring concerns about the foundation to the chair, members of the administration and other board members in a timely manner. Am I understanding that correctly?"

"Yes, you are." Percy sounded like a proud professor. "Your grandfather thought of it as a check on the board."

Jerry was right. Her grandfather had included in the bylaws checks on the foundation's board as well as the chair. "What does it require of the board?"

"That section requires *any* member who had a complaint about *any* aspect of the foundation to bring their concerns to the entire leadership team—chair, vice chair, administrative assistant and board members—in a timely manner. Your grandfather was adamant about that. He didn't want the members to go off in secret to complain about the foundation, then ambush him during a meeting. He dealt with enough of that in the corporate world."

Grandpa, I could kiss you. "How do the bylaws define a 'timely manner'?"

"It's quarterly." A clicking sound carried from Percy's end of the line as he moved through the electronic file. "Article Five, Section One explains that the leadership team will close out all old business each quarter. My father and your grandfather referred to it as the speak-now-or-forever-hold-your-peace section."

Symone flipped through her printout of the bylaws. It would have been helpful if her grandfather and Percy's father had created an index. She made a mental note to request one, perhaps after the board meeting that would decide her fate with the foundation.

"Found it. Thank you." She highlighted the passage. "Is there a penalty if a board member breaks any of these rules? If they meet separately to discuss their concerns or if they don't bring their concerns to leadership in a timely manner?"

"Oh, absolutely." Percy chuckled. "Your grandfather was big on enforcement. Penalties for various infractions—missing board meetings, missing leadership votes, discussing foundation business without authorization, et cetera—are all described under Article Thirteen, Section Six, Disciplinary Measures."

Symone flipped through more pages, searching for Article Thirteen, Section Six. "I can't believe you remember where all of this information appears in this document." Percy's laughter made her smile. She got to the pertinent section and skimmed the text. *Gotcha!* "This is just what I need. Thank you, Percy."

"Anytime, my dear. Call me if there's anything else I can do for you."

"Oh, I will." Symone gave Percy her best, asking him to give her love to his family, then ended the call.

She took a few moments to review the Disciplinary Measures more thoroughly before she remembered her promise to call Ellie. She filed the bylaws, then entered her administrative assistant's phone number by memory.

Her admin answered on the first ring. "This is Eleanor Press. May I help you?"

"Ellie, it's Symone—"

"Symone! Where have you been?" Ellie's voice rose several octaves. Symone winced. "We've been so worried about you. Percy said you disconnected the call abruptly."

"I'm fine, Ellie. I'm sorry you were worried." Symone paced the room. It was more spacious than her bedroom in the cabin. She stopped to again admire Zeke's original drawings of the Scioto River and the Park of Roses.

"But where are you?" The other woman sounded frustrated.

Symone smiled at her fussing. "Ellie, you know I can't tell you that."

Ellie exhaled a heavy sigh. "Symone, with all due respect, how much longer is this going to continue? It's been more than a week. What's taking Touré Security Group so long? Do they even know what they're doing?"

Symone's muscles stiffened. It surprised her how much her admin's criticism of Jerry and his brothers bothered her. Her face heated with anger.

"Yes, they do know what they're doing." Her tone was curt. "They have my complete trust and respect."

"How can you say that?" Ellie seemed equal parts angry and incredulous. "You barely know these men. What have they learned from their investigation?"

Her temper strained for release. Symone made an effort to keep it in check. "I don't owe you an explanation or update. Do you have any issues relating to the foundation you need to discuss with me?"

Ellie's sigh was softer. She brought her voice under control. "I'm sorry, Symone. I'm worried about you. And I'm running a lot of interference with the board. It's very stressful. They want to know when you'll be back in the office full-time."

"Once we find the person who killed my mother and who's threatening me." Symone turned back to the bed, and the folders, printouts and charts strewn across it. "Is there anything else?"

"How's the report coming? Do you need any more information?"

"It's almost completed." Symone settled back against the bed's headboard. She lifted her laptop's lid and reawakened the device.

"Really?" Ellie sounded pleasantly surprised. "Great. Do you want me to review it for you?"

Symone shook her head although Ellie couldn't see her. "No, I can handle it. In fact, I'd better get back to—"

Ellie interrupted. "I'm sorry, Symone. I didn't mean to upset you. I'm just worried about you."

Symone forced herself to relax. Ellie had apologized. She was irritated but accepting the other woman's apology and moving on was the right and mature thing to do. "There's no need to be worried, but thank you. Email if you need me. And don't let the board get to you. Tell them to call me if they need to discuss my return to the office."

She and Ellie ended their conversation cordially. The board must really be putting pressure on her admin. Symone tossed the burner phone beside her on the mattress. Once things returned to normal, she'd encourage Ellie to take a few weeks off.

"Eleanor Press and Xander Fence are fugitives." Mal dropped the bombshell at the start of the team's videoconference late Friday morning. Working from home, he wore a cream polo shirt, navy cargo shorts and athletic socks. "They're wanted by the FBI for bank, insurance and wire fraud."

Symone's mind went blank. "What?" She was seated to Mal's right at his circular blond wood dining table.

"Wait a minute. What?" Jerry spoke at the same time. Seated on Mal's left, he was similarly dressed as his brother in a jade polo shirt and black shorts.

"Excuse me?" Zeke spoke from the small blond wood conversation table in his office. He looked like the corporate executive he was in a white dress shirt and magenta tie.

"Now we know who Xander's partner is." Celeste sat beside Zeke, sipping coffee. The private investigator was wearing another black cotton T-shirt. "How'd you discover that?"

Mal lowered his pen to his notepad and leaned back against his chair. "When we searched farther than five years back, we lost the trail on Ellie and Xander. That made me suspect those were fake names. I used the trial facial recognition program we'd ordered—"

Jerry corrected him. "The one *you'd* ordered, geek."

Mal slid his brother a look but didn't take the bait. "We couldn't find anything on Xander beyond five years ago because his identity didn't exist. His real name is Norris

Hall. Hall and Dorothy Wiggans belonged to the same community theater group."

Symone's eyes flew to Mal's. "That's how he learned about the foundation."

"Apparently." Mal nodded. "As for Ellie, her identity is stolen. Her real name is Bonnie Rae." A few clicks on his laptop allowed Mal to share his screen. He uploaded two images. "These are Hall's and Rae's FBI wanted photos."

Zeke nodded. "Impressive work, Mal. Thank you."

Celeste squinted at the computer screen. "I agree. Good job."

Jerry patted Mal's shoulder. "You've got skills, Mal."

"Thank you." Symone could only stare at the images on the screen. Instead of Ellie's auburn hair and jade eyes, Bonnie Rae was a brown-eyed brunette. So was Norris Hall. Symone felt sick.

She stared at Mal but didn't see him. His voice was muffled beneath the pulse roaring in her ears. Her lips were parted, but her mind was blank. She didn't have the words.

Jerry leaned forward to catch Symone's attention from Mal's other side. His movement shattered her trance. "Are you all right?"

Symone shook her head. Her fingers trembled as she smoothed the shorts of her tangerine culottes. "I've worked with her for more than nine months. I never once suspected she was anyone other than who she said she was." She turned to meet Jerry's eyes. "And she killed my mother."

"We don't know that yet," Zeke said.

"Yes, we do." Celeste gestured in Symone's direction. "As the foundation's admin, she worked closely with Symone, Odette and Paul. She probably overheard snatches of conversation that could've included information about

Odette's heart condition. She could access Symone's phone and laptop to plant the bugs."

Zeke spread his hands. "All good points, but we can't jump to conclusions."

Celeste shrugged. The movement was jerky with impatience. "Okay. If it makes you feel better, we'll pretend two plus two doesn't equal four—yet."

Jerry addressed Symone. "You really need to talk with your background check services vendor."

"You're right." Anger chased the chill from Symone's blood. She waved a hand toward the computer screen. "Ellie or Bonnie or whatever she calls herself had access to all our bank account information and financial documents. I just spoke with her."

Celeste lowered her coffee mug. "Today? What about?"

Symone clenched her hands. "She wanted to know where I was. Of course, I didn't tell her. I thought she was being protective. It never occurred to me she could be Xander's partner—or a fugitive from the law. She also asked about the report for the special board meeting."

Zeke rubbed his eyes. "We have to take this to Eriq and Taylor." He dropped his hand. "They can bring Bonnie Rae in for questioning."

Jerry nodded. "She probably knows where Xander is."

"Please excuse me." Symone stood and started toward the stairs. Her legs felt shaky. "I have to call the foundation's lawyer and ask him to remove Ellie's—Bonnie's—access to the foundation's accounts."

Seconds after Symone ended her call with Percy, Jerry knocked on the open door to her guest room. The look on his face made her stomach drop. His expression was almost as grave as it had been when he'd broken the news that her mother had been murdered.

Leaning against the nearby dressing table, she dropped the burner cell into her pocket and braced herself for whatever he had to say. "What's happened?"

"There's been an accident." He paused. "Paul's in the hospital."

Symone's knees shook. If it wasn't for the dresser, she would have ended up on the floor. Her only thought was to get to her stepfather. Fast.

Chapter 17

"What happened to Paul?" Symone slid forward on the car's back passenger seat. She strained to keep panic from her voice and gory images from her mind. Mal was navigating his black SUV on the twenty-minute drive to Mount Carmel St. Ann's in northeast Columbus Friday morning.

Jerry turned sideways on the front passenger seat to see her. "Eriq called Zeke. Paul was hit by a car in a shopping center parking lot."

"Oh, my—" Symone covered her gasp with her right hand. "How is he?" Her palm muffled her words.

Jerry took a breath. "He was still unconscious when the ambulance arrived."

Dropping her hands, Symone closed her eyes. "Why didn't I insist he accept protection? I should have insisted." She felt Jerry's hand, warm and strong, cover hers where they rested on her lap. Her eyes popped open.

Jerry held them. "You tried to get him to change his mind, but you couldn't force him. TSG had an agent watching him, but from a distance. She was the one who called the ambulance and provided a description of the car."

Symone eased her hands free of Jerry's and sat back against the smoke gray cloth interior. Her skin was cold where she'd lost his touch. "Thank you for that."

Silence settled in the vehicle. The tension around her was like an inflatable ball, pressing against her as it swelled. Symone chased images of Paul's broken body from her mind. Desperate for a distraction, she concentrated on the view through the side window. Treetops were interspersed with shopping centers featuring upscale restaurants, fast-food stops, specialty stores and movie theaters. These neighborhoods were homes to warehouses, discount shops, gas stations and parking lots. And in the distance, the silhouette of the downtown skyline loomed.

Symone drew a calming breath. Mal's SUV smelled like vinyl cleaner, soap and pine needles. Jerry had been using a rental during the case. What kind of car did he own and what did it smell like? Probably coffee, fast food—and mints.

Mal merged onto Interstate 270 toward downtown Columbus. The sluggish traffic put her patience to the test.

She checked her watch, then looked up at the back of Jerry's tight curls and Mal's clean-shaven head. "I thought I was the killer's target? Why would they attack Paul, especially since we announced his resignation from the foundation?"

"I thought that was strange." Mal's response was almost inaudible.

Symone caught the look that passed between the brothers. She narrowed her eyes. "Are you using me as bait?"

"I'm sorry." Jerry shifted on his seat to look at her again. "We think the killer's getting impatient and is trying to draw you out. Eriq and Taylor agree with us."

"They're at the hospital." Mal changed lanes, moving closer to the exit in preparation of getting off the interstate. "Zeke updated them on Ellie's and Xander's real identities."

Symone removed her glasses to rub both eyes. "If you're going to set a trap with me as the target, you could have at least told me."

Mal glanced at her in the rearview mirror. "It was Jerry's idea, but I'm sorry, too."

"You have enough on your mind with Paul's accident." Jerry held her eyes. "I wouldn't put you in harm's way if I wasn't sure you'd be safe with Mal, Eriq, Taylor and me."

Symone adjusted her glasses. "You want to use me as bait. I want to see Paul. We both get what we want. Just next time, tell me."

"I'm hoping there won't be a next time." Jerry faced forward.

"So am I." Mal's voice was grim.

Symone's eyes brushed over the back of Jerry's head before she turned away. Once they solved this case, would her life have to be in danger before she saw him again?

Eriq and Taylor met them in the hospital lobby and brought them up to Paul's room. Symone's tension eased a bit when she saw the uniformed police officer stationed outside his room. The young man was chatting with a nurse who looked to be about his age. They made a good-looking couple.

Symone gave Eriq and Taylor a smile of gratitude. "Thank you for providing him with protection."

"Of course." Taylor wore a black, scoop-necked blouse and cream slacks. "He came to for a little while, but he's sleeping again now." She gestured toward the nurse who'd joined them. "Becky's one of the nurses assigned to your stepfather."

The young woman was about Symone's height. She returned her handshake with a firm grip. Her hot pink, short-sleeved top and matching pants clashed with her wealth of red curls. Her hair framed her peaches-and-cream complexion. Her brown eyes sparkled when she smiled. Symone instantly felt she could trust the medical professional.

Becky's voice was soft and kind as she explained Paul's condition. "Your stepfather has a headache. He doesn't show signs of a concussion, though. He has a few cracked ribs, some cuts and bruises. He's in pain, but the good news is we don't believe any of his injuries will lead to permanent damage."

"That *is* good news." But Symone couldn't stop worrying. "Would it be possible for me to see him? I won't stay long."

Becky shook her head. "He's sleeping, which is exactly what he needs. We don't think he should be disturbed yet. But we're going to check on him again in another hour. You could see him then."

An hour? That long? Symone sighed, gritting her teeth. "All right. Thank you and thank you for taking care of him."

"You're welcome." Becky smiled. "I'm familiar with The Bishop Foundation. Thank *you* for everything you do." She left before Symone could respond.

"All right, then." Eriq pulled out his notepad. "The TSG agent assigned to Paul told the officers at the scene it looked like the driver aimed for your stepfather." He gave Symone an apologetic look. "The driver struck him and kept going as though they were fleeing the scene. Other witnesses corroborated the agent's statement. We also have part of the license plate and a description of the car—a silver hatchback."

Symone froze. "A silver hatchback?"

Eriq smoothed his bolo tie. The copper slide clip was shaped like a walleye. He wore it with a white shirt and navy slacks. "We're way ahead of you. We checked for cars registered under Ellie Press and Xander Fence. We know Ellie owns a silver hatchback and the first three letters of her plate match witnesses' reports, GZH."

Jerry looked to Symone. "This hit-and-run's similar to the second threat against you and Paul."

Symone's eyes strayed toward Paul's room. Something didn't make sense. "When did the hit-and-run happen?"

Eriq flipped through pages filled with notes.

Taylor found the information in her book first. "About nine."

"That's right." Eriq nodded, stabbing a page in his book. "Why?"

"I was on the phone with Ellie—Bonnie, whoever—a little after nine." Symone frowned. She looked from Eriq and Taylor to Jerry and Mal. "I called her at the office. She answered the phone right away and we spoke for several minutes." She turned back to the detectives. "That may have been Ellie's car, but she couldn't have been driving it. She was on the phone with me."

Jerry's muscles tightened with surprise. He crossed his arms over his jade polo shirt. "Xander Fence."

"He's resurfaced." Like Jerry, Mal crossed his arms over his cream shirt.

"*He* must be the one trying to draw Symone out." Jerry addressed Eriq and Taylor. "We don't know if he's going to look like Xander or Norris." Will he be a green-eyed blond or a brown-eyed brunette?

Eriq gestured toward the officer outside Paul's door. "We gave Officer Mallard pictures of both suspects and their alternate identities."

Symone adjusted her glasses. "But if they're partners,

why would Xander try to frame Ellie for the hit-and-run? What's the benefit?"

Taylor shrugged. "He must be setting her up to take the fall. You've heard the saying there's no honor among thieves."

Eriq turned to Symone. "You said you were speaking with Ellie at the time of the hit-and-run. What did you talk about?"

Symone gave the detectives a succinct summary of her conversation with her admin-cum-FBI-fugitive. It was the same information she'd given him and his brothers earlier. Jerry watched her sharing the exchange with Eriq and Taylor. Her recap was clear and concise. Her voice was warm and soothing. Her arms were as graceful as a dancer's as she used them to talk. She was beautiful.

The four of them plus Officer Mallard stationed outside Paul's door were partially blocking the hallway. However, from the way Symone's eyes kept straying to Paul's room as though her stepfather would appear in the doorway, Jerry was sure she wouldn't willingly move to a more comfortable location. Her continued care and concern for her stepfather impressed Jerry. He'd been surprised and disappointed when Paul had deserted Symone after being told she was the killer's target. However, Symone remained by her stepfather's side when he was in danger. She didn't hold a grudge. She was motivated by decency and doing the right thing. Another reason he was in love with her.

After Symone brought the detectives up to speed on her conversation with Ellie, Jerry turned to them. "We need a favor."

Eriq gave the three of them a suspicious look. "What is it?"

At the same time, Taylor smiled. "Of course."

Eriq scowled at his partner.

Asking for this favor was worth the risk of rejection. If his plan worked, it would ensure Symone's safety and get Ellie/Bonnie and Xander/Norris out of her life for good.

Jerry continued. "Let Zeke and Mal watch your interview with Ellie. They could research her answers for connections to Xander or help us find him before he finds us."

Eriq seemed skeptical. "And where would you be?"

Jerry turned to Symone. She was watching him as though he was a stranger. That hurt. He worked through the pain. "Symone and I will search Ellie's office for anything that would connect her and/or Xander to Odette's murder, the threats against Symone and Paul, or maybe even Dorothy Wiggans's death. Maybe we'll even find something that lets us know where Xander is. But we'll have to do this after hours when the employees have gone."

"It's a good plan." Mal nodded in approval.

"Yes." Symone sounded surprised. "It's a very good plan."

Taylor turned to Eriq. "I agree. Teaming up with Zeke, Mal, Jerry and Symone would save us a ton of legwork on the back end, especially if Jerry and Symone find something in Ellie's office."

Eriq hesitated. "But if this hit-and-run is just for Xander to get to Symone, is it really a good idea for just the two of you to go off on your own?"

Symone squared her shoulders. "We'll be careful. Don't worry."

Eriq shrugged. "Well, if you're not worried, I'm not worried." He shifted his attention to Jerry. "Let's do it."

"Great." Jerry felt a surge of success. If they found evidence linking Ellie and Xander to these crimes, and could arrest both of them, they could close this case tonight and Symone would be safe. He turned to Mal. "Let's get Zeke."

Mal held up his cell phone. "I'll let him know we're coming."

Jerry turned to Symone. "Are you with me?"

"Always." Her eyes seemed drawn to Paul's room one final time before she led the way to the bank of elevators.

Always. He wished that word wasn't so out of reach.

Symone unlocked the side door that led from the parking lot to the lobby of the building that housed The Bishop Foundation Friday evening. With the longer summer days, the sun was still out although the temperature had dropped. Thankfully.

"This building's lack of security is insulting." Jerry seemed frustrated again by the lack of cameras. He held the door open for her.

Symone locked her knees in preparation for walking past his warmth and scent. She watched as he looked over his shoulder toward the parking lot, and up and down the sidewalk. His tension eased. Apparently, they hadn't been followed. Good.

Jerry joined Symone inside, making sure the door locked behind them. Then he submitted the lobby to the same scrutiny he'd given the building's exterior. Overhead lights were on all over the main floor. Symone suspected the extra electricity was the property manager's concession to safety. Of course, the company passed the cost of the all-night utility usage back to its tenants, including the foundation.

Symone led them to the elevators. "You said as much previously." She pressed the Up button, then gave him a smile. "In fact, you criticized the security one week ago today, the first day we met."

Heat shifted in his eyes. Symone caught her breath. His look reminded her of their night—and morning—of intimacy. Her skin tingled as though he'd touched her.

Jerry broke eye contact, shifting his attention to the elevator bank behind her. "We're the only two people here. It's not safe. Do you work here by yourself after hours?"

The elevator's arrival claimed Symone's attention. She entered the car and waited for Jerry to join her before pressing the button for the seventh floor. "I have the feeling that if I answer yes, you'll be disappointed."

"It's not safe, Symone," he repeated. "Promise me—"

Symone waited but Jerry didn't finish his thought. Was he going to ask her to promise him she wouldn't come to the building after hours? She clenched her fists at her side. Was he toying with her? Was she his charge and nothing more? Were they friends? She gave him a once-over from the corner of her eyes. She remembered what he looked like without clothes. There was no way they could ever be just friends.

The elevator doors opened, depositing them in the anteroom outside The Bishop Foundation.

Symone crossed to the suite's entrance. She sensed Jerry behind her. It was her turn to avoid his eyes. "I'll email the property manager in the morning about requesting an estimate from TSG."

Jerry held the door for her again. "We'd appreciate the contract, but this is about keeping you safe."

Safe from murderers, burglars and assailants. Symone was grateful for that. Was there a service that could keep her heart safe from him?

"This way." Symone gestured to the offices at the end

of the hall. "Ellie's office is beside mine." She caught his smile. "What's funny?"

"Nothing." But his smile remained. "This will be the first time I'll be able to walk this hall with you without members of your staff stopping you every three feet to say hello and tell you about their families."

Symone chuckled. "Those are some of the best parts of my day."

"I can tell. I hope you're able to prevent the board from voting you out."

Her joy vanished. "So do I." A few more steps brought her to Ellie's office. She pulled out her keys again. "We lock all the offices at the end of the day as a safety precaution. I have a master key that opens every room in the suite, though."

She unlocked the door and crossed the threshold into Ellie's spacious area. Like Symone's, Ellie's room was furnished in heavy, dark wood pieces, including a desk, bookcase, credenza and conversation table. The single window behind the navy blue executive chair welcomed a wealth of natural light.

Jerry looked around. "Your office is bigger."

Symone circled the desk. "What are we looking for?"

Jerry crossed to the credenza. "Anything that she's not supposed to have. A folder. A recording device. A checkbook for the foundation. An envelope taped to the bottom of a drawer." He looked over his shoulder at her. "I saw that one in a movie."

Symone wished he'd stop being so charming. She opened the center drawer and found pens, pencils, rubber bands and thumbtacks. Nothing seemed suspicious. "You were impressive earlier. When did you become a planner?"

"I've recently learned planning has its benefits." Jerry

flipped through the files in Ellie's credenza. His movements were practiced and efficient. This wasn't his first search.

She shook her head. "As a lifelong planner, I agree. I'm just surprised you've admitted it. You once told me you thought planning was a waste of time."

"People can change." His words were low, reluctant. Completing his examination of the credenza, Jerry moved on to the bookcase. The shelves held a dictionary, a thesaurus, medical industry journals and project binders, among other things.

"Hmm." *Would that include changing their minds about getting involved with their "charges"?* Symone pulled out the center drawer and turned it over. "There's no hidden envelope."

Jerry searched the credenza's exterior. "Keep looking. We need to find something that could help prove Ellie and Xander were involved in a conspiracy to defraud the foundation."

The desk had four other drawers. Symone moved on to the one at the top left. She found scissors, binder clips and a ruler. Bending over, she managed to wiggle the drawer free of its rollers. She turned it over—and gasped. "There's an envelope taped to the bottom of this drawer."

Two long strides brought Jerry to her side. "What is it?"

Symone turned the drawer upside down on the desk's surface so she could access the package. It was a nine-by-twelve manila booklet envelope. The return address belonged to the company that processed the foundation's background checks.

"It's addressed to me. Why did Ellie hide it?" She pulled the envelope free of the drawer and opened it. Inside was a thick stack of papers.

Jerry read over her shoulder. "It's the background check for Xander."

"Except this one comes with a recommendation to deny his membership to the board." Symone flipped through the pages. "Ellie intercepted the report and switched the real one with the one she'd falsified."

The quiet click sent ice through Symone's system. She looked up and found a gun pointed at her. Just beneath the sound of her pulse galloping in her ears, she heard Xander's voice.

"I'll take that envelope, please."

Chapter 18

"Norris Hall, I presume." Jerry's voice mocked him. He paraphrased the famous quote, substituting Norris's name for Dr. Livingstone. His bravado in the face of a gun wielded by a serial killer almost sent Symone into cardiac arrest.

Norris stood just inside the door to Ellie's office. He wore the curly blond wig and dark green contacts he'd established as his look for Xander. But tonight, he'd made a wardrobe change. Instead of an expensive three-piece suit and Italian shoes, he wore black sweats and sneakers.

"We haven't been formally introduced." Xander's thin lips parted in a smile—or maybe it was a sneer. He held the gun as though it was an extension of his hand.

Symone's mouth was too dry to swallow. She set the report on Ellie's desk and clenched her hands to stop them from shaking.

"Jeremiah Touré." Jerry's smile was cold. His eyes were sharp. "By which name would you prefer we call you, Xander Fence or Norris Hall?"

Jerry stood beside Symone, back straight, shoulders squared, legs braced. He'd shifted closer to the desk as though once again shielding her with his body—his body that seemed to be always in motion. Then why was he so still now? He could probably disarm the other man in two moves.

"Xander will be fine." His shrug caused the gun to shift just a bit.

Symone's knees almost buckled. She leaned her thighs against the desk, braced her hands on its surface and drew a shaky breath. The bitter scent enveloping her was fear.

Turning to Jerry, she widened her eyes, *Disarm him.*

He looked her over, then returned his attention to the man with the gun.

What did that mean? Her muscles shook from a disabling mixture of confusion, fear and anger.

Jerry cocked his head. "Do you prefer Xander because Norris is wanted by the FBI? Fraud, right? Bank, wire, insurance and a few others."

Xander's smile faded. "You've done your research."

Symone couldn't take this chatter any more. This wasn't going according to their plan. They were supposed to get in, get evidence, then get out. She hadn't envisioned being held at gunpoint. Perhaps she should have thought of that. But right now, she was having trouble controlling her breathing and she couldn't think straight.

"You killed my mother." Her voice was raw.

Xander shrugged again. "Collateral damage, I'm afraid."

Symone saw red. She wanted to climb over the desk and choke the feigned sympathy from his face.

Jerry shifted forward. "What was Dorothy Wiggans? Why did you kill her?"

"Step. Back." Xander pointed the gun at Jerry's head. He lowered it to Symone's chest when Jerry returned to her side. "You know about Dottie? Boy, you *are* good. I needed Dottie's spot on the board to make the plan work."

"Why are you doing this?" Her voice was more demanding than she'd expected. Anger was giving her strength.

Xander raised his eyebrows. "For money, of course. The foundation has lots of it."

Symone's temper was overtaking her fear. "Board members are paid a percentage of the profits from the products we invest in."

"I want more." He sounded so reasonable while making his unreasonable demand.

Symone concentrated on her breathing. She needed to collect her wits. "Defrauding my family's foundation won't be as easy as you think. We have safeguards in place."

"Like that safeguard?" Xander nodded toward the manila envelope in front of Symone. "*You* should be surprised by how easily I took control of your foundation. In less than a month, I convinced a simple majority of your board members to challenge your leadership. You've lost your company. Your stepfather left you. *You* should've left when I asked you to. But no. Instead, you decided to involve an innocent man in trying to protect your precious foundation. It's your fault he's going to die."

Symone turned to Jerry and again widened her eyes. *Please, do something.*

Again he looked at her, then away.

She didn't understand. She'd seen his strenuous workouts. His reflexes were fast. His punches were powerful. Why wasn't he using those skills on Xander now? Symone was certain he could disarm the other man in two moves, three tops. What was holding him back?

You are.

Symone's eyes had opened. Jerry was holding back because he was afraid the gun would go off in the struggle and she'd be hit by a stray bullet.

Think. Think. Think. What can I do to get us out of dan-

ger? "Do you really think killing me and Jerry will give you control of my family's foundation?"

How do I take myself out of the equation?

"My brothers and the police know what you've done." Jerry shifted his stance. "The detectives in charge of this investigation are interrogating Ellie right now."

"Ellie. That fool." Xander spit out his words. "She's become a liability."

Take myself out of the equation. Of course! Symone deliberately looked past Xander as though there was someone in the hallway behind him, then hurriedly returned her attention to him. He narrowed his eyes at her.

Symone cleared her throat. "Is that the reason you tried to frame Ellie for the hit-and-run that almost killed my stepfather?"

Xander gave a mirthless laugh. "You ask too many questions."

Now or never.

Symone looked past Xander. "Help us!" She shouted, infusing her words with all the fear and desperation in her body.

She saw Xander spin around to confront an enemy who wasn't there, turning his back to the adversary in the room. She saw Jerry leap at Xander.

Symone threw herself under the table. Digging her burner cell from the pocket of her culottes, she dialed emergency services.

"9-1-1. What is your emergency?"

"An armed shooter has broken into The Bishop Foundation. Please send help." She gave the foundation's address, then disconnected the call.

"Symone!" Jerry was breathless. "You can come out now."

She crawled out from under the table. Straightening,

she brushed off her clothes, then took a moment to get her breathing under control. Jerry stood a distance from the table. He held the gun aimed at Xander. The other man lay on his back at Jerry's feet. His arms were raised above his head.

"The police are on the way." Her voice shook slightly. The adrenaline that had kept her going through this threat was quickly draining. Forcing her legs to move, she circled the desk and headed toward the door. "I'll get something to restrain him." She hoped to find something suitable in their supply closet.

Jerry watched her walk toward him. He gave her a crooked grin. "Great improv."

She smiled into his eyes. "Thank you. Great save."

His expression softened. "We make a good team."

"I know." Symone continued past him.

She'd always known they were better together. They hadn't had to put their lives on the line to convince her. It was Jerry who'd encouraged her to push back against her board's attempt to oust her. She'd urged Jerry to tell his brothers the real reason he wanted to leave their company. Even their arguments over the suspects in their investigation had helped them arrive at the truth about her mother's murder, and Xander and Ellie's scheme.

But what difference did all that make when Jerry was certain they were from different worlds?

"She screamed 'Help us,' as though the world was coming to an end." Jerry hadn't shared details like that with Taylor when he'd given the detective his statement earlier at the precinct. But in his family home—now Mal's home—surrounded by his brothers and Symone, Grace and Celeste late Friday night, he needed to share the fear, anger, uncertainty and, yes, humor of the experience. He could smile about it now—barely—but he'd almost had a stroke when Symone had drawn Xander's attention to herself with her scream. He shut out the images of what could've gone wrong before he passed out.

Celeste turned to Symone. "What made you shout 'Help us'?"

Jerry looked at Symone seated beside him on the love seat. His heart clenched with concern. She seemed exhausted. It was as though she'd used the last of her adrenaline to file her report with Eriq and now she was coasting on fumes. Or perhaps the hot, sweet chamomile tea Mal and Grace had made for the group had something to do with it. Jerry was a little tired himself. The tea's herbal scent wafted up to him.

Symone spread her arms. "I was afraid if I shouted 'Get him,' Xander would think I was referring to Jerry."

Dry chuckles floated around the room. Mal and Grace leaned against each other as they sat on the near corner of the sofa like the lovebirds they were. Celeste had taken the far end of the sofa. Zeke had pulled one of the dining chairs into the living room and positioned it beside her. There was something going on between those two. Celeste had impressed him. Jerry was rooting for his brother's happiness.

Symone had all but collapsed beside Jerry. He'd wanted to see to her comfort, curl his left arm around her shoulder and tuck her into him. But he couldn't, not if he'd meant what he'd said when he'd told her they didn't have a future together.

Jerry turned his head, smiling into Symone's sleepy chocolate eyes. "Those weren't your only two options."

"Those were the only ones that came to my mind at the

time." Symone's voice was low and breathy. Was it fatigue? Or something else, something he'd foolishly rejected?

Zeke raised his mug toward her. "Thank you for choosing the one most likely to keep my brother alive."

Mal nodded. "Yes, good choice, Symone."

Symone blushed as Jerry, Grace and Celeste echoed Zeke's and Mal's gratitude.

His brothers were making light of it now, but it was obvious from the looks on their faces when he'd walked into the precinct with Symone that they'd heard what had happened. He hoped never to cause them that much anguish again.

Grace cradled her mug between her palms. "For Xander and Ellie, it was just about the money?"

Jerry nodded. "It was a confidence scam."

Mal interrupted. "All of their crimes were confidence scams. They'd earn people's trust, then take their money."

"True." Jerry brought an image of their arrest report, which Mal had provided, to mind. "Xander had gained the board's acceptance and convinced a simple majority of them to call for a no-confidence vote against Symone."

Symone shook her head with disgust. "Which he'd done with indecent speed."

Jerry continued. "Then he'd need a supermajority to vote her out."

"Wow." Celeste's eyes widened. "Do you think he would've gotten the supermajority?"

Symone adjusted her glasses. "I don't know. During our last board meeting, I could tell a few still supported me but a couple were unsure."

Grace sighed. "That was too close. It would be a great

loss for the health care industry if The Bishop Foundation ever lost the clarity of mission your family brings to it."

"Thank you." Symone nodded. "I agree."

Grace frowned. "But Ellie seems to have been the key to this plan." She shifted to look at Mal. "Xander wouldn't have been able to get a hold on the foundation without Ellie so how did she get in?"

"Identity theft," Mal said. "It took me a little while to find the connection—"

Jerry interrupted. "No one stays hidden from Mal for long."

Mal smiled. "Bonnie Rae had stolen the real Eleanor Press's identity so her background would be approved. But, according to Ellie, Xander was afraid they'd be pushing their luck if he also stole someone's identity. So they submitted a fraudulent background check for him instead."

"I was curious about something." Celeste leaned forward, resting her forearms on her lap. Zeke's eyes were drawn to her beside him. "Why did Xander think Ellie had become a liability?"

Symone rubbed her thumbs over her warm porcelain mug. "Because she refused to destroy the actual background report the foundation's vendor provided, which recommended *against* adding Xander to the board."

Jerry watched Symone's thumbs caress her mug. "Ellie was using it as leverage to keep Xander in line. She was afraid he'd cut her out of the money or make her the fall guy for their scheme."

Zeke gestured with his mug of tea. "That report is evidence of Xander and Ellie's conspiracy to defraud the foundation."

Celeste drank more of her tea. "Symone, how do you feel now that Xander and Ellie are in custody?"

* * *

Symone paused, considering her answer. How did she feel? Destroyed, alone, afraid.

She met Celeste's eyes. She tried, but failed, to strip the emotion from her voice. "It doesn't bring my mother back. They destroyed my family and for what? They were *never* going to gain control of The Bishop Foundation's accounts." She paused, blinking away tears and trying to steady her voice. "However, I'm glad I was able to confront them. That was so important to me. And I'm very grateful to all of you—Grace, Mal, Zeke, Celeste and Jerry—for helping me get justice for my mother. It means a lot. Thank you doesn't feel like enough. I'll never forget it. I promise."

"We're glad we were able to help you," Mal said.

Zeke nodded. "Absolutely. This was important. And thank you is more than enough."

Jerry's hand settled softly on her shoulder, drawing her attention to him. "Your family deserves justice. We were happy to help."

Silence settled over the room. Symone thought of her mother. She would have liked Jerry. She would have liked all the Touré brothers. Symone wished she hadn't had to meet them under these circumstances. Xander and Ellie had taken so much from her—her mother, her trust in her board members, her stepfather. And while The Bishop Foundation was out of immediate danger, she was facing a lot of heavy lifting to repair the damage the confidence scammers had done and to rebuild the foundation.

Grace broke the silence. She sent a smile around the living room. "It seems like the five of you wrapped up this case with a great big bow. This was a complicated—and dangerous—investigation, but you closed it in just one week. Congratulations."

"Thanks." Celeste sat back against her chair. "It was a long, hard week. But I agree with Grace. You Tourés run a tight ship."

"Thank you, Celeste." Zeke shifted on his chair to face her. "I knew you'd be a great addition to the team. I—we—enjoyed working with you."

Symone sensed the chemistry between Zeke and Celeste. She was sure everyone in the room did, including those two. They'd make a good couple. At least Zeke didn't seem as clueless as his youngest brother. Her eyes drifted toward Jerry before she dragged them back to the rest of the group.

Celeste looked at Zeke. "I enjoyed working with you, too. I hope we can do it again sometime." She stood, collecting her purse from the sofa. "It's late. I should get home. Great job, everyone. Thanks for the tea and chat. Have a good weekend."

"I should leave, too." Symone rose from the love seat. "The case is over—"

Celeste turned to her. "Do you want a ride?"

Jerry shot to his feet. "No!"

Startled Symone spun toward him. "Actually, I would like—"

Jerry interrupted again. "Celeste, it's too far out of your way and, as you said, it's late."

Symone's shoulders sagged. She would've loved some time alone to chat with the other woman but Jerry was right. It was too much to ask.

"Thank you for your offer, Celeste." She turned to collect her purse, which she'd left on the love seat. "I'll call a car service."

Jerry caught her hand. His fingers were long and warm as they wrapped around hers. "Wait. Why? All your stuff's upstairs. Why don't you stay the night and I'll take you home in the morning?"

Because I don't want to drag out this goodbye. I'd rather rip the bandage off tonight and wake up with a fresh start in the morning.

She turned her head but didn't quite meet his eyes. "The case is over, and I don't want to impose."

Jerry stiffened as though he'd read more into her protest than she'd intended. "You're not imposing, Symone. Right, Mal?"

"Not at all." Mal's reply was immediate and sincere. "Please stay."

"You seem tired, Symone," Grace added. "Why don't you go up to bed and Jerry will take you home in the morning."

Symone hesitated for a heartbeat or two. She was exhausted. It had been a long and emotional seven days. The group seemed determine to add another night. Fine, she'd go up to bed, shut her door and pretend her heart wasn't breaking.

She turned her back to Jerry. "Thank you for your hospitality, Mal. I'll take your advice and go up to bed. It's been a long day."

She watched Celeste leave, then bid Jerry, Zeke, Mal and Grace good night before dragging herself up to sleep. Just one more night. Then, in the morning, she'd start rebuilding the foundation and her heart.

"Thank you again for driving me home." Symone sent a brief look toward Jerry as he took State Route 33 to Upper Arlington early Saturday morning. She wanted to sear the image of his strong, clean profile onto her memory, but it hurt too much to let her eyes linger. "I'm going to put 'buy a new car' on top of my to-do list since Xander and Ellie bombed mine. I'll have to get a rental for the time being, though. Actually, there are a lot of things on the top of my to-do list."

Like stop talking.

But Jerry's silence was making her nervous. These were the last few minutes they'd ever spend together. What was he thinking about? Had he realized pushing her away was a mistake? She stared blindly at his dashboard. Or was he thinking about returning this rental car?

"I'm sure you have a plan for getting through all of your tasks in a timely manner." The smile in his voice tugged at her heart.

"And I promise to keep my word about asking my building manager to get a proposal from TSG." They'd earned the recommendation. And although she was paying for their services, she felt she owed them more.

"Thank you." Jerry stopped at a red light. "My brothers and I appreciate that."

Symone swallowed the lump in her throat. "I'm glad things worked out for you and your brothers, and that you've decided to continue working with your family's company. Family's important."

"I agree." Jerry glanced at her. "Speaking of family, have you gotten an update on Paul's condition?"

"I spoke with one of the nurses this morning. He was still asleep when I called. I'm picking him up after I get the rental."

"Is that the reason you wanted to leave so early today?" Jerry continued through the intersection after the light finally turned green. "Because you're picking up Paul?"

His question was like a punch to the heart. "No, Jerry. I'm leaving because there's no reason for me to stay."

When the silence settled into the car this time, Symone ignored it. Traffic on this Saturday morning was brisk. She watched the sunlight fall like diamonds on the Scioto River. Thick old trees and overgrown underbrush framed its banks.

"Are you ready for your board meeting next Monday?" This time Jerry broke the silence.

She nodded, keeping her attention on the scenery through the windshield. "I believe so."

"You'll be great." He made the turn onto Fishinger Road. "The foundation would be in trouble without you."

"Thank you." She risked another look in his direction. "That's kind of you to say. If I am able to pull this off, it will be thanks to you."

"No." His tone was firm. "Your success is all you, Symone. No one else."

She looked at him in surprise. "Thank you."

Jerry shook his head. "You don't have to thank me. You're stronger than you think. You're smart and capable and kind. You just need to have more confidence in yourself."

Symone struggled to keep her jaw from dropping. "You sound like my mother."

Jerry laughed. "Then your mother was even smarter than I imagined her to be."

Symone's laughter joined his. "She was very smart—and strong, capable, kind and confident." She hesitated. "She would have liked you."

A flush rose up Jerry's neck and settled in his cheeks. "My parents would've liked you as well."

Then why doesn't their son want to take a chance on us?

Instead of asking the question aloud, Symone directed Jerry to her house. He pulled into her winding stone driveway, bordered on both sides by well-manicured lawns, evergreen bushes and stubby, short trees.

Jerry turned off the engine and stared at her stone Tudor-style home. "Wow."

Symone stiffened. "I grew up here. When my mother and Paul bought their new home, I bought this house from her. She gave me a good deal."

She felt Jerry calculating the differences in square footage and costs between their childhood homes. To him, this would be a tangible reminder of their differences.

Symone shifted to face him as she unclenched her teeth. "Thank you for bringing me home." Looking into his eyes, she saw him pulling away. It hurt.

"You're welcome." He gave her a distracted smile. "It was my pleasure." He popped the trunk, then unfolded himself from the driver's seat.

Symone followed him to the back of the rental car. "I can get my bag. Thank you."

"I'll get it." His response was final. "And I'll have the rest of your belongings from the safe house brought to you by Monday."

"Thank you." In retrospect, she was embarrassed that she'd taken both of her bags to the safe house. Carrying all those clothes around probably made her seem like a diva, which may have given Jerry even more reason not to get involved with her.

With a mental shrug, Symone led him to her maple wood front door. "Would you like to come in for some coffee?" She held her breath, waiting for his answer.

"Thanks, but I'd better get moving. Like you, I've got a lot of stuff to take care of today."

She'd expected that response. Disappointment was like bile in her throat. Symone unlocked her door and pushed it wide open. Jerry reached around her to set her suitcase just inside the entrance. She noticed he avoided looking around. Was that because he didn't want the memory of her home?

Symone straightened her back and squared her shoulders. She braced her legs. "Thank you again for everything. I'll never forget what you've done for me and my family's legacy." *Or what you've meant to me.*

Jerry nodded. "It's been an honor. If there's anything we can do for you in the future, please let us know." His eyes swept her face as though committing her features to memory.

She was doing the same with his. "I hope I won't need you to keep me alive in the future."

He smiled. "I hope so, too."

Symone stepped back and offered him her right hand. "Good luck with TSG. Please give your brothers my best."

Jerry looked from Symone's face to her hand. He lifted his eyes to hers. She saw a light shift in them.

Symone's breath left her lungs with a whoosh as Jerry pulled her into his arms. He pressed his mouth to hers and swept his tongue between her lips. The moan rose from her gut. Her thighs tensed as her body began a slow burn. She sucked his tongue as memories of their lovemaking—never far away—rushed back to her. She tightened her arms around his shoulders. Jerry held her closer. His right hand slid down her back to press her hips to his. Symone felt his arousal.

She moaned again and pulled her mouth from his. "Jerry, I—"

And then he released her. Without a backward glance, Jerry strode to his rental car as though some crazy ex-girlfriend was chasing after him. He reversed out of the driveway and disappeared.

The tears came without warning. Symone stumbled into her home and shut the door. Her sobs grew louder as she crumbled to the floor and curled into a ball.

Jerry, I love you.

Chapter 19

"I thought you could use some moral support." Paul stood in the threshold of Symone's office early Monday morning, minutes before the special board meeting to hold the no-confidence vote for Symone.

She rose behind her desk and crossed to him. "It's good to see you, Paul. You look well."

In the ten days since Xander had struck Paul with Ellie's car, the cuts and bruises had faded significantly. Despite the discomfort of fractured ribs, Paul was dressed formally in a dark blue tie, dark blue pin-striped, three-piece suit and snow white shirt.

Symone had been taking him to his follow-up medical visits. Both Paul and his older brother were disappointed by this delay in Paul's relocating to North Carolina. For their sake, she hoped Paul had a speedy recovery. But she was grateful for the distraction of her stepfather's presence.

"I feel better every day." Paul leaned against the doorway. "What about you? Are you ready for the meeting?"

"Considering I'm on my way to it now, I hope I am." Symone's tone was dry.

She collected her manila meeting folder and six plain white standard business envelopes printed with The Bishop Foundation logo. Each one was addressed to a remaining board member.

"Yes, I'm certain you are." Paul watched her approach him. "You seem more assertive and bolder since that horrible mess with Xander and Ellie." He hesitated. "You seem sadder, too."

Symone stopped beside him. "I'm just anxious to get this meeting over with." *And I'm missing Jerry. Terribly.*

"Remember, no matter what happens, you've given it your best effort. You always do. Your parents were so proud of you."

"Thank you, Paul. That means a lot." She led him into the hallway, then linked her arm with his to provide him with support as they walked to the boardroom. Along the way, they picked up Jackie Emery, Symone's temporary administrative assistant, who would be taking the board meeting minutes in Ellie's place.

Symone led them into the empty room. Her watch showed they had seven minutes to wait. Board members slowly trickled in.

Tina Grand called the meeting to order at exactly 10:00 a.m. She read from what appeared to be a prepared statement. "Due to changes in the board membership, the board agrees to cancel this special meeting for a no-confidence vote for our foundation chair. The board also apologizes to our foundation chair for any perceived lack of support this scheduled vote may have signaled."

Preferring not to hold a grudge, Symone sent a smile around the table. "Apology accepted."

"Thank you, Madam Chair." Tina glowed with relief. "So, if there are no further matters, the meeting will be adjourned."

Symone looked around the table. When no one else stirred, she addressed the board. "Madam President, I have a matter for discussion. This pertains to several articles in our bylaws." She passed photocopies of the specific bylaw articles around the table. She shared her copy with Paul. "Let's start with Article Two, Section Three. This article requires each member of the board to bring concerns about the foundation to the chair, members of the administration and other board members in a timely manner."

She looked around the table. Symone saw dawning concern in the members' stiffening features and widening eyes. "In other words, if you were concerned about the manner in which my mother or I were handling the foundation's accounts, you were required to tell us much sooner than six years after my father's death."

Tina flipped through the copies. "The penalty for a member not reporting concerns in a timely manner is removal from the board?" Her voice ended in a squeak. "I was not even aware of these rules." She looked around the table. "Was anyone aware of them?"

Murmurs of dismay and confusion circled the table.

Symone's disappointment lay like a brick in her stomach. "That's the problem. None of you are committed to the foundation, not the way it needs you to be. We need board members who will be real partners. Members who are as enthusiastic about our mission as I am."

Kitty humphed. "We made a mistake, but we've apologized. I don't think there's any reason for you to take it to such drastic measures."

Symone stood and circled the table, delivering her personalized letters to the members. "Please don't misunderstand. I appreciate your apology. This action is not a reflection of my personal feelings. If this was a personal decision, I wouldn't dissolve this board." *Or at least I wouldn't remove most of you.* "I'm doing what's best for the foundation."

"I just got here." Wesley looked from Paul to Symone. "Isn't there like a probationary period? I could really use the money from serving on this board."

That was the kind of attitude from members that got them into this situation in the first place. "I'm afraid there isn't a probationary period."

Keisha's sigh was low with resignation. "I've enjoyed being part of this organization, but you're right. Every one of us had an obligation to bring the investment and grant approval process concerns to you immediately."

"Thank you, Keisha." Symone returned to her seat. "The envelope has information about the separation process. If you have any questions about the process or your compensation package, please feel free to contact the foundation lawyer, Percy Jeffries. His business card is in your envelope."

Julie sat back against her chair. "I'm disappointed, but I understand your decision. What's the process for reapplying?"

Symone frowned. "I'll have to research that, Julie. This is a new development for the foundation."

"I'd like to know about that, too," Aaron said. "I'd like to recommit to the foundation."

"Thank you, Aaron. That's nice to know." Symone turned to a blank page in her notebook. "I'll let everyone know about the reapplication process. If there aren't any other questions, we can conclude this final meeting of this year's board."

Tina glowered at her from the other end of the table. "The meeting is concluded."

The older woman swept out of the room without another word. The other members wished Symone well before departing.

Paul turned to her. "Congratulations, Symone. You've won."

"I don't feel like I've won." Symone watched the members and Jackie disappear beyond the conference room doors. "For the first time in the history of my family's foundation, we don't have a board."

"You had to follow the bylaws or risk setting a bad precedent." Seated on her right, Paul reached over and patted her shoulder. "But these changes you're implementing almost make me want to stay."

Symone felt a spark of hope. "You were in the administration, but if you'd like to be on the board, you're always welcome."

Paul shook his head, but there was a wistful quality to his smile. "Thank you, but I think I'd better leave. The foundation, our home, everything has too many memories of Odette for me to stay."

Symone felt that, too. But Columbus was her home and she'd rather live with those memories of her parents than without them. She stood and linked her arm with Paul's. "I understand. But if you change your mind, let me know."

Paul cleared his throat. "I really loved your mother, but Langston Bishop was a tough act to follow." He paused. "You know, there's something about Jerry Touré that reminds me of your father."

"I agree." Symone swallowed a sigh, thinking of Jerry. He was exciting. Larger than life. The ten days they'd been apart hadn't helped to diminish her feelings for him. Symone had a feeling even a year apart wouldn't make a difference.

"We've come to see for ourselves." Mal crossed the threshold into Jerry's house late Monday morning.

Jerry frowned at his brother's back. "To see what?"

Zeke strode in after Mal. "You've taken a three-day weekend to clean your house. We're here to document this event with photos, videos and interviews."

"Ha. Ha." Jerry locked his door. He was dressed in a baggy gray T-shirt and black canvas shorts. His feet were bare. Both Zeke and Mal wore dark business suits with jewel-toned shirts and ties.

Jerry had been cleaning for almost four hours today. He'd had trouble sleeping last night, but this morning, instead of being tired, he was filled with nervous energy. He'd channeled that momentum into cleaning his basement. He'd begun this unusual cleaning spree Saturday and had already cleaned the top and main floors of his two-story home. His house now smelled like furniture polish, floor wax and window cleaner.

Reluctantly, he trailed after his brothers, who'd made a beeline for his kitchen. This entire situation had shades of their childhood, good-natured taunting at his expense. At some point, wouldn't they have to outgrow that?

Jerry washed his hands at the kitchen sink. "Do you guys want coffee?"

He wandered to his coffee machine to prepare the brew although he didn't need the caffeine. Breakfast might be a good idea, though. All he'd had was an apple.

"I didn't know you had black-and-white marble countertops." Mal ran one large hand over his kitchen counter.

"You're in my way, Mal." Jerry's eyes strayed toward the clock across the room. It was after ten. Was the foundation's board still meeting? What was happening? Had they voted? Would they still vote after everything that had happened? He needed to know.

Jerry measured the water for the carafe, then poured it into the machine.

"Wow. I don't think I've ever seen this floor." Zeke stared at the hardwood beneath his feet. Jerry had polished it yesterday.

"Yes, you have." Jerry measured the grounds for the coffee. "You and Mal helped me put it in." He turned to face his brothers through the kitchen pass-through.

Zeke and Mal sat at Jerry's round, blond wood dining table. They'd taken off their jackets and hooked them over the backs of their chairs.

Zeke gave Jerry a narrow-eyed stare as though he could decipher all of Jerry's thoughts. "What's this really about, Jer?"

Jerry crossed his arms and leaned back against the kitchen counter. "What do you mean?"

Mal rubbed his forehead with the tips of his right fingers. "Not this again."

Zeke rested his right ankle on his left knee. "Jer, you took a vacation day to clean. For you, that's a cry for help."

Mal stretched his legs in front of him and crossed them at his ankles. "You've been uncharacteristically quiet and withdrawn since we closed Symone's case. Do you want to talk about it?"

Jerry glanced again at the clock on the wall across the room. A few more minutes had crawled past. "The Bishop Foundation's Board is meeting right now to decide whether to keep Symone as chair or replace her."

Zeke's eyebrows jumped up his forehead. "Are they going through with that vote? They were taking their orders from a confidence scammer."

"Have you spoken with Symone recently?" Mal asked.

Jerry's eyes dropped to the cream floor tiles in his narrow kitchen. "I haven't spoken with her since I brought her home." That was ten days ago. Ten very long days.

Zeke arched an eyebrow. "Not even to thank her for referring us to her building manager? Getting that contract would've been a perfect excuse to call."

Jerry ran a hand over his hair. "I'm not looking for excuses to call her. I'm trying to figure out how to function without having her in my life."

"Why?" his brothers asked in unison.

Jerry paced the kitchen. "I've told you. She's out of my league. You should see the house she grew up in. You could fit each of our homes inside of it."

Zeke shifted on his seat, exchanging a look with Mal. "What does the size of a house have to do with whether the two of you are compatible?"

Jerry's stomach roiled with frustration. His skin crawled with it. His brothers should understand how he felt. They'd grown up in the same home. In contrast, they'd seen Symone, with her pearls, expensive suits and matching shoes.

He swallowed his pride and admitted to the fear that plagued his mind and heart. "I can't give her the kind of lifestyle she's used to."

Mal arched an eyebrow. "Did she ask you to?"

Jerry swept out his arm. "Not yet, but—"

Zeke considered him with narrowed eyes and a furrowed brow. "So your plan is to picture a relationship with Symone, then fast-forward to some imaginary breakup?"

Put like that, Jerry admitted his behavior sounded pretty foolish.

Mal shook his head. "Jer, talk with Symone. Let *her* be the one to decide if you're good enough for her."

What if her answer is no?

"Do you remember what Mom told us after Dad died?"

Zeke asked. "Losing someone hurts like hell, but the time you spend with them makes it worth it."

Mal nodded his agreement. "She's right. When Grace broke up with me in Chicago, I thought I'd never get over the pain. But I didn't for one moment ever regret being with her."

Jerry thought about his time with Symone. What his mother and Mal said made sense. Even if Symone turned him away, he'd still have those memories. He'd like the chance to make even more.

"All right." Jerry strode out of the kitchen. "I'll ask Symone to take a chance on me." He hesitated. "But first I'll need a plan."

Symone sat at her desk Monday afternoon, doing what she did best, especially when she was stressed and overwhelmed. She was making a list. Topping the list was revising the screening process for employees and board members. She needed a replacement for Ellie, preferably someone who wasn't a fugitive from the FBI. She had to replace the board.

And she had to call Jerry.

She couldn't stop thinking about him. She felt him in her dreams. He whispered to her throughout her day. She was craving mints. And sometimes she would see him at random places around the city. Those sightings hurt worst of all because when she approached him, he'd turn out to be someone else.

Symone dropped her head into her hands. This had to stop. She had to convince him to give them a chance. He was being unreasonable.

Symone sat up and adjusted her glasses. She took a breath before reaching for her cell phone beside the landline on her desk. She didn't know what to say if he answered the call. She would wing it and hope for the best.

A knock on her open office door broke her concentration. Symone looked up. "Jerry?"

Good grief. Was she dreaming again? He looked so real. He stood in her threshold in a gunmetal gray suit, maroon shirt and black tie. His right hand was still pressed against the door. His left hand held a bouquet of long-stemmed red roses.

His smile was uncertain. "You don't look like someone celebrating reclaiming control of her family's foundation."

He was really here? The pulse at the base of her throat broke into a sprint. "How did you know about that?"

Jerry crossed her threshold and closed her door. His loose-limbed strides brought him to her desk. "I spoke with Paul. Congratulations." The caution clouding his eyes belied the smile curving his lips.

"Thank you." Symone was beginning to believe he really was in her office. Her eyes dropped to the bouquet. "Are those for me?" The scent of the roses filled her office. She'd much rather smell him.

"Yes." He extended them to her.

"Thank you." Symone took them and buried her face in the roses. "They're beautiful."

The bouquet was really here. Maybe the man was, too. Her heart felt ready to burst from her chest. She couldn't stop smiling.

"Symone—" He came around her desk, offered her his hand and helped her to her feet. He drew a breath. "Symone, when I look at you, I see someone with intelligence, courage, integrity and kindness."

Her pulse fluttered like a butterfly in her throat. She set

the bouquet on her desk. "Not a bank account?" Her voice was a whisper.

Jerry shook his head. "No. I used that as an excuse to push you away because I thought I wasn't good enough. But being 'good enough' isn't about a bank account. It's about what's in here." He pressed her hand against his heart. Its beat was strong and steady against her palm.

She raised her eyes to his face. His image was blurry through her tears. "Why didn't you tell me this before?"

His throat muscles flexed before he could answer. "I was afraid." His chuckle was wry humor. "I can confront an armed serial killer, but the thought of disappointing you makes me shake in my shoes."

Symone laughed. She pressed her palm against his chest again. "You could never disappoint me, Jerry. From the first day we met, you've been saving me. I love planning with you. I love being spontaneous with you. I love arguing with you. And I absolutely love falling in love with you."

Jerry's heart slammed against her palm. He lowered his forehead to hers and exhaled. "I love falling in love with you, too."

Symone gasped. "You do?"

He nodded, his forehead rubbing against hers. "I cleaned my house."

Symone's lips parted. "Jerry," she breathed.

He lifted his head to look at her. His smile was uncertain. "I'd planned to come to your office and take you to lunch. Then, I'd plead my case to you."

Symone beamed up at him. "I prefer acting on impulse." She rose up on her toes and kissed him.

* * * * *